ACCIDENTAL MAGIC

MODERN MAGIC - BOOK ONE

NICOLE HALL

To Eli, for believing

1

SERA

THERE WAS a man under her kitchen sink on his back, and not in the fun way. At least, Sera Allen was pretty sure it was a man. The legs sticking out from the cabinet wore jeans and work boots that seemed masculine enough, but it was when the cursing started that she was sure. His voice was low, rough, and vaguely familiar, though she couldn't quite place it. She awarded him some extra points for creativity, but didn't lower her bat. A girl had to protect herself.

"Excuse me," she said.

The cursing stopped abruptly as his head thunked on the underside of the counter. He twisted and started to slide out. Sera bit her lip. There was a whole lot more of him than she'd expected. *Run back out to the car and slam the door, or stand still and wait to be murdered?* Her lizard brain urged her to panic, but she'd had plenty of practice convincing her brain that panicking was a terrible idea.

His head cleared the cabinet, and he stood, turned to survey her, then leaned back against the counter, arms crossed over an impressive naked chest. Sera sucked in a breath. He wasn't bulky, more lanky corded muscle, but he took up a lot of the space in the little kitchen. Still, Sera was ready to clear the bases using his face if he made any moves toward her. It would be a shame too because his face was all lean angles and pretty brown eyes. He raised a brow as she stared at him for several more seconds.

"Not that I don't mind a little break, but maybe you could lower the bat and we could use our big girl words?" His voice matched his stance, deceptively mellow.

Sera didn't move. "Who are you and what are you doing here?"

He shrugged. "Thought I'd see how much I could get for the sink on the black market."

She tightened her grip on the bat. "I'm calling the police."

He grinned. "Looks like you got your hands full from where I'm standing."

Sera wondered if hitting him would be considered self-defense if all he'd done was stand there. Probably not, though he *was* trespassing. He didn't seem inclined to injure her, and Sera wasn't naïve enough to think that the bat was keeping him at bay. Sure, he probably didn't want any bruises, but he had a good half a foot on her and he looked like he was all muscle. If he wanted the bat, he could probably take it from her.

She shifted the bat into one hand and reached into her back pocket for her phone.

He put his hands up in surrender. "C'mon, Sera. I was kidding. You seriously don't remember me? You've seen me naked."

Sera lowered the bat and took a closer look at his face. "Jake?" As a teenager, he'd been lanky and a little awkward.

She'd found it adorable until he'd let her leave without a single phone call. He'd grown up a lot in seven years. *Too bad.* "You seem to be in the wrong house."

He ran a hand through his unruly hair and muttered, "You got that right." He glanced at the sink behind him. "Look, I came by earlier to make sure the water and electricity and whatever was turned on. Evie gave me a key years ago. When I checked the water, something funky was happening with the sink. Thought I'd be nice and fix it up for you before you got here." He glared at the sink. "But I can't find anything wrong with it."

His explanation rang true, but she got stuck on one point. "Evie gave you a key?"

"Yeah. I did odds and ends for her." He met her eyes, sadness swimming in his. "I'm sorry about her passing."

Sera swallowed hard and nodded. She hadn't seen her grandmother since the summer she'd turned seventeen. At the time, her grandma insisted that everyone call her Evie. *Grandma makes me feel so old.* She'd smiled as she said it and pulled Sera in for a hug. Her lonely teenage heart had soaked it up.

After Sera'd left, they'd talked on the occasional holiday, but it had never been enough. A need deep inside her wanted Evie to ask her to return, and a fear just as deep ensured that she'd never broach the subject herself. It stung that Evie'd maintained a relationship with grown-up Jake instead of her own granddaughter.

The boy she'd known had been wild. He'd pushed the limits every chance he got, and somehow, it never came back to bite him in the ass. Sera frowned. This Jake, half-naked in Evie's house, her house now, looked different, but acted the same. So maybe he hadn't grown up so much as gotten bigger. His brown eyes were the same. Vibrant and mischievous. It surprised her that she hadn't recognized him before, but to be fair, she *had* been distracted staring at his chest.

Sera set the bat on the kitchen table and narrowed her eyes. "I distinctly remember you refusing to learn how to fix things around the house despite your dad's best efforts. You said that was his thing, and you were destined for something more. I'm pretty sure that's an exact quote."

Jake winced. "Well, it turns out teenage me didn't actually know everything. It wasn't long after you went back home that I started working for my dad's company."

Sera raised a brow. "He let you near his tools?"

Jake chuckled. "After a while, yeah. Clems left, so Dad ended up with more work than he could handle. I started picking up the slack a little, helping him out."

Sera nodded. "Always the hero. So, now you claim you know how to fix a sink?"

"Yes. I can fix a sink." He rolled his eyes.

"What's wrong with this one that necessitated an evening shirtless visit?"

Jake crossed his arms in response. "I always fix sinks shirtless if I can. They get drippy, and I believe I already mentioned that I can't find anything wrong with this one. It's the damnedest thing. Nothing is blocked, but it's draining slow, then fast, then slow again." He frowned at the sink again.

Sera joined him and reached for the faucet. She really wanted the sink to be fixed so she could send him on his way. Her brain was tired and even more mixed up with grief after all the traveling, making it hard for her to remember why she wasn't supposed to touch his chest. The metal was cold, but heat rushed across her hand and down her fingers. For a second, golden light spilled over the sink from the window, but then Sera blinked and it was gone. Water rushed into the basin and down the drain in a steady flow. They both watched it for a few more seconds, then Sera turned it off again.

She looked up at him. Her words were dry. "Good job. You fixed it."

He huffed out a breath. "Awesome. If you have any more problems, please call someone else."

Jake reached past her for the toolbox on the counter, and Sera almost leaned into him. A habit from long ago that she'd thought buried. She took a stumbling step back instead. He quickly steadied her, his hands gentle on her upper arms, and searched her face.

"You okay?"

A few deep breaths calmed her racing pulse, but it took off again when she met his eyes. *How inconvenient.* "I'm fine," she said. "Just tired."

The half-lie rolled off her tongue easily, and Sera hated that it came so naturally. She backed away and shoved her hands in her jeans pockets.

Jake held her eyes for a moment, and Sera wondered a lot of things. Were his parents still next door? Was he in a relationship? Was he married? Did he have kids? Did he still slide his hands into a girl's hair when he kissed her? Warmth crept up her cheeks, and Jake chose that moment to drop his eyes. There was no way he didn't notice her blushing.

He busied himself with his tools. "It shouldn't take long for you to pack up Evie's stuff, and the house is in good shape, so it won't be too hard to sell," Jake rambled.

Something glimmered in the dark cabinet, distracting her, so it took a second for Sera to process his words. She glanced up in surprise. "I'm not selling the house."

Jake stopped packing up his tools. "Renting it out then?"

"No, I'm moving in. Tomorrow, actually. Isn't that why you came by to check on the utilities?"

He shrugged. "Rumor mill said you were coming to stay tomorrow, but I assumed it was temporary."

"It's not. This is my home now."

Jake took a long look at her and nodded. "Okay."

Sera got the feeling he didn't believe her, but she didn't give a crap. Evie had wanted Sera to have her house, and Sera was going to take good care of it. The house was more than a means to an end; it was a new beginning in a place she'd been happy. She'd loved her grandma, despite the distance.

Jake's easy smile had vanished, and Sera was surprised she missed it. It was habit to be closed off and unwelcoming, easier to make people leave her alone that way, but maybe her therapist was right and it was time she put some effort into building, or even rebuilding, friendships. Even if she'd been the one to torch them in the first place.

"Thanks for your help, Jake."

He snapped his toolbox closed. "*De nada*." He turned to go, but words popped out of her mouth, surprising both of them.

"Does Maddie still live at your parents' house?" Sera cringed. *Why couldn't you just let him leave?*

Jake looked over his shoulder to answer her. "Nah, she moved to the other side of town a while ago, and my parents are gone."

Sera's brow furrowed. "Oh, Jake, I'm so sorry."

He winced. "Not like that. Mom made a bunch of money investing, and they retired early. They gave me the house so they could travel around Europe. They're in Norway right now, terrorizing the local wildlife."

Sera let out a relieved breath. "Well that's something, but Maddie's still around?"

Jake turned fully to her, but his voice was still hesitant. "She is, but I don't know what she's into lately. We don't really hang out other than when she invades the house to steal my food."

"Too bad. I could use some friends." Sera mumbled quietly.

Jake ran his hand through his hair again. "Maybe you'd still have some if you hadn't run away without looking back. Besides, town is maybe a five-minute walk from here. She's hardly living across the country."

He wasn't wrong. That summer had been the first time she'd spent more than a few days at a time with Evie. It had been full of surprises, and she'd let events beyond her control scare her away. Initially, she'd tried to contact them, but not very hard. And it's not like any of them had tried either. That last thought was bitter. Eventually, it had been easy to let her mom break those connections. Sera forced herself to meet his eyes. "I'm hoping for a fresh start. It's...it's one of the reasons I'm moving back."

Jake studied her intently for a long moment. The grin that bloomed across his face did funny things to her insides. "Okay, but you asked for it."

"I'm going to regret this, aren't I?"

He pushed away from the counter and invaded her space again. This time she held her ground. "Probably, but it might be fun."

The heat in his eyes excited her and made her nervous at the same time. They'd been friends first, once upon a time, and Sera hoped they could be again. No matter how distracting she found this grown up Jake to be, she definitely wasn't looking for anything more. She was still dealing with the fall-out from her ex-husband, and she needed to figure out who she was on her own. There was no need to pile on more complications, especially not with their history and with this town being her new home.

Jake ripped a piece of paper off the pad on the fridge and scribbled two numbers down. "The first is my private cell. If you have any non-sink related problems, give me a call. I'm across the yard. The second number is Maddie's. I can't speak for her taste in friends, but she'll probably be happy to hear from you." He traded the paper for his toolbox and opened the back door.

Sera put her hand on Jake's arm before he could head out. "Thanks, Jake. For real."

"See you tomorrow, Sera." There was a challenge in his voice, but she refused to rise to the bait. He would see her tomorrow. And the next day. And the next. She was staying put this time.

She nodded, and the kitchen door closed with a soft click behind him. Sera couldn't help but watch out the kitchen window as he walked across the yard and disappeared into the shadows at the property line. Sera shook herself. If she couldn't get a handle on her body's reactions to him, living next-door to Jake was going to get very awkward in the near future.

———

SERA CROUCHED DOWN to close the cabinet door under the sink and remembered the glimmer. Something shiny had caught her eye during their conversation, but when she stuck her head under the counter, there were only pipes. *Huh.*

Sera sighed. She'd planned to go into town and hit the

diner, but it was late and dealing with Jake had drained her. Her overnight bag was still by the front door where she'd left it. Evie's baseball bat had been in the umbrella stand as usual, and she'd felt it prudent to not be encumbered while defending herself. The bat could stay in the kitchen. She latched the back door and killed all the lights except the one over the stove. An archway opened into the living room, and the big front windows let in the glow from the streetlights. It wouldn't have mattered. The house hadn't changed much in seven years, and Sera could navigate it with her eyes closed.

She rubbed her face, eyeing the stairs. *Or I could just crash on the couch.* It was newish and looked comfy, but she really needed to stretch out on a bed and maybe sleep for a week. Sighing, she snagged her bag and saw another glimmer out of the corner of her eye. It was on the console by the stairs. When Sera turned to face it, it winked out. There was no denying something had been there this time. Fireflies? In the house?

It wasn't beyond the realm of possibility that she was hallucinating. She'd driven twenty-three hours straight from Orange County, California to Mulligan, Texas. Somewhere around El Paso, she'd thought about stopping for some sleep, but it'd been mid-afternoon at that point and the comfort of Evie's home was calling. The console didn't hold anything that looked like it would reflect golden light, and the cabinet definitely hadn't. Neither had her hand.

There was a green ceramic gourd lamp, some art books, and a collection of pictures in plain white frames. Even the pulls were simple matte black against the wood. Sera picked up one of the frames and took a closer look. It was of her teenage self hugging Evie. Sera was in some of the other pictures as well. Photos she didn't remember sending. They were mostly major life events, her high school graduation, her wedding portrait, and one of her with Will, her ex, at a black-tie event. She turned that picture face down and looked around the room more carefully.

Evie had a lot of pictures on the walls and on every flat surface. Sera walked past them, trailing her fingers over the glass. Some were pictures of Evie in town with people she didn't recognize, some forest-y landscapes that appealed to Sera, and at least half of them were pictures of Sera herself. The room was full of her, of her achievements and her life.

Sera rubbed her chest as a sharp pang spread through it and down to her stomach. She'd wasted so much time trying to make the wrong people love her, and apparently, she'd missed her chance to have it right here. The room was filled with her grandmother's love for her. Tears blurred Sera's vision as she turned her back on the photos. Evie'd had her own way, pragmatic and patient, but Sera hadn't appreciated the love that encompassed all of it. *And now it's too late.*

———

THE ROOM to the right at the top of the stairs had been hers. Sera held her breath and opened the door. The switch turned on the nightstand lamp, and in the soft glow, Sera was glad to see the big bed was still made up with sheets and a blanket. There wasn't even any dust. Pretty blues and whites made up the color scheme, but the abstract patterns could have been picked out by anyone. Sera was almost disappointed that it was decorated as a generic guest room. *What were you expecting? A shrine? Time to get your head out of your ass.*

Her window overlooked the backyard, and in front of it sat her old campaign desk and chair. The antique low dresser and mirror she remembered faced it against the opposite wall, and across from the bed was the closet. No TVs in the bedrooms for Evie. Bedrooms were for resting. Sera smiled. Tomorrow, she'd have to brave Evie's room and see if she followed her own rules, but for tonight Sera needed to let her overwhelmed brain and body rest.

She turned to shut off the hall light, but didn't see the switch and didn't feel like looking so Sera just closed the bedroom door. *I'll remember where it is tomorrow.* She dropped her bag at the foot of the bed and undressed, leaving her clothes in a jumble on the floor. Evie would have sassed her about it, but Sera was more than fading fast. It was a struggle to keep her eyes open. She didn't even bother with pajamas, just crawled under the blue quilt into cool sheets and let her body go limp with a deep breath. There was so much to deal with tomorrow, but that could wait for...well...tomorrow. She remembered the lamp and cracked an eye open. The glimmer was back, next to the light this time. Suddenly, the room dropped into darkness. As Sera watched, the glimmer faded out a few seconds later. She reminded herself to check the wiring on the lamp in the morning.

JAKE

JAKE PULLED Sera's door closed softly behind him, even though he wanted to slam it. *She wasn't supposed to be there until tomorrow.* He knew Evie had left the house to her, he even knew Sera would have to show up at some point to pack it up and sell it off, but this had been too soon. Jake strode across the lawn as fast as he could without actually running from his far too sexy neighbor.

It was warm out for October, and he'd forgotten to turn the AC back on when he'd left that afternoon, but whatever, what was a little more sweat. When he'd turned and seen Sera standing over him with that bat, he'd nearly tumbled back into the cabinet in surprise. He told himself if he'd been a little more prepared, the sight of her wouldn't have affected him so intensely, but it didn't sound convincing, even to himself. How could the sight of her after so many years still do that?

Jake dropped his toolbox inside the back door and sighed at the mess that greeted him. Milk out on the counter, crumbs and bits of food everywhere, dirty dishes caked in who knew what next to the sink. Not even in the sink. Maddie was such a slob.

He sniffed the milk before putting it away and noticed that his leftover lasagna was gone. *Dammit, that was supposed to be dinner.* "Maddie? You still here?" He hollered.

His little sister appeared in the archway between the kitchen and living room and gave him a big smile. "What? Oooh, you're back. Get the sink fixed?"

Jake brushed past her and sank onto the couch, trying not to let his annoyance show in his voice. "Yeah, but I don't think I did much. It went from not working one minute to working the next. I told Sera to call someone else if it acts up again."

Maddie looked up from picking at her dark blue nails. "Sera was there? She's early."

"Ya think?. She found me under the sink cursing at the damn pipes and threatened to—nevermind, it's not important." Jake stretched his arms along the back of the couch and beckoned her closer. "Don't think I didn't notice you ate all my lasagna."

She walked past him and ruffled his hair on the way to the front door. "I regret nothing. It was delicious."

"That was my dinner, Mad."

"Maybe label it next time. Or hide it better."

"Why would I hide food in my own house? Oh right, because I have a mooch sister who doesn't understand personal boundaries."

She shrugged. "What's yours is mine."

That was the problem with Maddie. He'd give her the earth and all the stars if she asked, but she never asked. It was partly his fault for spoiling her, but his parents had been way worse. After they'd moved to Europe and given him the house, Maddie had taken to coming and going like she still lived there, even though she'd moved out before they had.

"Mad?"

She stopped in the middle of tying her Converse and looked up. "What?"

"Sera says she's staying. Planning to live in Evie's house. Her house now, I guess."

Maddie's face shifted from mockery to pity. He hated the pity, but she'd been there when Sera had left the last time. "Maybe she's different? A lot of time has passed."

Jake scrubbed his face with his hands. "Yeah, maybe."

Maddie's arms came around his head for a quick squeeze, then she was back to her normal self, prancing to the door. "Well, maybe don't sleep with her again and she'll stick around this time."

He threw a couch pillow at her, but she ducked out the door before it could make contact. That was the thing about Maddie. She loved with her whole heart and tried to make the people around her happy, even if her mouth got in the way sometimes.

Jake heaved himself off the couch and went to the kitchen for a beer. He didn't feel like cleaning up Maddie's mess, so he turned the light out and left it for the morning. Beer for dinner wasn't the best life choice, but seeing Sera then losing his lasagna made it good enough for tonight.

It was dark in the living room without the kitchen light, so Jake turned on the tv in search of the Texans game. They were having a shit season, but it was better than thinking about shoving his hands into long dark hair and wondering whether her skin still tasted faintly of peaches.

Ten minutes later, he was up one touchdown, down one beer, and wishing he'd tried to convince Maddie to stay a little while. He couldn't concentrate, at least not on the game. His eyes kept wandering to the window that over-looked her property. There were lights still on.

What was she doing? Was she thinking about him? He couldn't get his mind off of her. She was supposed to arrive tomorrow, go through Evie's stuff, then leave again. He'd planned to avoid being home for a couple of days and then go back to his life, sadly with one less awesome old lady in it.

Evie'd respected his wishes not to talk about Sera, even though she'd obviously kept tabs on her granddaughter. He noticed the new pictures of her that appeared in Evie's house. The sight of Sera in a wedding gown on some other guy's arm had knocked the wind from him the first time he'd seen it, but he'd learned to avoid certain places on Evie's walls. They'd had plenty else to talk about, and Sera's move to town and abrupt move away were old news.

He'd known Sera since they were kids when she'd come to visit her grandma, but she'd never stayed very long. The summer before his senior year, before he went to work for his dad's construction company, she'd moved in with Evie and changed everything. They were inseparable for three fantastic months. But by the time fall rolled around, she'd been gone, and he'd been neck-deep in building Mr. Anderson's new deck and trying not to fail out of school. He threw himself into it because when he wasn't working, his chest ached with missing her.

He didn't pine for her anymore or anything like that, but at the time, he'd been so sure that she loved him back, right up until the day she left. Sera was his first. First love. First heartbreak. Not his first time having sex, that honor went to Vanessa McIntyre in junior year, but his first time making love. Underneath it all, she was his. He'd felt it all the way through him. She'd belonged with him. Or at least that's what he'd thought.

Clearly, she hadn't agreed. Over the years, he explained those feelings away as hormones or fanciful thinking, though he'd only admitted that last one to Ryan one night after too many drinks. But seeing her tonight, it was a gut-punch. All the way through him.

Jake switched the game off, who cared if the Texans were finally winning one. They sucked at distracting him. As a last resort, Jake pulled out his phone and dialed Ryan.

"Hey Jake, what's up?"

"Wanna sit in my living room in the dark and get drunk?"

"Uhh... as fun as that sounds, no. What's going on?"

Jake could hear video game sounds in the background indicating that Ryan had stopped playing, but Ryan didn't seem to care that his avatar was being murdered. *See? That's a good friend, right there.* "Sera's back."

Ryan whistled low. "The infamous Sera. Think I'll get to meet her this time before she takes off?"

"That's the problem. It looks like she's staying."

"How is that a problem? You've been pining for her for like seven years."

"I don't pine, dumbass. It's perfectly normal to miss someone you cared about."

"Sure. Then why aren't you out searching for a new lady instead of calling me on raid night?"

Jake shut his eyes and dropped his head back on the couch. "Because I ran into her tonight, and I'm trying to stop myself from heading back over there."

It took a second to process that Ryan was laughing. "I don't understand how you can still have feelings for this girl. You told her you loved her, she left, then refused to see you or talk to you."

"That's not—ugh, nevermind. I'm regretting ever telling you about this."

"Okay, fine. Seriously though, you don't know anything about her. The current her. I get you had real feelings for her before and got hurt, but there's nothing stopping you from talking to her and seeing what's up now."

"I don't want to see what's up. It was a long time ago, and I have no intention of going through all that again."

"Uh, huh. And two seconds ago you said, and I quote, 'I'm trying to stop myself from heading back over there'. So *now* you're saying you don't want to get in her pants?"

"More than just about anything at the moment, but it's not like she's the only option around."

"Right, because you're a strong, independent man, and you don't need no woman?"

"I super hate you right now."

Ryan was laughing again, and Jake heard a familiar chime in the background. "Look, I gotta go man, but if you really don't want to go over there, go booty call Chelle or go to bed. Either way, you need to make up your mind. Oh, and if you have any other pressing emotional needs to work through, call Maddie."

The call cut off on Ryan's hyena laughter, and Jake wondered why he'd ever befriended Ryan in the first place. Nah, Jake knew why. Ryan was a good guy; it was just that his version of help skewed towards computer references and snarky comments. Not that he'd expected any help. He'd just needed...something. Anyway, Jake knew what that chime meant. Zee was reaching out to Ryan and that was a mess Jake didn't want to get involved in. Dealing with the Fae almost always resulted in Zee fiddling with his head.

He had no idea if Ryan had similar experiences, but the few times they'd talked about it, Ryan had been clear that he disliked the Fae. And Zee in particular. Jake and Ryan shared some pretty hefty secrets, but Ryan was almost fanatically silent about his history with Zee. Not Jake's problem currently. *Thank god.* Magic wouldn't help him deal with Sera or his traitorous body.

Jake opened his eyes and glared at the specks of golden light floating around the window facing Sera's. He didn't need or want their help.

"Go away."

One by one, they blinked out, and Jake went upstairs to try to get some sleep.

2

SERA

THE NEXT DAY dawned bright and way too early. There were only flimsy sheers over the windows, and the tree was shading the wrong part of the room. Sera groaned and rolled over, covering her face with her pillow. Her back hurt from being in the car so long the day, *days?* before, and after the first blissful hour of unconsciousness, she'd woken up over and over again to dreams of being eaten by a half-dead tree.

A buzzing noise from the nightstand penetrated the pillow shield, and Sera suddenly remembered the lamp going out on its own the night before. If it was a fire hazard, she was chucking it out the window. She peeked, but the lamp was still and silent. Her phone, on the other hand, was about to vibrate itself onto the floor. A glance at the screen confirmed what she feared.

Her mother was calling.

Nope. Sera hit cancel and tossed the phone on the foot of the bed. She wasn't going to ruin her morning quite yet. She needed coffee, her toothbrush, and some clean pants. Not necessarily in that order. A quick rummage through her bag and a few minutes later, she was ready to tackle the coffee.

Evie's house was comforting in its sameness. Ocean colors were everywhere. Blue and green watercolor paintings hung next to a lush fern that sat next to a plush navy sofa. The items themselves had changed, but the placement and tone of the room remained the same as it had always been. Sera'd visited many times before, but she'd only lived there for the one summer. It hadn't mattered, she'd burrowed in and made it hers too. Tears threatened to fall, but Sera blinked them away.

She wanted to walk into the white kitchen and find Evie at the stove cursing at her eggs. Sera's steps faltered in the living room as a quiet snick came from the kitchen. It sounded like the fridge closing. Sera frowned.

No one else was supposed to have a key, but Jake had proved that wasn't true the night before. As far as she knew, the bat was still on the kitchen table. In the kitchen. Next to the fridge. Her car was out front. She could leave the trespasser to Evie's weeks old food.

Sera straightened her back and marched into the kitchen. No one was going to mess with Evie's stuff, even if she wasn't here anymore to use it.

"Hello?"

The room was empty. Fridge closed. Bat still in place on the table where she'd left it, back door still locked. A bit of gold glimmered next to the coffee maker in her peripheral vision, but when she turned her head it was gone. More hallucinations.

Sera closed her eyes and took a deep breath. There was no panic anymore, just a deep-seated sadness. She knew the glimmers were tricks of the light, and not hallucinations, but years of being told she was imagining things were hard to forget. Being in Evie's house brought back the memories of her mother and then Will insisting she wasn't well. That the things she saw weren't real. That she needed medication, silence, rest. Sera opened her eyes and looked around the bright kitchen, quiet and alone. Screw them and their pop psycho-babble. And screw their medication that made her fuzzy and compliant.

She'd take hallucinations over Will any day.

The coffee maker was one of those pod kinds, and Sera opened every cabinet and drawer looking for the pods, but no luck. She leaned against the counter, toying with her phone. Coffee was necessary to life on the best of days, and this was going to be a rough one. A paper next to her elbow fluttered to the ground. There in Jake's loopy handwriting was Maddie's number. Jake would probably have coffee, but Maddie was the safer choice. She'd call Maddie, who she hadn't talked to in seven years, and ask her to come over with coffee. *What could go wrong?*

Maddie didn't answer. *Would Jake?*

She shook her head. The situation wasn't that desperate. She could drive into town and have her own coffee in less than five minutes. Loud brakes and a metallic noise squealed from the front of the house, so Sera tucked her phone into her back pocket and went to accept her moving container delivery. Coffee or no, it was time to do the things.

The driver was professional and quicker than Sera would have liked. Now that the time was nigh, she wasn't sure she was ready to start all over in a new place. Like Jake had said last night, she could sell the house for a good amount, but then what? Start over in a different new place? She wasn't willing to stay with her mom any longer, and she didn't have any friends who had lasted through the divorce.

light stayed with them on the path, but they disappeared every time she turned her head to look at them. She'd thought fireflies came out at twilight, but they didn't have fireflies in California so what did she know? The smell of the pine straw rose from the forest floor, and she breathed in deep. It was a spicy scent she hadn't realized she'd missed. That and fireflies and Jake and Evie's muffins. *No! Not Jake, muffins.* How many other things had she missed out on because of fear?

Her thoughts turned dark, and she asked the first question that popped in her mind to change that direction. "Who summoned me?"

She almost wasn't expecting an answer after all the reverent silence, but Ryan glanced back at her. "I'm not sure if it's better to tell you or leave it as a surprise."

"Well that was cryptic and unhelpful."

"The Fae," Jake answered quietly behind her.

Sera almost stopped, but the pull was filling her chest like a balloon and making it hard not to run. "The Fae? What the heck is that, a book club? A motorcycle gang? A band of merry men?"

Ryan snorted. "Actually, I'm pretty sure they'd love to be described as a motorcycle gang."

Jake grinned. "That *was* an interesting choice."

"Yeah." Ryan stopped walking and moved to the side. Past him, was a clearing with a circle of waist-high stones set upright into the top of a wide, low mound.

Sera couldn't stop. She moved right past him, up the mound, and stepped through, into the stones. As she reached the center, the pull drained from her, and she slumped down onto the grass. She glanced around. Ryan and Jake stayed at the edge of the clearing, once again silent and unhelpful.

"Took you long enough."

Sera jerked her head back around. From her sitting position, she was now at face-level with a small creature hovering on little gossamer wings in front of her.

It was a fairy.

A. Real. Live. Fairy. There was no other word for it. Delicate, translucent wings, pointed features, and a light, gauzy gown that almost glowed against her rich copper skin. It was like she'd stepped out of a kid's movie. The fairy perched on a shorter rock inside the circle and folded her wings behind her. Sera refused to believe this was a dream or some kind of shared hallucination. Looking around, she realized Ryan had joined her in the circle, but Jake had faded back into the trees a little.

The fairy inclined her head at Ryan. "You've served your summons."

Ryan nodded back. "Why not send someone she knows? I thought Jake was going to deck me when I touched her."

"I'm not here," Jake yelled from the trees.

The fairy glared in his direction. "That's good because you weren't invited."

Sera climbed to her knees. "What the—"

Ryan clapped a hand over her mouth. "Be careful what you say around them."

The fairy moved her glare to Ryan. "Let her speak. I have no intention of twisting her words."

"Bullshit."

"Vulgarity is no substitute for wit," she shot back.

Ryan rolled his eyes. "You stole that from Downton Abbey."

She shrugged her tiny shoulders haughtily, and Sera ripped Ryan's hand away as her brain caught up with the conversation. "You speak English... and watch Downton Abbey?"

The fairy smiled, but even with her small stature, it felt predatory. "First, we do as we please. Second, Downton Abbey is amusing, and third, Zee."

Sera blinked a few times. "I'm sorry?"

"It's my name. Zee. You keep calling me 'the fairy', but I much prefer my name."

Panic started to rise up her throat, but Sera swallowed it down. "Stay out of my head." She stumbled to her feet. "Actually, stay out of all of me. I don't know what you did to get me here, but it sucked and I'm out."

Sera made it as far as the surrounding stones before she hit an invisible wall and lost her balance. Her hand came down to steady herself on the closest rock and pain tore through her head at the touch. She snatched her hand back, but it was too late. The pain radiated and grew, making her gasp and squeeze her eyes shut. It felt like something inside her was tearing open.

A soft sigh of wings or breath, she wasn't sure, brushed the side of her face. "Humans are so fragile." Zee's cool hand pressed against her temple. "The magic in the stone brought your own to the forefront. It broke the seal that's been keeping it asleep."

Sera cracked her eyes open. The dim light filtering through the trees made more pain shoot through her head, and the fireflies were back in force. "Magic isn't real."

Zee snorted. "Sure, and neither are fairies."

"I don't have magic." Sera gritted through clenched teeth.

The small hand on her temple stroked again and the pain receded for a moment. "You do, and a vast reservoir of it, if the amount currently trying to break free is any indication."

Another wave of stabbing pain made her whimper, and a strange glow drew her attention to her hands. Cracks appeared in her skin as she watched, beginning to panic, but instead of blood, it was something golden seeping out, like liquid fireflies. Her hands didn't hurt nearly as much as her head, but they felt tingly as if they'd fallen asleep. The pins and needles sensation spread up her arms, and Sera's heart stuttered into full-blown panic.

"Make it stop. Please," she gasped.

Zee's smile was there and gone in an instant, but she nodded. "I can forge a bond between you and an anchor for your magic. It will allow you to share the power when it begins to overwhelm you."

"An anchor? Another person?" She'd thought the idea of being tied to someone again would be the worst hell, but the tingling had reached her shoulders, and in that moment, she could admit there were worse fates. "Would it be permanent?"

"No. It has to be a willing person, but eventually, you'll learn control and the bond will no longer be necessary."

"Do it," she whispered.

Zee looked past her to Ryan on the edge of the circle, and a look of pain crossed her features so fast that Sera might have imagined it. But Ryan was shaking his head vehemently, and before he could say anything, Jake spoke up from right next to them. Sera hadn't even known he'd moved to stand beside her.

"I'll do it." His hand slid into hers, and she felt the warmth but not the touch.

Zee nodded, then flew to touch their joined hands. A few seconds later a searing heat materialized in Sera's belly.

Jake gasped, but he held tight to her. The pain in her head receded, the cracks closed, and Sera could feel Jake's thumb rubbing across the back of her hand. The tension left her shoulders, and she slumped to her knees. Sera was so exhausted and overwhelmed she almost gave into the temptation to lay down right there in the grass and give up for today.

So that just happened. With her eyes closed, she fervently wished that she'd slept in that morning. Jake rubbed her hand until she straightened and reluctantly opened her eyes.

Instead of Jake, she was face to face with Zee. "You owe us payment."

Sera stood all the way up and glared at the fairy. "Payment?"

Zee's wings fluttered and she flew up until she was still eye level with Sera. "Yes, payment. We've provided you aid, and you'll return the favor. It's our way."

"You summoned me because you needed my help, and now you want me to help you *and* pay you?"

"Don't fight it. She's going to win in the end," said Jake from her other side, still holding her hand tightly.

Sera glared at him and tugged her hand away. "You and I are going to have a very serious discussion about keeping secrets when we get back."

"It wasn't my secret to tell." Jake shrugged.

Sera shook her head. Mind-reading fairies with magical powers were not on her agenda for the day. She'd planned to unpack her stuff, pack up some of Evie's things, cry for a bit, grapple with the big blank space where her future should be, and maybe call her mother back if she was feeling especially masochistic. Instead, magic was real, and now she was anchored in some Fae bond with Jake, her first, and possibly only, love slash hottie neighbor, whom she was trying - albeit thus far unsuccessfully - to avoid. She'd probably still fit the crying in later.

Sera squared her shoulders and focused on Zee again, still hovering in front of her. "What do you want?"

Zee looked a bit cagey. "We have a little problem." She motioned for Ryan to join them looked like she was stalling, having trouble knowing where to start. Sera decided that she'd give the fairy one more minute, but then she was out of there. Sera needed to head back to reality, where she had her own problems to tackle. If Ryan or Jake wanted to stay and play errand boy, good for them. It was nice to have hobbies.

"Evie isn't dead."

Sera's train of thought stopped mid-track. "What?"

"Evie isn't dead," Zee repeated. "She was tricked by a Dark Fae named Torix, who—no, there's too much." She hesitated. "Let's say we're the good guys keeping him trapped and powerless. Only... mistakes were made and now he's significantly less trapped and powerless."

Sera glanced at Jake, then Ryan. They looked as shocked as she felt. It was a lot of new information in a fairly short amount of time. She had no reason to believe Zee, though her own experiences that day tended to support the 'magic is real' part of the explanation.

But the police had found Evie's body outside her house on the front walk. Pretty close to where she and Ryan had been standing earlier. Sera'd been trying not to think about her grandmother dying alone in her front yard. They'd said it was an aneurysm, that she'd gone quickly and with no pain. Per Evie's will, they'd cremated her body and scattered the ashes, all before Sera could make it out to Texas.

"Her doctor identified the body. The dead body. There

was definitely someone dead who looked exactly like my grandmother."

Zee's face softened. "I'm sorry to bring you this news so abruptly, but your grandmother is alive."

Jake wrapped his arm around her shoulder, and Sera leaned into him without thinking. "I'm living in her house. They gave me her house. I couldn't find her coffee this morning, but her creamer was still in the fridge." She shook her head. "Who died?"

"No one."

"But—"

"It was a bit of Fae magic. Not a small bit, mind you. Golems have always been complicated, but we... I... felt it was necessary. Torix was trapped in a tree in this forest many generations ago by my ancestors. Our barriers prevent him or his magic from escaping, but we need to renew them periodically for them to maintain their strength. Once something passes those barriers, there's no way to retrieve it."

"What does that have to do with my grandmother?"

Zee winced. "The renewal was a little delayed, and Torix was able to get her to go through the barriers."

"What was she even doing out here? How do you know her?"

"The same way we know Ryan and Jake. We needed something, so we asked nicely." Ryan snorted and Zee glared at him before continuing. "As for why she was in the way? Only she can answer that in full, but I suspect she was attempting to curb Torix on her own."

Sera's anger surged to life. "You mean you guys screwed up, my grandmother tried to fix it, and instead of helping her, you let her get trapped with a dangerous, magic-wielding dark fairy."

Zee looked a little chagrined. "That's mostly accurate, except also some of Torix's magic escaped while the protections were weakened, and he's infected someone."

"Infected someone? What is wrong with you people?"

Zee ignored her interruption. "Someone, a human, is sharing his magic and doing his bidding. We thought we'd replenished the barriers in time at first, but it's become increasingly obvious that it wasn't fast enough."

"The car accidents?" Jake asked.

"Yes, also the vandalism, and the thefts. We think it's the beginning of something much darker. Torix feeds off of negative emotions. The more his minion can produce and capture for him, the stronger he becomes. We need you to find whomever it is and bring them here so we can break the bond."

Jake nodded, but Sera didn't get it, and Ryan was stubbornly silent.

"Why can't you do it? Summon this person the way you summoned me?"

Zee gestured at the trees around her. "The Wood is an elemental forest, ancient and powerful in its own right. It protects us, but we're forbidden from leaving. It was the pact we made for fleeing our homeland and creating the barriers here."

Sera must have looked confused because Ryan chose that moment to jump in. "And they needed me to touch you to activate the summons."

Sera glared at him. "I'm still not clear on how you're involved."

He shrugged. "It's not relevant or your business."

She pointed at him about to argue, but her hand was glowing. "What in the actual hell." Sera shook her hand like she was trying to put out a match.

Zee sighed again. "I'll teach you some basics before you go so you don't injure others... or yourself. But remember that you'll need Jake to help anchor your magic if you want to do anything beyond the basics."

"How am I supposed to learn anything beyond the basics?"

"You're welcome to ask for help, but it will require further payment. You are, of course, free to test your abilities at your own risk."

Sera pushed herself away from Jake, eager for the first time since she'd driven away from her mom's house. "Fine. Practice with Jake and you teach me some basics. Got it. To be clear before we start, this is a freebie. I won't owe you anything extra after this."

Zee smiled slowly. "You're learning already. Good, and agreed. This is a freebie. I'll teach you two things: how to sense magic, and how to sense people. You may close your eyes if you wish."

Zee waited a moment, but Sera left her eyes open.

"Very well. Let your eyes and mind relax and look inside yourself. Your power lies dormant, and it takes a nudge to wake it up."

Sera had no idea how to nudge her new-found power. Less than five minutes ago it was trying to kill her, so she wasn't entirely sure she wanted to wake it up. Zee raised a brow at her but didn't say anything. Sera narrowed her eyes. The mind-reading thing was getting really annoying.

She tried imagining an internal nudge, like poking herself in the chest, but from the inside. To her surprise, warmth unfurled from her middle and spread out along her limbs.

"Excellent. Now cast it out in the stone circle and see what you feel."

Cast it out. Right. Sera pushed somewhere near her diaphragm and breathed out. Her senses landed on Jake and Zee, but Ryan had stepped back out of the circle. They were distinct presences in her power, and she could feel something else shifting under the surface. When she focused on Jake, heat pulsed in her and she started to blush. Better to focus on Zee.

Sera met her eyes, and Zee nodded. She shifted her focus there, and suddenly, Zee felt completely different. She was infused with a prickly sensation that felt green, as if she were made from fresh leaves in spring. While she was admiring how verdant Zee seemed, Sera let her power creep further past the stones and into the trees unchecked until it ran into something else. Something cold and angry.

Sera recoiled. Her power followed her lead, the feeling shut off abruptly, and her eyes snapped open. She hadn't realized she'd closed them. Her power curled back inside of her, content to sleep some more.

"Well done. You have a natural affinity for searching. That'll come in handy. What you sensed in Jake is between the two of you, but what you sensed in me was my magic."

"It was green." Sera felt weird saying it out loud.

"Magic manifests itself for many people in color. Humans can't see it with their normal vision, but you can be trained to recognize it."

"What if something felt angry with no color?"

"You felt something else?" Zee immediately zipped higher and scanned the trees surrounding them.

"It was an accident. I didn't realize I needed to control where my magic net thing went, so it sort of oozed into the trees."

Zee opened her mouth, hopefully to explain, but a long wolf howl cut her off. Granted, Sera hadn't spent a lot of time in the east Texas woods, but she was pretty sure there weren't supposed to be wolves around. Zee froze, and all the hair stood up on Sera's arms. It felt like a lightning storm was coming in.

"Go," Zee said, and a path appeared in front of them. One second it was trees and brambles, the next everything had shifted to reveal a dirt track extending into the forest.

Jake and Ryan shared a look, and both reached out for her. Jake was faster. He grabbed her wrist and jerked her toward the path. "Always a pleasure, Zee."

Sera dug in her feet and tried to turn back to Zee, but the guys were pulling her forward. "Why summon me? And how do I turn off my freaky glowing arm?"

Zee ignored her questions. "The sprites will protect you in the trod. Don't venture off the path." And with that cryptic message, she disappeared from the circle in a shimmer of light.

The wolf howled closer, and over her shoulder, Sera watched it appear from the shadows on the far side of the clearing. At least waist high on all fours, it had mottled grey fur that stuck up along its back. It skirted the stones, walking around the outside of the clearing along the edge of the trees in a low crouch. Sera could barely hear the growl, but she could see its lips curled back over yellowed fangs. It was the glowing eyes, golden in the sunlight, that finally got her to move on her own. Wolves didn't have glowing eyes.

She shifted her weight and ran, pulling in front of the guys.

The path twisted ahead, and Sera ran through a group of fireflies that exploded into tiny sunbursts. She blinked, but didn't slow her pace. Not fireflies, Zee had called them sprites. If she made it out, she'd have to Google what the hell a sprite was. Or ask Jake, as long as he didn't get himself killed trying to wrestle the wolf into submission to help them escape. *Stupid hero complex.*

Both guys were pounding up the path behind her, but it was only wide enough for one person at a time. She wasn't concerned that she'd hold them up, she'd been a cross-country runner in high school, but a glance back confirmed what she'd suspected. Jake had put himself between Ryan and the wolf. *Insert eye roll here.*

Ryan was huffing, but he was keeping up. An itchy feeling crawled up Sera's spine, so she looked back again. The wolf was definitely chasing them, but it looked like it was keeping pace instead of gaining, and its eyes were locked on Sera. She slowed, and between rapid glances over her shoulder, the wolf slowed too. Sucking in a ragged breath, she shifted off the path and ran parallel through the trees. Ryan passed her, but before Jake could, the wolf shot up through the trees in a burst of speed.

Sera dodged back onto the path in front of Jake, and the wolf slowed back to his previous position. As long as they stayed on the path, it either couldn't or wouldn't get any closer. *Hmm.*

"Sera, stop playing dodge tree and move your ass," Jake called.

He was on her heels, but Sera was eighty percent confident that they were safe. That twenty percent uncertainty kept her running. She wasn't sure she could sprint the entire path out of the forest, and the back of Ryan's neck was turning an unhealthy shade of violet. Maybe he *was* actually a sprinter and not an endurance athlete.

"Have to slow down." Unlike Jake, who didn't sound winded, Sera wanted to conserve her oxygen.

She'd intended to slow to a distance pace, but a pained yell from ahead on her left spiked her adrenaline. Ryan was still a few feet ahead of her, and he was panting too much to yell.

"Sera, help..." It was Evie's voice, and Sera didn't hesitate. She plunged into the woods to her left. After a few steps, the golden light from the path disappeared. To her surprise, she didn't hear heavy footsteps or a wolf crashing through the underbrush after her.

It was a lot darker under the thick canopy without the sprites to light the way. Tall pines and scrub oak let in enough light for thick brambles to grow in whatever clear spaces they could find. Sera pushed through a bush bigger than herself and slid to a stop on loose pine needles.

She'd emerged into another clearing. This one with a giant gnarled oak in the center. The underbrush simply stopped in a circle around it. Sera listened for another call, but the lone sound was her labored breathing.

Why hadn't the wolf chased her and where was her grandmother? The hair on her arms stood up as she noticed the runes carved into the tree. Zee had told her not to leave the path. Sera looked up, but despite there being no other trees nearby, no sunlight shone on the oak. Silence enveloped her. What mistake had she made this time?

Welcome, child.

A shiver skittered down her back. The voice slid into her mind like oil, definitely not Evie. She had a bad feeling she knew who it was. "Where is my grandmother?"

She is with me. We bide our time in small amusements. Did you enjoy my wolf? The glowing eyes were a nice touch I thought. It's been so long since I've tasted fear this close.

"Release her," Sera demanded. Stupid bravery had gotten her this far, she had to try.

Perhaps if I had a better offer. Say, a young divorcee with questionable sanity and trust issues?

"You'd trade my grandmother for me?"

Power begets power, as they say. I'd much rather have you and all your delicious emotions.

A phantom breath wafted across the crease between her shoulder and her neck, like an open-mouthed kiss but bitingly cold. Sera shivered and rubbed the spot warm again.

Your grandmother is resilient, offering me but a sip of fear, a soupçon of despair.

An image of Grandma Evie, dirty and slumped over in the dirt, flashed through her mind, then was gone. Sera's fear urged her to run forward, to offer herself up as sacrifice to protect the only woman who'd accepted her whole. Tears pricked her eyes as she held her feet still.

Ahh, yes. Such lovely anguish. Does this help you choose?

Another feminine grunt of pain echoed in the clearing, and a tear trickled down Sera's face. It would be such a small loss and Evie would be free.

All you need do is step forward to the tree.

His mention of the tree reminded Sera of Zee's warning about the barriers. That once something has passed beyond them it couldn't be brought back. How could he have the power to release her grandmother but not himself?

"You're lying. She's trapped exactly like you are."

The feeling of smug certainty dropped from around her, and the temperature plummeted. Cold anger pushed at her, sliding up her legs and arms to gather around the base of her neck.

The Fae don't lie, and I won't be trapped much longer. Come Samhain, I'll find you myself.

Frigid pressure pushed against her throat and made it hard to breathe. Sera clenched up and tried to suck in air, wishing desperately for warmth, but expecting to eventually black out. Instead, golden glimmers appeared around her and settled against her skin. The sprites seemed to push the threat away, and she could take a full breath again.

From far away, she heard Jake's voice calling her. "Sera, I can't reach you."

She silently thanked the sprites and took a step back, out of the clearing.

3

SERA

REALITY SNAPPED back into place like an elastic band. She could hear birds and wind in the trees, and Jake was standing right in front of her. He grabbed both her shoulders and pulled her against him.

"You run very fast," he said as he gulped in air.

Sera wrapped her arms around his waist and buried her face in his torn shirt, stupidly glad that he was there. "He's torturing my grandmother."

His arms tightened. "Torix?" She nodded into his chest. "We'll get her out."

"Yeah? Are you going to help by taking your shirt off, keeping secrets, and saying nothing?" She pushed away from him.

Jake sighed. "Sometimes you learn more by listening."

Sera's body lit up in a flash of anger. "And what did you learn while listening?"

"That the Fae asked you specifically to bring back the person working with Torix. That Ryan is way more connected than I thought he was. That Zee didn't give you a straight answer about Evie. Really, I learned a lot."

Sera dropped her shoulders in defeat. "Me too. My grandmother isn't dead. Magic is real. Fairies are assholes, and everyone knew about it but me. Speaking of assholes, where's Ryan?"

"I swear he's not usually an asshole. He hightailed it out on the path. That wolf wasn't joking around. As soon as I followed you off the path it lost interest in me, but it sped up after Ryan. He was probably making sure it left us alone." Jake held up a hand. "Before you ask, no, I don't know what that was about. I've never seen a wolf before, and I damn near had a heart attack when you disappeared. Ryan will be fine though. Zee said the path would be safe, and Ryan wouldn't step foot off of it."

"I heard Evie."

"Of course you did."

Her hackles rose, but the warm spot inside her insisted he believed her and wasn't being sarcastic. Instead of snapping at him, she said, "I'm not imagining things. I found Torix's tree, and my grandmother was in there with him. He tried to trick me into joining them."

"Looks like it didn't work, but just in case, what's my middle name?"

Sera thumped him on the shoulder. "Leslie, because your mom was obsessed with regency romances. Take this seriously." She snickered.

Jake rolled his eyes, but slid his hand down her arm and linked their fingers. "I am, and I believe every word you've said. I could feel you in the woods, but I couldn't find you. At some point, we're going to have to talk about what Zee did to us." He leaned forward and touched his forehead to hers.

Sera jolted back at how intimate that felt, but also at the

words he used. They were so close to the ones in her head. "I don't see why that's necessary."

"Well, I couldn't sense you before Zee did her magic hands, but now there's this internal GPS that won't turn off. Also, your hand is glowing again." He held up their joined hands, and sure enough, hers was giving off a faint golden light.

"Dammit," she muttered.

"C'mon, I'll walk you home and you can yell at me some more about it there."

She wasn't sure how much more of the weird stuff she could handle, and Jake seemed to sense that. He kept a firm grip on her hand, even though she tried to pull free, and started talking about some of the people she'd known before. Sera tried to hold onto her anger, but it faded as he walked with her through the woods. For a while at least, she could pretend that everything was normal and her biggest worry was keeping Jake at arm's length. He chattered about his parents living their best life in Europe, his little sister blowing off college, his construction business. Nothing about the Fae or people-eating trees or magical paths through the forest. She could still see the sprites blinking at the edge of her sight, but there was no trail to speak of. Only pretty lights under the long shadows of the trees.

Shadows, she realized with a jolt, that fell in the wrong direction if they were headed back to her house.

Sera pulled Jake to a stop. "The light is wrong."

"I know."

"*What* do you know?"

Jake sighed. "Fine, you'll figure it out soon enough. Time works differently in the fairy trods. Their words, not mine. It's probably right around sundown now."

"We were in the woods for a full day?"

"Sort of. A day's worth of time passed, but I'd say we were tromping around for an hour and a half or so. Maybe two hours tops." He tugged until she started moving again.

"I think I must be in shock because at this point I'm accepting every weird thing you tell me."

"And letting me lead you to your doom." He cackled evilly.

"That's not funny."

"It's totally funny." He looked her over, and his eyes turned serious. "You're taking this pretty well actually."

"I've been plagued by strange occurrences my whole life. While this is by far the strangest, at least it finally offered an explanation for the rest of them."

They walked out of the woods two doors up from where they'd gone in. When Sera looked, she couldn't see any sign of the trod, but then again, the sun was dropping behind the houses shrouding everything in darkness.

Jake stopped short of the road. His house was closer, but he was staring at hers. A new car had replaced Ryan's in her driveway. Clearly, it was a day for visitors. A man stood on her porch, and though she couldn't make out his face, she knew it was pinched in annoyance. Will hated waiting for anything except himself.

The air wasn't really chilly, it was Texas after all, but Sera shivered as the sun set. It had been one hell of a day, and her ability to deal with any more bullshit was down to nothing. She hadn't given Will her new address, hadn't even told him she was moving out of her mom's place. Fifteen hundred miles wasn't enough to get away from him apparently.

"Someone you know?"

"Yes." Sera belatedly realized Jake was still holding her hand and drew away. He let her this time. She'd gotten so used to the warmth of him that the cool air against her palm felt strange.

"You want me to come along?"

"No."

"Now who's talkative."

Sera raised a brow at him. "Don't think you're getting off easy. I appreciate the reprieve, but when I'm done dealing with Will, you and I are going to have a real discussion."

Jake watched her with knowing eyes. "You don't have to do everything yourself, you know."

"This is none of your business."

"What if I want it to be my business?"

"We don't always get what we want."

He looked at her porch again, then nodded. "Fine. Come over after for dinner and a beer, and we'll talk."

"Okay, but no stuff about magical bonds or things that happened seven years ago. And I'm not staying out late, I'm already wiped."

Jake saluted and marched back to his mower. She noticed he didn't agree to her conditions, but she also had no intention of giving up or running away this time, and they'd have to talk about their past at some point. He also had volumes more knowledge about the Fae than she did, and it was time she was brought up to speed. There were plenty of things Jake had that she wanted, but she had to be careful not to offer more than she was willing to give. Friendship, yes, but she had a feeling he'd like more than that.

Sera squared her shoulders and blew out a breath. Will first, then Jake.

The mower roared to life as she made her way home. She could feel Jake watching her as he circled the yard again. Will spotted her as she walked past Jake's mailbox and onto her property. He stayed where he was, slouched against a pillar on the porch, but his face smoothed into a look of worry rather than annoyance. His grey suit was rumpled, and anyone who didn't know him would probably find it disarming. She knew better than to believe any image he presented.

"Sera, there you are. I've been waiting for hours. I was getting worried you'd had another episode."

She figured today could be called that. "So you thought you'd loiter on my porch?"

He straightened up and fixed his tie. "Is that any way to greet your husband?"

"You're not my husband. You're not my friend. Get off my property."

"Wouldn't you like to know why I'm here?"

"No. Go away." She climbed the steps past him as the porch light came on. There was a subtle glow inside the window, and Sera wondered if sprites could turn lights on and off. Will moved into her space, and whether it was sprites or a timer, all that mattered was she was no longer standing in the dark with him.

"Why don't we go inside and talk like adults?" His tone was tender, but Sera could hear the annoyance underneath. He didn't wait for her to answer, just crowded her out of his way and turned to open her door. The doorknob twisted smoothly under his hand, but the door wouldn't budge.

Sera knew she hadn't left it locked and silently cursed herself for not taking such a basic precaution. It wasn't something she'd forget again, especially since Will now knew where she lived. He jerked the knob a few times, then tried shoving it with his shoulder. No luck, and Sera couldn't help her smile. She guessed sprites could lock doors as well as turn on lights.

Score one for the sprites.

Will blew out a frustrated breath and turned on her. "You think this is funny?" The gentle concern was gone, revealing the anger she'd known was there.

"Yes, and if you don't leave in the next thirty seconds, I'm calling the police."

She was out of practice, but after Torix, Will seemed small and pathetic. Although, he *was* still bigger than her, and she'd forgotten not to stand too close. His hand wrapped around her upper arm, and he pulled her against him. Pain that was too familiar shot through her shoulder, and she had to fight down the fear that was threatening to take over.

"You're still my wife, papers or no, and the police will believe what I tell them. That you got confused, just like before." He glanced at the house then shook her hard enough to rattle her teeth. "You never could listen. I have documents that give me half of your inheritance from your grandmother. We weren't officially divorced when she died, so it's legally mine. You're going to sign them, then you're going to get your ass in the car and we're going to go to a nice dinner. If we can even find a decent restaurant in this backwoods hell hole."

Sera gritted her teeth. Evie had died five weeks ago, and the final divorce papers had come about the same time. She really should have paid better attention, but there was no way he was getting his hands on Evie's house.

"Kiss my ass, Will." She was seconds away from kicking him in the balls when Jake shouted from the yard.

"Hey! Get your hands off her."

Will's grip loosened. Sera pulled her arm back and took a couple of big steps away from him. It was kind of reminiscent of the scene that morning. Before the world had gone crazy. Jake leapt up the three steps, and Sera put both hands on his chest to keep him from going right at Will.

"Jake, calm down." A part of her shriveled at being reduced to pacifying someone's anger again. She braced for Jake to push past her and take a swing at Will, but he shifted his focus. His blazing eyes met hers and he lifted a hand to brush his thumb across her cheek.

"Are you alright?"

Sera nodded as his hand slid down her neck, leaving tingles in its wake. Her arm throbbed, but she barely noticed it. Her adrenaline was hyped up for a battle, and instead of the thrill of finally fighting back, she was wrestling with her attraction to Jake. Something she'd been sure she'd purged years ago.

Will cleared his throat, and they broke eye contact. Jake stepped between her and Will, who was still standing at her door. Sera hadn't noticed before, but Jake looked big standing in front of Will's more academic build. *Huh.*

"The lady asked you to leave," Jake was deceptively calm.

Will gave him a small smile that didn't reach his eyes. "You misunderstood. We're in the middle of a discussion, and Sera can sometimes get hot-headed." He looked past Jake to address Sera directly. "We can finish this later. I have other business here anyway. Enjoy your dalliance. It'll be worth it to watch you crawl back to me."

Sera's eyes narrowed, and Jake kept himself between them, turning with Will as he strode past them and down the front path without a second glance.

She liked to think he would have left even if Jake hadn't intervened, and without calling the police, but experience said it was unlikely. It wasn't until Will's car started and he drove away that Sera's shoulders relaxed.

"That's twice now I've had to ask a man to take his hands off you today," Jake said.

Sera's racing heart was returning to normal and with it came exhaustion. "Guess I'm just popular."

"Was that your ex-husband?"

She ran a hand through her tangled hair. "Yes. He has a problem respecting personal space. Or people in general."

"Sounds like a real piece of work. What was your plan if I hadn't been here?"

The question sounded like basic curiosity, but Sera heard the undertone of scolding. She wasn't about to be accosted by one man then berated about it by another. "It doesn't matter, does it? You were here to play the mighty hero. Thanks for that, by the way, but next time mind your own damn business. I can take care of myself."

His eyebrows shot up. "Yeah, you really looked like you had it handled. I should let him toss you around then? Maybe more? Didn't know you were into that kind of thing. My apologies."

"Don't be a dick. There are more options besides damsel in distress or kinky sex games."

Jake threw his hands in the air. "I was trying to help."

"I didn't ask you to help. I'm not a child."

His gaze trailed down her body, lingered on her curves, her lips, then settled on her face. "I'm well aware of that fact, Sera."

Sera was angry and tired, but his gaze left fire in its wake. Where Will had been predatory and possessive, Jake was caring and appreciative, and that made all the difference. That and the magic that bound them together. She should have asked Zee for more details about the effects of the bond, but one thing was clear. It gave her a one hundred percent accurate reading on Jake's intentions.

They were both still for a moment. The sprites twinkled around them on the porch. Wind rustled the trees in the pregnant silence. They were on the edge of something, and it wouldn't take much to fall over.

"I have to be able to take care of myself. You won't always be around." Her voice sounded husky. She was pleading, but she wasn't sure what for.

Jake moved closer. Sera stepped back until she bumped against the door, but Jake didn't stop until he was directly in front of her, standing in her space. She wondered if the bond told him how much she liked it the way it told her how much he was trying to hold back.

He shook his head. "It hasn't always been that way. There was a time I would have followed you to the end of the Earth."

"That was years ago, things change."

Sera caught her breath as he gingerly lifted her arm and looked at the finger-sized bruises blooming there. "I can see that." His thumb caressed the skin above her elbow. "You've always been fiercely independent, but I wish I'd gotten here sooner all the same."

Sera never realized her elbow could be so sensitive. It had never failed before, so why should it be any different now? Give them five minutes alone together, and they'd have their hands on each other.

She wanted him. Sera didn't want to, but she did. It was stupid not to admit it when the bond wouldn't let them hide. He crowded her against the door, both of them breathing hard, and all she knew was need. She wanted his hands on her, his mouth, his body. It had been a long time since she'd felt this way. Maybe not since their last night together before she'd run.

Jake let go of her arm and put both palms flat on the

door on either side of her. He dropped his head down and took a couple of careful deep breaths. Sera clenched her fists to keep from grabbing him, but his scent surrounded her. His mouth was inches above hers, all she had to do was tilt her face up.

"I missed you." Jake's admission whispered through to the heart of her.

She tilted.

Her lips met his and sparked an explosion of movement. His hands slid into her hair and held her head still as he demanded entrance to her mouth. Her arms circled around his waist, fingers digging into the cotton on his back, and she opened for him. He tasted like she remembered, like cinnamon gum and home. Sera made a noise deep in her throat, and he lifted her thighs to brace her against the door. She wrapped her legs around his hips and arched into him.

Jake's lanky body had changed into broad shoulders and lean muscles, and Sera couldn't get enough. She was frustrated by the layers of clothes between them, and groaned in approval when his hands slipped under her shirt. Her legs tightened as his calluses caught her skin, his thumbs rubbing along the bottom edge of her bra.

She squeaked as the door swung open behind her. They fell inward, but Jake shifted at the last second and took the brunt of the fall against the hardwood floor. His chest shook underneath her, and Sera realized he was laughing. The moment was broken, but she was strangely content to lie on top of him in the foyer.

"Never a dull moment around here."

"I swear that door was locked when Will tried to open it."

"Your house is infested with sprites."

"I didn't realize they could make things happen in the real world."

"They're magic. Only the Fae know what they can really do. Then again, they might be limited to opening doors."

Sera laughed. "Think they'll close the door for us too?"

With one quick movement, Jake flipped her under him, and her laughter faded at the look in his eyes. That was all it took to reignite the fire. His body covered hers from ankle to chest, and she could feel his hardness pressing against her center. They were both teetering again, but now neither seemed eager to push it further.

He trailed his fingers down her neck, and she shivered. "I always loved this spot on your collarbone." His hair tickled her face as he laid a soft kiss on the place his fingers had vacated.

"And the spot under your ear that makes you moan." Another kiss. She pressed her lips together to keep from making the noise he'd known would happen.

"And—"

She stopped him with her fingers against his lips. If he kept going, she was going to regret it. "This is too much. I haven't even been back a day, and it feels like everything and nothing has changed. I've only been divorced for a little over a month, and I'm not the same person I was before. We don't actually know anything about each other anymore. I... I need some time."

He kissed her fingertips, and she let her hand fall back to her chest. "Okay."

Relief and disappointment washed over her in equal measure. Most of it was hers, but some of it was his too. "I think you need time as much as I do," she whispered.

"Maybe. You're right that this is going at breakneck speed, but it doesn't matter if I know this version of you or not. If you need me, I will always be there for you. You tell me when you're ready."

Sera knew he was waiting for some kind of answer. He wanted a clear sign of how to move forward. It was so tempting to give in to Jake. To not have to fight for a little bit. She'd lost years of her life being told she was incompetent, weak, crazy. Then pills had kept her foggy and compliant during her last bit of time with Will. In the end, she'd clawed her way back to herself, and it terrified her to give any of that kind of power to another person again.

There was barely a breath between them, but Sera couldn't make herself cross the distance. "I need you to go home, Jake."

"Okay." He brushed his lips against hers, once, twice, then levered himself up.

Sera propped up on her elbows. She couldn't leave it at that. "You still owe me an explanation."

He grinned. "You still owe me a dinner."

"What? You invited me!"

He kept on grinning as he walked out. The door shut soundly after him, and the lock clicked into place. Sera stared at the spot where he'd disappeared for one more moment, then flopped back on the floor, arms spread eagle, and blew a lock of hair out of her face. Tiny golden glimmers fluttered around. Sera shook her head. The sprites were clearly going to be trouble, but at least they had good taste in men.

JAKE

JAKE'S SMILE lasted well after he crossed the lawn back to his place, well after dinner and the dishes. Even well into a show he turned on but didn't feel like watching. His mind circled around and back to Sera. Always Sera.

In frustration, he turned off the tv and tossed the remote onto the coffee table. He was too wired to sleep, but he didn't want to bother Ryan for a second night in a row to talk about what Ryan would probably just call his 'lady troubles.' Besides, he had to teach in the morning and was most likely sleeping off the afternoon. Apparently, it took being chased by a wolf for Ryan to add some endurance when he ran.

The sprites were gathering near the window facing Sera's house again. He didn't know why they didn't go over there instead of hovering in his place. According to Ryan, sprites didn't do anything beyond appear and float around like moths. But it definitely seemed like they'd opened the door earlier, and he could have sworn they were laughing at him and Sera sprawled on the floor of her entryway.

That had been some quality sprawling.

Jake blew out a breath and headed to the garage. If nothing else, he could work on his side gig. He'd taken over the woodworking shop from his dad long before they'd left for Europe. The man was brilliant at construction, but his art was terrible. Jake's was much better, at least that's what his clients seemed to think.

The garage was meticulous. His dad may have taught him the woodworking skills, but his mom had instilled a sense of order and cleanliness that had somehow missed his sister completely. There were several projects in various stages of completeness tucked away in bins under the counter, but Jake wasn't feeling any of those. He wanted something new.

He ran his hand along a piece of mahogany the same color as Sera's hair that he'd been saving for something special. Maybe a Celtic knot around a dragon. Or a phoenix. He'd seen the tattoo peeking out from under the shoulder of Sera's tank top. It was something new.

Before he had a chance to do much more than gather his tools, his phone rang. His heart sped up, but it wasn't Sera calling him back over. His mom's number flashed on the screen.

Jake squinted at the clock, 10:48 pm in Texas, so... really stupid early in Norway, but his mom had always been up with the sun. He wondered how she was dealing with a place where the sun never went down.

"Hey Mom, what's up?"

"I saw the most marvelous thing."

"Another moose?"

"No, honey. Although that would also be marvelous."

"I'd really prefer if you stayed away from the moose, Mom."

"Noted, but they're really very gentle creatures."

Jake rubbed his eyes with his free hand. "Don't make me have another talk with Dad about boundaries. It feels super weird."

"I'm not sure when you forgot that we're *your* parents, not the other way around, but we can handle ourselves."

"I know. What'd you see?"

"A troll!"

Jake shouldn't have been surprised. His mom was essentially a fairy-tale princess, attracting all kinds of animals and potentially mythical creatures. Considering the afternoon he'd just had, he wasn't sure he should discount that she'd actually seen a troll. If trolls were going to be anywhere, he'd bet they'd be in Norway. It was something he'd have to ask Zee about the next time he saw her.

He belatedly tuned back into the conversation that his mom had continued without him. "—said it was a mossy rock, but I knew better. Your dad told him, and now we're staying in Oslo for another couple of weeks with this adorable couple at their Airbnb. She says they've been together for fifty-six years, started going steady in upper secondary, that's high school for us. It made me think of you and Sera your senior year. I heard she's moved back to town." She paused for a breath, but Jake wasn't fast enough. "And she's single, no kids. It's such a shame. A sweet girl like that, well I guess she's a woman now isn't she, but a woman like her should have a family to wrap her in love."

"You're not subtle, Mom."

"All I'm saying is she's had it rough. Her sorry excuse for a mother..."

"Last I heard she was a successful lawyer."

"Yes, but a terrible mother. It was so obvious before that she was love-deprived. Sera, not her mom. She soaked it up like a sponge. A love sponge."

"Please don't ever say that again, Mom. I'm begging you."

She ignored him. "It was too bad she had to leave Evie and go back to that harpy."

"I'm sensing a story here that has nothing to do with Sera."

There was a shuffle on the other end of the line. "No one was ever good enough for that woman. Not even her daughter." Jake could hear her tsking in the background, but then she changed tacks. "I was so sorry to hear about Evie's passing. She was such a beautiful soul. Will you give Sera my condolences?"

"Yeah, I will." Evie was a force for good on everyone she

met. Jake shook his head. They had to find a way to free her from Torix. "She asked about you, by the way."

"Of course she did. She's a good girl, and she'll make a wonderful mother."

Jake groaned. "Not this again, Mom. I'm only twenty-five. I have plenty of time to make babies later."

"You're right. You should focus on your relationship with Sera first. Make a strong foundation, then babies."

Jake groaned again for his mother's benefit, but rubbed at the mild ache in his chest. He'd felt pulled to Sera before the binding, but now it was a physical sensation. "There's nothing going on between Sera and me."

"Mm-hmm. This is my skeptical voice, just so you know. I remember you two before. You thought you were so sneaky, but a mother knows."

"I don't want to talk about my sex life with you, Mom. Besides, she's been back a day. I think I can afford to give her time to at least unpack before I propose and attempt to fill her with grandbabies."

"Don't take too long, you're not getting any younger."

Oh my god, seriously? Time for a subject change.

"I think maybe Maddie is seeing someone," Jake blurted.

I'm a bad person.

His mom gasped. "She told you that? For how long? Do you know him? Is it a him? You know I've never been entirely sure with Maddie."

Jake pinched the bridge of his nose, then sank down into his work chair and made random circles on his notepad. "I'm pretty sure she's into guys, but now that you mention it, we've never directly talked about it." It didn't matter who his sister loved, but she was his *baby* sister, so he made an abrupt one-eighty from that line of thought. "She didn't actually *tell* me she was dating, but she's been happier than usual. You know how she gets. And she's been over mooching food a lot less."

"It's not mooching. We told her she would always be welcome at the house."

"It's my house now, Mom, and my food. She always goes for the good stuff. I've had to start hiding the steaks."

"Pssh, she'd never go through the effort of making a steak."

Jake snorted. "Okay, yeah, but I have to hide the chocolate...and lasagna." He added bitterly.

She laughed. "Now, that I believe."

Jake was silent for a moment as that made him think about belief and all the stuff Zee had said this afternoon. He'd learned not to trust the Fae to be straight, but the incident with Sera and the binding made things pretty fucking serious.

"Do you need us to come back?" His mom was way too perceptive.

"What? No," he barked, then tried to soften the abruptness. "Besides, I don't want you to miss the igloo light thing you have planned next month."

She hesitated. "It *was* non-refundable, but my children always come first. Are you sure? I can feel that there's something..."

"Please stay in Norway, Mom." He needed her far away from Mulligan if things didn't go well with the Fae. On second thought, maybe he should send Maddie to her. Bonus, Maddie would hate Norway.

"Okay, we'll stick with our schedule. For now, anyway. Anything else to report?"

Jake flipped through the pages of swirls and lied to his mother. "Nope. Everything's great."

"Well get some sleep, honey. I'll try to call again next week. We love you."

"Love you too, Mom."

It was easier to lie when she couldn't see his face, but she was usually able to figure him out anyway. He tossed the pad back on the counter and picked up the wood. Maybe he was getting better at lying? He started sketching a phoenix in the center and tried to shake off the feeling that he'd been lying to more than just his mom.

4

SERA

SERA OPENED her eyes to a blinding light and quickly shut them again. Either there was a sprite sitting on her face or the sun had already reached her windows. She groaned. That meant it was afternoon and she'd slept all day.

She flipped over and checked her phone on the night-stand. 4:03. Late afternoon then. Her stomach growled aggressively, and she realized that she'd failed to eat the day before. After Jake had left, her energy levels had dropped to nothing. She'd crawled up the stairs and into bed, where she'd proceeded to have dreams alternating between happy naked time with Jake and fighting off a tiny evil fairy that looked like Will with a flyswatter.

It wasn't quite a nightmare, she'd have loved to squash him flat, but Torix's voice kept echoing her mind. *Come Samhain, I'll find you myself.* She shivered, not entirely sure it had only been a dream. And what the hell was Samhain?

She dressed in her last set of clean clothes, brushed her teeth, and pulled her long hair back in a ponytail before she admitted that she wanted to linger on the sexy Jake dreams. Seven years had changed a lot, but not her body's reaction to him. Will paled in comparison in every single way, and Sera was feeling bitter about each wrong decision she'd made that had led her to him. Nothing like trusting someone to take care of you then having them turn around and drug you into compliance. And while it wasn't the same, being bound to Jake almost against her will was rubbing her the wrong way.

Now that she knew the truth about magic, she wondered if the Fae had been punishing her. The glimmers she'd tried to explain had been sprites, and it seemed some people could see them and some people thought she was crazy. She was unclear if it was the sprite or the person who decided what was visible. The idea that magic was real... well, it hadn't truly sunk in yet. It was all so far-fetched that she wanted to ignore the whole thing. Mundane issues like breakfast and coffee jumped well above learning to turn mice into horses or whatever magic was good for.

Halfway down the stairs, Sera remembered that there was no coffee in the house. True punishment at its finest.

A look out the window confirmed that Jake's truck was gone from his driveway. The mower was put away, and his yard looked more or less finished. There were a couple of sections that were significantly shorter in a circular pattern. She guessed that was from him trying to keep an eye on her and Will. There went her brilliant plan of begging Jake for coffee. Maybe it was time to venture into town. She needed to get some food besides coffee anyway.

WILSON MARKET WAS STILL the de facto place to get groceries. Mrs. Wilson nearly threw her back out pulling Sera into a hug when she tried to check out, and Mr. Wilson insisted on carrying her bags to her car. She smiled when he suggested she come out for dinner, but didn't commit. Who knew how long it would take to deal with Zee's assignment.

The sun was already setting behind the one-story buildings that surrounded the square when she pulled into Rosie's Pizzeria. Cheerful lights blinked in the window as the businesses started rolling up their awnings for the evening. Normal lights, not the sprites she'd gotten used to seeing everywhere. Glimmers had followed her around the market, the liquor store, through the single stoplight, and gathered in the square behind her, but none ventured into Rosie's. *Huh.*

She'd managed to avoid thinking about naked Jake for the last two and a half hours, but she couldn't avoid that she'd sort of promised him dinner. Seven years ago, they'd spent a lot of time at Rosie's. As far as they could tell, no one named Rosie had ever worked there, but they made the best New York pizza in Texas.

It hadn't taken long for the news to get around that Evie's granddaughter was back in town because Jim Hogan wasn't surprised in the least to see her in the restaurant. He rang up her regular without asking, and threw in a slice of her favorite cheesecake as a welcome back present. It was almost like no time had passed at all.

Back at the house, she put away the groceries while cleaning out the expired stuff. It brought up vivid memories of doing the same thing with Evie. Two days ago, all she'd wanted was to settle into her grandmother's house and start a new life for herself. She wasn't sure what she was going to do for a job once the trust ran out, but she'd always found something. Waitressing, temp work, retail...anything that didn't require a commitment. College hadn't worked out for her, but she was smart and organized, and she'd be a valuable employee. Especially now that she knew she wasn't crazy.

It was supposed to be simple. House, job, future. She hadn't considered Jake, or Will, or a town that didn't forget, or magical forest creatures with ulterior motives, or Evie. *Or Evie.*

Sera stilled. More than anything else, she wanted to rescue Evie. The best way she could see to do that was to learn as much about magic as she could... and figure out a loophole that a powerful Fae hadn't been able to come up with in generations, with magic that she couldn't learn or use on her own. *Suuure. No problem.*

Guess it's time to confront Jake.

Armed with a six-pack and a steaming pizza box that smelled like heaven, Sera crossed her yard toward Jake's house. If he was nice, she'd consider sharing her cheesecake with him. The traitorous part of her brain insisted it would be a lot more fun if he was naughty, and now she desperately wished she'd only had nightmares the night before.

Sera half expected him to answer the door shirtless, but he was in jeans and a dark tee that made it hard for her to look away from his brown eyes. He leaned against the doorjamb and crossed his arms. Relaxed was his default, but his smile looked distracted.

She held up the pizza box. "Dinner, as demanded."

Jake's grin widened. "Rosie's." She could see the effort it took to put away whatever was bothering him as he stepped back and motioned her in.

Not much had changed. The couch was new, as was the big flat-screen over the mantel, but it looked like his parents had left most of their stuff behind when they left for Europe. She guessed he hadn't even noticed. It seemed both of them were living steeped in the past.

"To be clear, I'm always grateful for pizza, but what made you head out to Rosie's?" Jake asked as he led the way to the kitchen.

Sera put the food and beer on the table and went looking for plates. "I was already in town, and I figured why not."

Jake sat down and pulled out the first slice. "Ah, beautiful, it's been too long."

Sera's head jerked around, but he wasn't talking to her. He was chewing with his eyes closed, lost in cheesy bliss. A warm feeling spiked through her. *Now is not the time.* Sera tried to convince her traitorous body.

The dishes were where she remembered them, in the cabinet next to the fridge. She grabbed a glass of water before heading to the table in the hopes it would cool her down. He'd already finished his first piece and was halfway through his second when she finally joined him.

"I have questions I want you to answer."

Jake swallowed and stole her water glass to take a swig. "For this, I'll tell you every secret I have."

"Why didn't you tell me before?" Her voice broke on the last word. It wasn't the question she'd intended to ask, but her brain had spit it out without warning.

For the first time since he'd opened the door, his eyes locked on hers. "Zee is very specific about who knows about the Fae. I agreed not to share their secret, and then I couldn't. If I tried, my mouth stayed closed. Literally. You felt their magic. You know how hard it is to fight it."

"I guess I'm on the approved list now. How did you find out?"

His lips tipped up. "They needed a builder. I can't say more than that."

"What about Ryan?"

"What about him?"

"How did he get involved? Why did they send him after me instead of you? How well do you know him?"

Jake put a slice of pizza on her plate. "Eat. I've known Ryan since high school. He moved to town not too long after you left. Smart guy, real into computers. Solid. He once defended Maddie against some meatheads on the football team."

Sera blew on her pizza before taking a bite. "You were on the football team."

He shrugged. "That's how I knew they were meatheads. Anyway, it was impressive since they had at least sixty pounds on him each, but he talked them down and walked away with Maddie. Far as I know, they never even tried to retaliate."

"Must have been nice for Maddie."

He pushed his plate away after a third slice. Not that he'd ever slowed down enough to use it. "Yeah, although I was never convinced she didn't start messing with those guys first. I don't know when Ryan found out about Zee, but they've definitely called him in for tech support before."

"Support for what?"

"Wi-Fi, the time I knew about. You'll have to ask Ryan if you want more info than that. Or Zee, but she's really good at telling you what she wants you to know and nothing more. As for why they sent him, I have no idea."

Sera opened her mouth to argue but he held up a hand. "I really don't. I don't even have a guess. I've seen a summons exactly once before, and it involved Mr. Hogan.

Honestly, I think they wanted pizza delivery, and you know how he feels about that."

"That... makes a disturbing amount of sense. You think we can trust Ryan?"

"Yes." Jake crossed his arms again and leaned back in his chair. "What else?"

Sera chewed silently for a moment, then swallowed. *Now or never.* "You let me go. It hadn't been twenty-four hours, you abandoned me for a whole day, and then you didn't even try to call."

"What?" Jake leaned forward and braced his arms on his thighs. "That's bullshit, Sera. As I remember it, I left you a note, spent the day walking on air at pre-season practice, and the next day when I came home from work, you'd moved away. No goodbye, nothing." He laughed without any humor. "I did call. I even tried to follow you. I got your mom's address from Evie and planned to drive out there in my shitty old Corolla one weekend. My parents thought I was crazy. Evie convinced me I should at least call first. I was dying to talk to you, but your mom answered. She wouldn't let me talk to you and told me in no uncertain terms that if I showed up she'd have me arrested."

Sera shook her head. "What? It wasn't—"

"I was going to come anyway." Jake reached over and took one of her hands, playing with her fingers. "But something she said finally stopped me. You were having nightmares. You'd wake up screaming my name, terrified. I'd bust through a thousand doors to get to you if you needed me, but I wasn't going to be the reason you were afraid."

She remembered those nights. Those dreams. She'd been reliving her last night in town, what she remembered of it. The night with Maddie that she'd never told him about. All these years he'd thought she was afraid of him, but he was only partly right. The dreams had terrified her, not because she was afraid *of* him, but because they'd all ended with Jake dead.

"I was never afraid of you." Jake looked away but she gripped his fingers until he met her eyes. "Never."

"Then what? What happened, Sera?"

She took a deep breath, but the kitchen was closing in on her, so she got up to pace the length of the room. "I can't talk about it because I don't remember most of it. Every time I try, I panic. My mom thought something was wrong with me since I was having panic attacks about nothing as far as she could tell. She convinced me I was sick. That I couldn't handle things myself, and I needed her to help me." Tears choked her. "I tried college, but Mom never let me get far away, then Will..."

Sera sank back into her chair, all her muscles tensing up. "Evie took my side. She said it didn't matter if I remembered anything, and she didn't care what I did or didn't see. She believed I wasn't delusional. But I wasn't here with her, I was stuck there. I owe Evie every scrap of confidence and love in me."

Her shoulders dropped. "And now in the end, it looks like my mom was right. Will was right. I can't handle this myself. I have no idea how to help her. I don't even know where to start."

Jake leaned forward again and grabbed her hand. "You don't have to handle this yourself. I know we'll find a way to get her out."

"How could you possibly know?" Sera's breath was coming in quick gasps. "You don't know what I'm capable of, even Zee said I wouldn't be able to use my magic on my own. How useless is that? What if Evie's stuck in that horrible tree until he kills her for real?" Sera couldn't get enough air. Her heart was pounding and black spots danced in front of her eyes.

Jake scooped her out of her chair and carried her into the living room. Tears started to fall as she tried to calm down. He settled them on the couch with her in his lap and leaned back until she was mostly laying on top of him.

"Breathe," he said. "I've got you. Breathe."

He took a deep breath, and she followed. Some of the tightness in her chest receded. Another breath and the black spots went away. They continued to breathe deeply in sync together for long moments.

She hadn't always had panic attacks. They'd started after she'd left Mulligan, then as time passed, they'd stopped happening. After her marriage, they returned. She'd try to take initiative with a work function or a dinner, and Will would intercede. He'd take over, and she'd be relegated to arm candy. Even something as simple as picking out her clothes became a battle. Nothing she chose was ever good enough. Then the pills.

After that, it had been easy to let him take control of everything. She'd floated along for months before she'd realized she couldn't remember what she'd done the day before. The week before. Her whole life was a blur. She was embarrassed it had taken her so long to realize he was drugging her. Then she'd wanted nothing but out.

Her body calmed, pressed against Jake's, taking deep breaths together. She'd forgotten the strength he offered. Not to take over, but to support and give her a place to rest when she needed it. The freedom was a balm to her soul.

Her cheek rested against his shoulder. Tucked into his lap, she let her body relax and her eyes close. His hand rubbed up and down her back, but never ventured into more interesting territory. Sera was both grateful and disappointed. She breathed him in. Warmth and wood and cotton. *There it was again. Home.*

"Just like old times, huh?" he said.

"Yeah, except your parents aren't pretending to sleep upstairs, my grandmother isn't peeking out the window, and Maddie isn't in her room watching tv way too loud to cover for us."

"And I'm wearing a shirt."

"That *is* weird."

His chest moved under her cheek as he chuckled. "I can take it off if it makes you feel better."

"Mm-hmm, because you know I always feel better when you're naked."

"Half-naked."

"I think the distinction is unnecessary."

"Maybe, but I didn't hear you denying it. You want me half-naked."

"And that's my cue to get off the couch, away from you and your wandering hands."

Jake squeezed her gently, holding her in place. "Stay. I promise to keep my hands G-rated."

"Not to yourself?"

"If you're lying on me, my hands are going to be on you." His fingers flicked her shirt up so he could trail them up her bare back. "Where is up to you."

Her skin burned where he touched her. She'd never realized her back was so sensitive. Elbow, back, maybe it was just him. He stopped before reaching her bra and splayed his hand. She didn't move. Didn't breathe.

Warmth rushed up her neck into her face. She wanted him to keep going. Wanted to take the easy road and follow where he led. His hand moved, but away from where she wanted it. A whimper escaped, and he pulled her shirt back into place and settled his hand at the small of her back. Completely G-rated.

Frustrated and defiant, she turned her head, brushing her lips against his collarbone. It was his turn to suck in a breath. It was probably a terrible mistake, but Sera wasn't ready to stop yet. He wanted her to decide? *Done.*

Another brush and his arm tightened around her. She pressed a kiss to his neck and felt his racing pulse. It had always been this way with Jake. One touch and she was lost.

Or maybe found.

Sera levered herself up to see his face, seating herself more firmly in his lap. His eyes blazed, but he waited. It was her choice to leave or stay, and he'd been almost right.

She didn't want him half-naked, she wanted him whole-naked.

Her smile grew as she slid her hands up his chest, taking his shirt with them. He leaned forward, flexing those glorious abs, and reached back to help pull his shirt over his head.

"Told you," he said.

Sera laughed and smacked his bare shoulder. "Keep talking and I'll take my toys – I mean cheesecake – and go home."

He tossed his shirt somewhere, and made better use of his hands by sliding them into her hair. She leaned forward to kiss him, but he stopped her. "Be sure, Sera."

For once, everything in her was in agreement. He was taut underneath her, muscles hard from holding himself still, but his hands were gentle on her face. There was no more panic or fear, only scorching anticipation for a man that should always have been hers.

Sera covered his hands in hers and met his lips.

One moment, she was dragging her hands down his

chest to his pants, the next he'd rolled her beneath him. His weight settled between her thighs and she moaned. There were too many clothes between them. She tried to unsnap his jeans, but he gathered both of her hands in his and lifted them above her head. His mouth left hot streaks down her neck where he lingered.

"Jake..." She didn't know what she was asking for.

His mouth immediately came back to hers. She arched up, pressing against his hardness, and tried to tug her hands free. She wanted to touch him. She wanted to see if what she remembered lived up to reality.

Jake groaned.

In the back of her mind, Sera heard a jingling noise and thought she should probably focus on it, but Jake had let go of her hands and there were much more interesting things to focus on. She curled a leg around Jake's hip, and the front door slammed open.

Sera yelped and shoved Jake off of her, sitting up. He hit the rug as Maddie flounced in and kicked the door closed behind her.

"Hey bro. Sorry, didn't think you'd be busy." She hadn't changed much. Her dark hair was longer and her style more boho, but she was still a big, brash personality in a tiny, little body.

Jake rubbed his elbow from the floor. "You could call next time. Maybe send an email."

Maddie ignored him and swung her gaze to the couch. "Sera. I heard you were back. Didn't take you long, did it?"

Sera's mouth dropped open. "It's not what you think."

"Last week he had Chelle pinned to that couch, but I guess you do you—"

"Maddie." Jake's growled a warning.

"What? I'm not the one horn-dogging it all over town."

"Don't be mean. You know I'm not with Chelle anymore."

"Does *she* know that?" Maddie didn't wait for an answer before she breezed into the kitchen. "Ooo, pizza."

Jake heaved himself up to standing and pointed at Sera. "Don't move. I'm going to deal with this real quick."

He followed Maddie into the kitchen, and Sera's head flopped back against the cushions. *Chelle?* She wasn't surprised Jake was seeing someone. It was a little more concerning that Maddie hadn't been surprised to see him with someone else. *What was I thinking?*

It had been two days – *two days* – since she'd driven in from California, and it seemed like she'd spent every moment of that time with Jake. Sure, they'd talked some, but it didn't make up for seven years of silence. Had she really gone through all that to regain her independence only to toss it away again at the first opportunity?

Sera scooted over on the couch until she could see partway into the kitchen. Jake had his arms crossed and was watching Maddie inhale pizza. She hadn't seen Maddie since that night, though Evie had told her Maddie's broken wrist had healed nicely. Sera wondered what she remembered.

Jake disappeared from view, and Sera got up off the couch. She should thank Maddie for interrupting them. Things were moving way too fast, and though Sera had been all about it in the moment, she realized she didn't know the grown-up Jake. Teen Jake, yes, but people change.

The nostalgia of the house, of someone who believed her, the relief of knowing once and for all that she wasn't crazy, it was all making her soft. She's forgotten that the only person she could count on was herself.

It was time to armor up.

JAKE

JAKE WAS GOING to strangle his sister.

"I need to borrow your truck," said Maddie.

"No. Go away." She wasn't going to leave, but it was worth a try. Maddie never did anything that wasn't Maddie's idea. It reminded him of another stubborn female.

"Is that any way to treat your favorite sister?"

"Who says you're my favorite sister? You didn't even knock. We talked about that."

"I have no memory of that conversation."

"Of course you don't. Go away." She was finishing off the last of the pizza, but it was a small price to pay if it meant she'd leave him alone the rest of the night.

"Well give me your keys and I'll let you get back to not cheating on your girlfriend."

Jake ran a hand through his hair and admitted defeat. "I told you. Chelle and I broke up over two weeks ago and we were never serious anyway. You know that. Why do you always have to be a brat?"

"If I promise to be nice can I borrow your truck?" She looked so hopeful with her big puppy dog eyes, but he knew her tricks.

"What happened to your car?"

"It stopped working and I'm broke-ass."

"Stopped working how?"

She wouldn't meet his eyes. "It may have had something to do with the yield sign I hit, but in my defense, it jumped out in front of me."

Jake sighed. "Were you drinking again?"

"I'm twenty-three. I'm allowed to drink. It's legal in all fifty states and everything."

"Yes, but it's not legal to drive after. Maddie, I'm worried about you. How am I supposed to lend you my truck when you won't even take this seriously? It's my work truck."

This time Maddie sighed. "You ruin all my fun. No, I wasn't drinking. It was late and the road had gravel all over it. I took the turn too fast and the yield sign stopped the car from sliding into the ditch."

"Where's your car now?"

"At the auto shop in Kilgore. Danny said he couldn't get to it for a few days."

"Is he going to let you work off the cost again?"

She shrugged. "Probably. I'll deal with it after he fixes my car."

Jake shook his head. "You can't take my truck, but you can borrow the Corolla."

"Ugh, the Corolla is in worse shape than my shitty car."

"No, it's not. It's just older. I wouldn't let you drive a car that wasn't safe."

She glared at him, and he noticed she was wearing more eye makeup than usual. "It doesn't even have power windows. I have to manually roll the windows down like a peasant."

"You *are* a peasant."

"You're a peasant."

Jake tuned her out. It wasn't the first time they'd bickered in the kitchen, so he could do it asleep if he needed to. His mind wandered to the makeup and where she might have been going on that road. There wasn't much out there between Mulligan and Kilgore, but he supposed it was possible she had friends he didn't know about. It was even probable, considering how busy he'd been at work lately.

She'd been rattling on while she dug in the refrigerator for more food, but Jake stopped her when she reached for the cheesecake. "No. That's Sera's. Touch it and I'll let her shank you herself."

Maddie lifted her hands in surrender and grabbed a banana from the bowl on the counter instead. "I'll take pity on you and accept your shitty Corolla."

"Why is that taking pity on me?"

"Because you're clearly hoping to get back in there and lose some more clothes and I'm in the way."

Jake rolled his eyes. "I've been saying that for the last five minutes."

"Yeah, but by now she's come to her senses. Good luck with the deflowering. There's probably some condoms in my old room on the off chance you still end up getting lucky."

Maddie ducked out the kitchen door before he could throw something at her. It slammed closed and he shook his head. Maddie liked to announce her presence coming and going. Although, she used to at least say goodbye.

Jake decided to clean up the mess before heading back to Sera. As much as he was hoping she hadn't come to her senses, he thought maybe he'd come to his. They'd been through a lot in the last couple of days, and there was all that history between them they should probably work through before starting something new. The part of him that was panting at the little bit of skin he'd gotten to taste wanted him to forget though. Whatever they'd done to each other when they were younger, Sera wanted him now. But how long would it last this time?

5

SERA

SERA WAS STANDING by the fireplace on the other side of the room from the couch when Jake walked back into the living room. He grabbed his shirt from the floor, pulled it on, and sank back down.

"Sometimes I hate my sister," he said.

"She loves you, even when she's tormenting you." Maddie had always been friendly before, so the undertone of meanness was new.

Jake was quiet for a moment. "She was rude to you. I don't know what that was about, but I'm sorry."

Sera could guess what it was about, but she wasn't ready to share that with Jake so she shrugged. "No biggie. Besides, I have more questions. For you and Ryan. Magic stuff this time."

Jake glanced at the clock over her shoulder. "He's usually messing around on his computer at this time of night. If he has his headset on, he won't hear a damn thing, but I can try calling him if you want."

It wasn't what she wanted, but her wants were proving to be dangerous. Talking was way safer than sexy time on the couch.

She nodded.

Jake got up to pull his phone from his pocket and gestured for her to follow him back into the kitchen. Ryan answered on the first ring. "If this is about Fae crap, I told you I don't want to be involved. They already own my ass."

"Hey buddy, you're on speaker. Sera is here," said Jake.

"Awesome. A little more warning next time?"

"It's not my fault you answer the phone like a dumbass."

"If Sera is there, I assume you're either calling about a three-way or you need help with Fae crap, despite my wishes."

"C'mon man, a three-way?" Jake scolded.

"Right. Well then why don't I come over and you can ply me with beer to make me talk. You guys are at your place, right?"

Jake agreed, and they ended the call.

"How long before he gets here?" Sera asked.

Jake looked at his watch. "Five minutes or less? He can be fast when he wants to be."

"About earlier..." Sera fiddled with a jagged nail on her thumb. "I'm sorry I lost it. And I'm sorry I keep giving you mixed signals."

"You don't have to apologize." Jake reached for her, but she side-stepped him.

"I'm not entirely sure what's happening here." She gestured back and forth between them. "But it's for sure outside my comfort zone. I've only been divorced for a few weeks, but it was a long time before that..." Sera trailed off and shook her head. "I can't seem to decide if I want to jump you or run from you."

Jake's jaw tensed. Sera had been trying to lighten the mood, but remembered too late how that would sound given their history. He nodded. "Sounds like a tough choice. Let me know what you decide."

She wanted to say something to fix it, but her brain stubbornly refused to help. Jake pulled a couple of beers from the fridge and took the seat furthest from where she'd dropped into a chair at the table. He could have been giving her space, but it felt like a snub. Still, he slid one of the beers down the table to her.

It seemed like time slowed to a crawl, but it must have been only a few minutes of heavy silence before Ryan came in through the back door.

"Took you long enough," Jake muttered.

"Hi guys. Nice to see you again. Yes, I'm fine after you disappeared on me and I had to convince an apex predator to follow my ass. I was literally chased out of the woods by a damn wolf."

Sera scowled at him. "Poor you. My grandmother is trapped in a tree with a sadistic fairy, how do you think she feels?"

Ryan laughed. "Probably rested. She's not exactly trapped *with* Torix. It's more like she's trapped near him. Zee put her in an enchanted sleep when she figured out what had happened."

"But I saw her. She was in pain."

Ryan hesitated. "How did you see her?"

"Torix showed me in my head. She was bent over and clearly in pain."

"He had to be messing with you. It was probably from some other time. Torix can't interact with her at all. Think of Han Solo trapped in carbonite but with less space slugs.

Extremely unfair, by the way, that the bad guy gets mind powers. Worst superhero story ever."

"So he lied? I thought Fae couldn't lie?"

"They can't. They also can't break bargains, for good or ill. He manipulated the truth so you'd see what you saw."

"Why should I believe you?"

"You called me." Ryan shrugged and grabbed a beer from the fridge, twisting off the top. "Look, believe what you want. I've been dealing with Zee and her kind for a long time, and even I don't know what they're up to most of the time."

"He's right. He's known Zee the longest out of everyone, as far as I know. Except maybe Evie... " Jake trailed off.

Sera turned on him. "Why didn't we call him in the first place then?"

Jake shrugged. "You said you had questions for me. Figured I was special."

Sera dropped her head. She'd been on an emotional roller-coaster for the past couple of days, strike that, the past couple of years, and the panic attack tonight hadn't helped. Although, if Ryan was right, then Evie was safe for the moment.

"Are you sure Torix can't touch my grandmother?" she asked quietly.

The smile slid off Ryan's face. "Yes. Evie is as safe as she can be while trapped in stasis. She's probably safer than we are if Torix is on the verge of breaking free." Sera appreciated the reassurance without the snark. *Good to know he took some things seriously, even if it was few and far between.* She could see why he and Jake were friends.

She took a deep breath and tried to focus on the next thing. "What is Samhain?"

Ryan tilted his head. "What?"

"*Sah-ween.* Samhain. It was something Torix said."

Ryan closed his eyes, so she looked to Jake. He shrugged, shaking his head.

"Ryan, buddy? What're you doing?"

"Hold on, I'm trying to figure out where I've heard that before."

"Something Zee said, maybe?"

"Yeah..." Ryan was silent long moments more while they waited. Then he opened his eyes. "Something to do with Halloween, I think."

Sera's head was starting to pound, so she abandoned her beer for a glass of water. When she got back to the table, Ryan had his phone out. "What're you doing?"

"I'm Googling it."

"Of course you are," said Jake.

Sera cocked her head. "Why didn't we think of that?"

"He's smarter than we are."

It didn't take Ryan long to smirk in triumph. "Found it. Of course, it's spelled all funky, it's a Celtic word. You'd think we'd be used to that here, but it still trips me up. S-A-M-H-A-I-N. How do you get a W from a M-H?"

Jake threw a wadded-up napkin at him. "Focus, dude."

"Fine. It's a pagan holiday in October that celebrates dead people, apparently Halloween was based off it or something."

"Or something?"

"I'm speed reading as I talk. I know the washboard abs and dorky good looks can fool you, but it's harder than it looks."

Sera rolled her eyes. "Uh huh. So what day is it?"

"It's on Halloween, ooh and get this, that night, supposedly the veils between worlds are weakened. Want to bet that includes the Fae barriers keeping Torix in place?"

Sera exchanged a look with Jake. It seemed really convenient that there was a day of the year that made shields or veils or whatever thin. "Does this happen every year?"

"Looks like it."

"That doesn't make any sense. If this thinning happens every year, then why hasn't he used it to escape before? It seemed like he'd been in that tree a long time."

Ryan shrugged. "That's a question for Zee. And she probably won't answer it straight."

"What did Torix say to you?" asked Jake.

Sera had never been a good liar, but she was going to give it her best. If Jake knew the context, he was going to become overbearing. She could take care of herself, but the guys deserved to know Torix planned to use Samhain somehow. A half-lie then.

"He said he would be free on Samhain." It was really close to the truth.

Jake leaned back from the table. "Well, at least now we know how long we have."

"What do you mean we?" said Ryan.

Jake scoffed. "You think Torix doesn't know about you and your close personal relationship with the Fae?"

"Hey, you guys were the ones who went and got yourselves bound and in their service."

Sera held up a hand to stop the back and forth. "Torix is a threat to all of us, and last I remember, Zee owned your ass."

Ryan looked away and took a long swig of his beer. Sera understood. She'd much rather be dealing with her mundane problems. On the surface, the whole situation should be absurd, but it felt real in a way much of her life hadn't.

Jake's leg brushed hers under the table as he stretched

out, and warmth erupted from the contact. She tried to calm the flush, but judging from the way Ryan was looking at her, she'd failed. Maybe it was fifty-fifty which problem she'd less like to deal with.

Sera tapped on her water glass and both guys looked at her. "I'm a firm believer that information is power—"

"Says the girl literally brimming with power," muttered Ryan.

She glared at him. "—so I think we should combine all our information."

"Isn't that what we've been doing?" said Jake.

"A little at a time. We're supposed to find Torix's minion or servant or whatever to cut off that source of power in some way we haven't figured out yet. How do we do that? Is there a tattoo or a code word that would mark that person?"

Jake raised a brow at Ryan. "I'm out of my element here, but I think that's more of a Hollywood thing. Torix knows who his person is, and as far as I know, there isn't a cult out there waiting for his resurrection."

Ryan shrugged. "I don't think so. There's a lot Zee doesn't tell me, but I think something like that would make it on the list."

"Just great." Jake's phone rang. He checked the number then got up. "It's work. Excuse me a minute."

Sera tried not to watch him walk out of the room. When she focused on Ryan, he flashed a knowing smile. *Screw him and his knowing smiles.* "Okay, so we're looking for an individual person doing... what? What benefit does Torix get from this person?"

"This answer, I *do* know. The minion creates chaos which produces negative emotions. The more anger, fear, hate, bad stuff his minion can capture for him, the stronger he becomes. Eventually, once they've gathered enough power, they'll have to call a circle to release him, like a magical place out of time."

"Like that place in the woods with the stones?"

"Like that, but it would have to be near or around his tree. It's not enough to make a circle physically. The person would have to have enough power to call it into existence."

"I don't know what that means."

"Enough belief backed by enough whatever is inside you to make the circle real instead of using a collection of stones."

Sera glanced after Jake. "Have you ever met anyone else with power? A human I mean?"

"In Mulligan, yes. Other places, not so much. It's unusual but not impossible. We have more than our share in town. Zee says like calls like. I say we're more forgiving here when people get freaky."

Their eyes met and held. It felt like Ryan was trying to tell her something. She remembered Jake mentioning there were some things they physically couldn't say.

Sera shook her head. It would have to wait for another time. "We're looking for someone with power then."

"That's the only way I can see this working, but like I said, there are a lot of people here with varying degrees of power. I don't know how much it would take to make the circle for Torix. I don't know what else they would have to do. I don't know if they can suck up some of his power like a demented sponge. That's one of my theories, not Zee's. I don't know—"

"Sounds like you don't know much," Jake had returned and was leaning against the doorway. "but I bet you have a spreadsheet."

Sera glanced at Ryan in time to see him blush. "A spreadsheet?"

Ryan flipped Jake off but explained, "I may or may not be tracking the people with power in town, levels of ability, skills, how they're connected... That kind of thing." He wouldn't meet her eyes.

"That seems really...useful right now."

Ryan shrugged. "It's also probably morally questionable since I'm doing it without anyone's permission. I wasn't aware anyone even knew about it." Another glare at Jake. "Zee asked me to start it years ago. She didn't tell me why, but I suspect it was so she could keep tabs on anyone who might pose a threat. She takes her responsibility to her people seriously."

Sera sensed a tone. He sounded admiring maybe? And his blush hadn't faded yet. Something else to untangle later. "Sounds like we have the beginnings of a game plan. Ryan can bring over the list of all the people in town with power, but then how are we supposed to figure out which one it is?"

"It might not be someone from town." Jake pushed away from the wall and ran his hand through his hair. "That call was from the job site on Magnolia. Someone was messing with the equipment. The guys were closing it up for the night, and one of the trucks got loose."

"What do you mean 'got loose'?" Sera asked.

"It was switched to neutral and pushed from the front so it rolled backward down a hill toward the site. Jimmy noticed in time and managed to get it stopped before it could do any damage, but it could've been a lot worse."

"Are you sure it wasn't someone forgetting to put it in park?" Ryan asked.

"No way. My guys know their jobs, and the truck was there for most of the afternoon before it started rolling. They said there was a new guy hanging around the site. He was asking questions about me, trying to be all casual, but he stuck out because he was wearing a suit. You know there's nothing over on that side of Magnolia where you'd need a suit."

A sinking feeling invaded Sera's gut. "You're thinking it was Will?"

"I think we need to consider all the possibilities."

Ryan raised his hand. "Who's Will?"

"My asshole ex-husband."

Ryan blinked. "Is it possible he could be the one working with Torix?"

Sera shook her head no as Jake nodded. "He's a dick, he's self-centered, and he's stubborn."

Jake's jaw tightened. "Don't forget abusive."

Sera ignored him. "But he's never shown any signs of power."

"He could be hiding it."

"He tried to convince me, and the court, that I was unstable because I saw little golden lights that no one else did."

Jake gritted his teeth. "I knew I should have punched that guy."

"It's easy to look back and see what was happening now, but at the time, I seriously questioned my sanity." Sera cleared her throat. "We can talk about that part later."

"You can bet your sweet ass we will."

Warmth filled her, and she had to question how low her bar had sunk for compliments. "The point is that I don't think it's him."

"Well, I find it hard to believe that one of my neighbors would try to flatten my guys for fun all of a sudden. Who else could it be?"

Frustration coursed through her. Sera had lived most of her life with people not believing her, sometimes even herself. Jake held her gaze from across the room, and Sera pressed her lips together. The best response was always to stop trying to convince them and do what she was going to do anyway. Jake could believe what he wanted, but Sera knew Will didn't have any power.

Ryan glanced back and forth between them. "I wasn't going to bring this up, but since we're talking about vandalism... Someone broke into the school today."

Jake finally broke eye contact to stare at Ryan. "Wasn't school open today? How do you break in when the doors aren't locked?"

"The science lab was locked. The 4H kids let the science classes borrow their prize rabbits to study genetics, but there weren't any labs scheduled today. When the kids went in there to feed them, all but one of the rabbit cages were open."

"I have a bad feeling about where this is going," said Sera.

Ryan shook his head. "That's the thing. Nothing bad really happened. There were three missing rabbits, but nothing else. And there was some valuable stuff in that lab. As far as anyone can tell, someone picked the lock and could have helped themselves but didn't. Just let the rabbits go. Or took them."

"What about security cams?"

"You've been to the school, Jake. Do you think we have money for security cams on the rabbits?"

"What does the administration think?" Sera asked.

"That it was probably the student club that keeps protesting the use of the rabbits in the labs, but they seem more likely to start a petition than to pick a lock, especially since they were borrowed from the 4H kids."

Sera held up a couple of fingers and ticked them off. "We

have a trapped evil fairy, his servant slash minion, a runaway truck, three missing rabbits, an entirely useless magic-user, and a not very forthcoming fairy queen."

Jake held up a finger. "You forgot an asshole ex."

"Can't forget him. And a list of most of the people in town with power. I'm going to be honest, a few of these don't sound like they're connected."

Ryan chimed in. "There's something else we're not talking about."

"I'm considering my grandmother a whole different issue."

Ryan flashed her a quick smile. "Probably for the best, but that's not what I was talking about. I've been watching the people in this town for a long time, and I've never seen or heard of anyone who could do what you did in the woods."

Sera looked down at her hands. "I don't even know what that was."

Ryan looked serious. "You've never had full access to your power before, so that makes sense, but no one else has ever needed an anchor. And definitely not strong enough to need to be bound to it."

"Hey," Jake protested.

"Sorry Jake, but for the purposes of this conversation you're an it. Why you, Sera?"

"I don't know."

"You have to know something."

"I don't." Sera pushed away from the table and paced to the back door. "I don't know anything about anything. I came here because I don't know how to be a normal functioning adult. Turns out I'm not, so that's a relief, but I'm still just fumbling around in the dark. I don't know why I am the way I am."

Both guys were staring at her hands, so Sera looked down to see herself glowing. Again. *Dammit!* She shook them, but the glow remained, so she held them up. "See, what *is* this? I can't even be upset without weird stuff happening on accident."

Ryan didn't move, but Jake came closer and wrapped his hands around hers. "Take a deep breath. It's going to take practice like any other skill."

Sera stared at his shirt and breathed in and out a few times. The scent of pizza mixed faintly with grass and sawdust. The combination was a comforting reminder of better times in that kitchen. When she peeked at their hands, the glow had faded. Her hands looked strangely tan, but she wasn't creating her own light source anymore.

"Thanks."

His hands slid away and he returned to his side of the room. "Anytime."

Ryan stood and threw his bottle in the recycling. "That was thrilling, but I need to head home. I've got a super exciting pop quiz for my 9th graders to prep for tomorrow. Think about it, Sera." He looked pointedly at Sera's hands, and she got the feeling again that he was saying more than she understood. "Why did Zee pick you? I'll send Jake the list and get back to you guys if I hear anything. Try not to blow anything up in the meantime."

"Ha ha. Wait, is that possible?" Sera looked at Ryan in alarm, but he rolled his eyes. "Jerk." She moved out of the way so he could leave.

"Later," he called. They both waved, and the door closed behind him.

Sera blew out a breath. "I should get home too. I'm beat, and I still have to unpack the moving container tomorrow."

Jake grinned. "Are you sure? You could try doing something useful with your power."

Sera smiled. "So far all I do is make a great night light, but that's not a bad idea. I may mess around with it, but not until tomorrow. I really am beat."

Jake lost his teasing tone. "Okay, but wait until the afternoon. I have to visit the job site and work for a while tomorrow, but I should be free by then."

Sera stiffened. "I'll see what I can do."

"Please, Sera. I'm your anchor for a reason. I don't want you to get hurt."

"Well maybe I should just sleep until you come to get me like a good little princess. I'll for sure be safe then." She didn't wait for a response, but she did refrain from slamming the door behind her.

The cool night air was a welcome respite from her anger. How dare he treat her like she was incompetent. This was all new to her, sure, but she was an adult. Last time she checked, she'd gotten married, divorced, and moved back to Mulligan all on her own. Jake and Will and her mother could all kiss her magical ass, and if she wanted to learn how to shoot flaming energy arrows from her eyes, by god she'd do it her-damn-self.

The walk across the grass didn't give her a lot of time to cool down, but the sight on her porch doused her anger instantly. The light had been broken, shards of glass glittered on the porch floor in the street light, but the wet lumps on the welcome mat were still visible. Matted fur stuck up in spikes, and globs of goop were smeared across the floor littered with chunks she didn't want to think about. She could identify three sets of rabbit ears among the carnage.

The smell hit her at the same time she realized these must be the missing rabbits from the high school. Sera turned away and swallowed heavily. Those poor animals. Her first thought was to call Jake over and let him take care of it. But his constant insistence that she needed his help firmed her resolve. She could handle this herself.

Sera detoured to the back door, and breathing shallowly through her mouth, she went in search of bleach. Her heart hurt for the rabbits and for the students who'd be missing them. As she gathered rubber gloves, rags, bleach, and hot water, she thought about the rabbits she'd once seen at a petting zoo party in a friend's backyard. They were harmless and cuddly, and Sera bet the students thought of their rabbits more as pets than as specimens or livestock.

She had a detailed image of a couple of teenagers holding speckled rabbits with twitching noses stuck firmly in her brain when she opened the front door. The smell was gone. Not two minutes ago she could smell the rotting bodies from the yard, but now it smelled like pine. More accurately, like warm pine wood chips, but the sun had gone down hours ago.

Someone had cleaned the porch. Sera looked toward Jake's house, expecting to see him puttering around through the windows, but his house was dark. Either Jake had snuck over here and done the quickest, most thorough cleaning job she'd ever seen or she'd imagined it. No one else had been around when she'd walked across the yard, but she had been distracted.

Could she have imagined it?

Once, not too long ago, she would have accepted that and called her therapist, but times had changed. She'd changed. The days of hallucinations and pills were past her. Sera reminded herself firmly that none of it had been imagined, not even then.

She dropped the cleaning supplies by the door and

walked to the porch steps to look back at the house. Not a single smear of blood, but the porch was still too dark. The glass from the broken bulb was gone, but the bulb hadn't been replaced. She peered up at the light fixture and made out the jagged edges of the remaining glass on the bulb.

Warmth rushed through her. Not her imagination. Not a hallucination. The proof made her almost dizzy with relief. She'd been prepared to power through, but it was so much better to know for sure.

She looked toward Jake's house again. If he hadn't cleaned the mess, who had? And how had they gotten rid of the smell? Come to think of it, if the rabbits had gone missing that afternoon, how were they already rotting? The memory of that smell was enough to put her off meat for the foreseeable future.

A rustling noise in the grass at the bottom of the steps made Sera jump back and reach for the bleach spray. It was a pitiful weapon, but there weren't a lot of options. When no one appeared, she moved to the edge of the shadows and snuck a glance around the porch pillar. There weren't any cleaning ladies hiding in the yard, but the grass was moving. Sera walked down the steps and her mouth dropped open.

There were rabbits in her yard.

Three speckled rabbits were nosing around in the grass. They'd been blending into the shadows, but now she could see that they were smaller than ones she'd imagined. Older than babies, maybe teenage rabbits.

She looked down at her hands still holding the bleach spray. Was she glowing again? They were maybe a little easier to see than they should be. Had she done this? Had she brought rabbits back to life? Sera stooped to pick one up but stopped before touching the soft fur. Were they zombie bunnies? She slowly stood back up. This was way beyond her understanding, and she wasn't sure she was entirely comfortable with the knowledge that she could resurrect wildlife. Though if she *had* accidentally used magic to clean up a bloody mess on her porch, it would make unpacking much easier.

6

SERA

SERA WAS in the stone circle again. It was light out, but she couldn't tell if the sun was coming or going. Everything felt surreal, the sky too blue, the trees too green. Her brain was having trouble focusing on any of the details of her surroundings, and she was pretty sure the trees were shifting places on their own.

All at once she knew she wasn't alone. She'd yet to take a step, but slowly spun, looking for whoever had joined her. It was like swimming through gel. She moved, but slowly and it took a long time for her body to react to the orders she was shouting in her mind. The trees made her dizzy, so she closed her eyes for a moment while her body caught up. When she opened them, the wolf was sitting at the edge of the clearing.

He cocked his head at her and let his tongue loll out while he panted. She should have been too warm outside, Sera remembered that much, but she felt completely comfortable in her jeans and tee. The glowing eyes looked less menacing when he was calm and docile.

Sera cocked her head at him, mimicking his stance. Why wasn't she afraid? Where was the panic that came with this feeling of helplessness? She let her gaze drift past him to the path that was in the process of reversing its curve.

It was the lack of sprites that snapped her out of her lethargy. She shook her head and tried to focus on the path. The details were still fuzzy, but it was clearly empty except for the wolf. It felt like he couldn't cross into the clearing, which was good because her legs felt so heavy she wasn't sure she could move them. How had she gotten there? The last thing she remembered was dropping her head back on the couch in the living room and wishing...what had she been wishing? Something about Jake and zombie bunnies.

The wolf dropped his head and nosed a stick toward her. Sera's eyebrows shot up.

"You want to play fetch?"

His head popped back up and his tail wagged. It made him look like a giant dog. With glowing eyes. And a strong predatory urge.

"No." His head dropped again and he whined.

"You chased me through the woods the last time I saw you, and now you're sad that I won't play?"

The wolf laid down with his head on his front paws and looked up at her with puppy eyes. Sera remained unmoved. She'd always been more of a cat person. Torix was playing a game where she didn't know the rules, so there was no way she was leaving the stone circle to play fetch with a demon wolf.

"Not a demon, an animal forced to do Torix's bidding."

Sera spun around at the voice behind her and almost fell over. A statuesque woman with dusky skin and amazing cheekbones had joined her in the circle. The whole situation was very reminiscent of the last time she'd been there, but she was somehow less disturbed by the prospect of someone reading her thoughts this time.

The woman rolled her eyes, and it reminded Sera of someone.

"First of all, it's not reading your thoughts if you're shouting them at me. Second, of course I'm familiar. We talked a few days ago. Humans. I swear you're going to stupid yourselves out of existence."

"Zee?" The Amazon in front of her didn't look like Zee. This woman looked like a model or a queen. Or a superhero. If Sera squinted, the sleeveless dress looked sort of the same with shimmering fabric and trailing bits, but she was pretty sure there were tawny leather pants under it.

Zee crossed her arms, highlighting the golden bands around both of her impressive biceps. "I'll do explanations first, but listen to me now because I hate this speech and don't want to give it again." She paused, and Sera realized she was waiting for some kind of agreement.

"How—"

"I'll take that to mean you're paying attention. Appearances are deceiving, especially among the Fae, but I feel like it's true everywhere to some extent. When we first met, I was using a glamour to help put you at ease. We've learned that humans are much more comfortable with the idea of magic if they think they can squash the wielder flat. This..." she spread out her arms, "is much closer to my true form. Though you did add some interesting accessories that I plan to incorporate."

"I added?"

"Yes. We're in your dreamscape." Zee peered at her closer. "You hadn't figured that out yet I see."

"Wait so this is all a dream?"

"No. You're asleep, and I called to you because we have matters to discuss. If you hadn't already come to the circle, I would have been unable to reach you."

Sera glanced over her shoulder, but the wolf was gone.

"Yes, he's real too." Zee's brow furrowed. "I'm not sure how he was able to connect though."

"So you and Torix can just pop into my head whenever you feel like it?" *Ah, there's the panic.*

"That wasn't Torix. Simply the wolf under his control. Though now I suspect there may be more to him... but no matter."

Sera was barely listening. She was leaning against the rock beside her attempting to take deep breaths.

Zee snorted. "Humans. If you had any shields at all, we wouldn't be able to intrude. It's one of the first things Fae learn to do. Guard their minds."

The tightening in Sera's chest started to loosen. "Can you teach me?"

Zee looked her over once. "Yes. I believe I can, but not right at this moment. I have something else to discuss first. Walk with me."

Zee gestured toward the woods, and Sera hesitated. "Are we safe?"

"We're in your mind. You get to decide that."

Sera nodded. That was an evasion if she ever heard one. So probably not safe, but if Zee was willing to leave the circle, it must not be immediately dangerous. Sera stepped past the stones and waited for Zee to join her. The path hadn't been wide enough for two people before, but they were able to walk side-by-side easily. Unlike the last time, there was no cheerful twinkling, but at least the trees appeared to have stopped moving.

Zee was right though, there was a lot to discuss. Their gang of misfits really needed something more to go on than the person serving Torix might occasionally glow while doing magic. *They also needed a better name than 'gang of misfits'. Focus.* Sera in particular wanted an explanation of how her power worked. Of course, none of that came out of her mouth.

"I think I made zombie bunnies."

Zee stopped short. "That's a new one."

Sera stared down at her hands, now back to their normal color. "Someone left mutilated rabbits on my porch. I felt so bad, and I couldn't stop imagining the poor high school kids cuddling their bunnies and how sad they'd be. I went inside to grab cleaning supplies, and when I came out it was clean and there were three fresh new rabbits hopping around my yard."

Zee chuckled. "You have a soft heart, like your grandmother."

"I don't want the power to raise the dead."

"That's good because you can't. Clean up a disturbing mess, yes. Bring life out of death, no. Those rabbits you saw were probably living somewhere nearby and came when you called them."

"I didn't call them."

Zee started walking again. "But you did. Your power is settling in, so if you're not careful, you'll be doing accidental magic left and right. You cleaned the porch and you called the rabbits because you wanted to fix the hurt you imagined."

Sera followed. There were no sounds in this wood, not even their footsteps. She wondered if it was because none of it was real or because her mind craved the silence. "What happened to the bodies?"

Zee sighed. "My best guess is that they're now buried in your yard where the rabbits were hopping around. You can't make things disappear, there are rules even in magic, but you can move them, move their energy. Their loss distressed you, but they'll feed the garden and create new life."

Sera wasn't sure she liked that explanation. The garden didn't need mutilated rabbits to thrive, but she supposed Zee had a point. They were already dead, if they could do some good, why not?

"You have other concerns."

Sera took a deep breath and picked one. "How long do I have to be bound to Jake?"

Zee raised an eyebrow. "Are you so eager to be rid of him? I was under the impression that it would be a pleasurable cage."

"A cage is a cage. Jake is... yeah, I'm not ready to talk to you about that yet. I'm grateful you stopped whatever was happening to me, but I want control over my own life. Especially my own body."

Zee stepped over a large branch and nodded. "I can understand the sentiment, but the power inside you is unsteady still. Unrefined. Without an anchor, it could cause irreparable harm to you and those around you."

Sera shuddered. "What if I'm willing to risk it."

"I'm not. What's done is done, and there are more pressing concerns."

Sera looked through the blur of the trees and fought her frustration. She never should have agreed to the binding, pain or no pain.

"And yet you did. Perhaps you should see what you can learn from the experience instead of fighting it. All that struggle must be exhausting. Don't you think that strength might come in handy when you try to save Evie?"

Sera's eyes swung back to Zee's. She needed those shields. "What did you want to discuss?"

"You have a deadline."

"Samhain. I know."

Zee didn't react, but Sera sensed she was surprised. "He'll try to get you close enough to drink in your power."

A chill went down Sera's spine. "What do you mean by that?"

"Fae aren't simply humans with magic and wings. We don't have to eat or drink. We consume emotion to survive."

Sera fought the urge to step further away. "Like psychic vampires?"

"I wouldn't describe us that way, but I can see how humans would. We take a small amount, a sip if you will. And not from people."

"How do you do that if you can't leave the woods?"

"Emotions travel far and small amounts get absorbed by the nature around you. We harvest from the Wood. It gives freely, and we protect it in return. Torix does not. Plus, your power is tied to your emotions, a veritable feast."

Sera remembered the feeling of Torix on her skin and shuddered. "How do I stop him?"

"Those shields would be helpful, and using your bond with Jake."

"I'll build shields, but I'm not bringing Jake into this any further."

Zee shook her head. "You won't have a choice. Without him, you'll fail."

"Is this the real reason you won't remove the binding?"

"In small part. You don't need to be bound to use Jake."

"I'm not using Jake."

"My apologies, a poor choice of words. Emotional bonds

strengthen you. Even with all that's inside you, it's not enough to protect yourself from Torix."

"There's something you're not telling me."

"Yes."

Sera's anger rose. Zee's cryptic help wasn't very helpful. "What happens to him if Torix succeeds and Jake is with me?"

Zee stopped walking. "He consumes you both."

Sera looked around and they were in the clearing again. Time to get to work. "How do I build a shield?"

"First, shields are not magic. They're a natural part of your mind that you can reinforce with magic. But like magic, you have to imagine it, visualize it, and believe it. Wrap it around your thoughts. You'll need to concentrate to maintain it at first, but eventually it will become second nature."

Sera tried several times to imagine a shield, and it appeared quickly in her mind, silver and round, but it was always followed closely by Captain America fantasies. Damn Marvel and their superior story-telling.

Zee chuckled. "That's a good start, but you need a shield that's yours."

Sera closed her eyes and tried one of the calming techniques she'd developed for her panic attacks. She imagined herself as a dragon flying high above the world, sunlight glinting off her golden scales. The wind caressed her face as she spread her wings wide to glide through the clouds. Her dream body relaxed and the wind picked up in the woods. Hair whipped her in the face as she pulled the image of the dragon closer to her. Wings folded into her back and shiny golden scales settled over her skin. The low hum in the world around her quieted. She hadn't even noticed it before.

Zee cleared her throat, and Sera opened her eyes. The

clearing was still there, but every tree was crystal clear. She could see specks of moss growing on the stone circle. The grass under her felt soft, and for the first time, she realized she'd been barefoot.

"Sera." The voice was fading.

She looked up, expecting to see a beautiful dark Amazon walking away, but she was alone. "Zee?" Her concentration dropped as she scanned the trees, and Zee appeared in the circle again.

"Very good. Those are magnificent shields, even for a Fae."

"I've always been a quick learner. Why didn't you talk like this last time?"

Zee grimaced, a barely perceptible blush staining her cheeks. "Ryan has an unfortunate effect on me. I can't seem to help messing with him when he's around. It's a distraction." She shrugged.

Sera wanted to ask more, but she wasn't sure if girl talk was appropriate. Were they becoming friends? Teacher and student? Acquaintances that sometimes hung out in dreams? She'd never been close to other women, other people in general really, so she was rusty on the social cues. Maddie had been her only real example, and that hadn't turned out great. Zee scared her a little, but she wanted to try again. One look at her imposing profile, and Sera decided she'd start with an easier target, like Ryan.

A wolf howled somewhere in the distance, and Sera shuddered. She wondered briefly if the wolf had killed the rabbits, but it seemed unlikely the wolf could open the cages without thumbs. Maybe in tandem with Torix's servant? The thought reminded her of the most important question they'd discussed the night before.

"How do we find Torix's servant? And why hasn't he

used Samhain to get free at any other time?"

Zee smiled and nodded. "Now you're asking the right questions. He needs a conduit for the power that's going to crest on Samhain. As long as he's behind the barriers, he can't access it. If the servant maintains the connection with him and calls the circle on Samhain night, he'll be able to manipulate it to his will. And this year, we won't have Evie to shore it up."

"Wait, you needed my grandmother, a human, to help you keep him trapped? What did you do all the years before she was around?"

Zee's smile dropped. "Luckily, it wasn't a problem before she was around. There was a glitch in the shields. We've since fixed it, but it was too late to stop Torix from inserting his power. Think of it like a tiny hole in a balloon. Your grandmother provided the patch every Samhain since then, when it was most vulnerable."

Sera couldn't believe the Fae were unable to patch it themselves. Zee was still holding information back, and she'd be super pissed if it got her or anyone she loved killed. "Well then what are you going to do next year?"

Zee raised a brow and gave Sera a once over. "We're hoping to find a replacement. As for how to find the servant. I'd suggest finding whoever murdered innocent wildlife outside your door."

The woods darkened for a moment, like a cloud had passed overhead. "Yes, I'd figured that one out on my own. But how do we know when we have the right person?"

"You feel with your magic and your mind. Like the bond between you and Jake, the servant has been bound to Torix. Become accustomed to finding your bond, and you will be able to find other bonds. Theirs will be dark where yours is light. Use your power."

"Are you seriously telling me to use the force? Can't you tell me something that doesn't sound like you ripped it off from Star Wars?" The twilight fell again, but didn't lift. Sera looked up, but everything outside the circle was fuzzy. "What's going on?"

"You're waking up. You have all the information I can give you. I'll leave you with a warning." Zee's image faded but her voice remained. "Until you have control, be careful who you trust."

Sera rolled her eyes at the emptiness. "Great. Thanks. Totally useless. Like I even know how to learn control or know when I've achieved it."

In a blink, the trees were replaced by her living room ceiling. Her eyes felt gritty, and her neck ached. One whole leg was asleep, which made it hard to get off the couch. Sunlight streamed through the windows as she shuffled to the powder room.

She relieved her aching bladder and splashed water on her face. The woman in the mirror looked the same as always, but Sera felt different. She closed her eyes and imagined her happy place. There she was, shoulder-length brown hair, circles under her blue eyes, no makeup, clad in dragon armor and fully shielded. Connected to the golden scales was a thick, shimmering rope stretching off to the distance. She poked it and felt a tingle go through her. It was like someone had stroked one of her emotions. A pleasant one.

It reminded her of the feeling of sitting on a blanket in Jake's backyard with his arms around her. She'd stared at the stars peeking through the trees while they'd talked about everything. He was safe and warm, and every inch of her was convinced that he would stand by her no matter what.

Sera pulled herself back and opened her eyes. Still in the powder room. Still feeling different, but a good different. The low electric hum she'd never noticed was gone, like in the dream, and she could relax completely for the first time in...well, ever.

Relief coursed through her. Did this mean no more random visits from Fae, good or bad? No more minor headaches? She wished she'd learned this trick years ago. Despite the neck pain, Sera felt rested. She stretched and went upstairs to get ready for the day.

Twenty minutes later, she was once again cursing the lack of coffee. One of these days she was going to remember to actually buy coffee pods when she went to the store. Her phone chimed while she searched the kitchen again, except she couldn't find her phone either. A couple of seconds later another chime sounded, definitely from the pantry.

She dug behind several cereal boxes and came up with her phone and a box of dark roast coffee pods. "Oh, hell yes."

The phone chimed again while she was holding it. Three new messages from Ryan. She didn't remember giving him her number, but she didn't remember leaving her phone behind the cereal either. *And thank god for that oversight.* She popped a pod in the coffee maker.

Sera read the messages while the machine worked.

One included a link to the list. One was an apology for the early text. And the last one was a borderline indecent GIF she hoped was for Jake, who was also included on the text. Sera skimmed the list and whistled at one of the names. Wouldn't the local parish be surprised to learn their close-minded pastor could wield magical powers?

The machine beeped, and Sera didn't waste any time. She blew on the steaming coffee, then scalded her tongue with a sip. Once upon a time she'd put enough sugar and creamer in her coffee for it to qualify as a milkshake, but Will had insisted that coffee should be drunk black or not at all. She snorted and pulled milk out of the fridge, adding a healthy dollop. Her day would *not* be ruined with thoughts of her ex. *What a tool.*

For once, Sera was glad she was unemployed. Evie's "death" had left her with a small trust that would hold her for a while, and the house was paid off. That meant she had a lot of free time on her hands. The moving container was still outside waiting for her to empty it, but she had limited time before she, possibly they, became a human buffet.

Sera realized she didn't know what day it was. She opened the calendar app on her phone and frowned. Eight days until Halloween. It didn't feel like late October.

Texas didn't seem eager to let go of summer. The kitchen was already heating up in the morning sun, but the shade trees she could see through the window were starting to look a bit less green. As she watched, a huge brownish squirrel climbed up the trunk of the tree closest to her kitchen window. It stopped on a branch at eye level and stared at her, tail twitching. Before they could resolve the staring contest, she caught movement out of the corner of her eye and the squirrel jumped into the leafy branches out of her sight. Beyond the tree, Jake was leaving his house.

Sera was annoyed to realize that she spent a lot of time staring out that window toward Jake's house, even as she continued to watch him climb into his truck with a backpack in his hand and a waffle in his mouth. Of course, he had to work. She'd woken up with this half-assed plan to lure him into the woods and find out what else she could do with her powers.

Sera smiled. That sounded dirty even to herself, but

then she remembered she'd yelled at him about not needing to wait for him and doing the exact opposite. Something about helpless princesses and shooting fire arrows from her eyes. That last part might have just been in her head.

Her phone chimed again. Man, she was popular this morning. Her grin faded. It was her mom, not Jake with a response.

Mom: I got a call from the moving company about when they can come pick up the container. Have you unpacked? Evie leaving you enough to be lazy doesn't mean you should be.

A suffocating show of love and affection, as usual. Or not. It was a miracle her mother had agreed to handle the funeral, but Sera hadn't been in the right frame of mind to take care of it. She'd also been broke. The fact that there were appearances to maintain after all was what she thought had swayed her mother in the end. Then they'd had a fight when she'd told her mom she was moving into Evie's house instead of selling it. After much discussion, ok, Mom talking at her while she'd stubbornly refused to engage or change her mind, her mother had acquiesced. Eventually, probably when Mom had finally realized she couldn't stop Sera, she'd offered to pay for the moving container. Money was one of the few ways she showed love.

Sera: I'm working on it. The house is already full. There's a lot to go through. If they call again, give them my number. I'll take care of it.

Mom: If that's what you want. You have two more days until you have to pay extra.

Sera: I'm aware. I'll deal with it.

Her mother didn't text back after that, and Sera was relieved they had been able to handle the issue without a call. Direct conversations between the two of them always ended in frustration. They didn't know how to talk to each other. She was mostly sure her mom didn't think she was incompetent and lazy, but she couldn't help feeling like less of a person after one text message. Well, that and because her mom had thought drugging her because she was crazy was a solid plan of action...

Fae powers or not, she'd have to figure out what to do with her stuff now that she knew Evie wasn't dead. Her fingers tightened on the coffee cup. As far as she was concerned, Evie would be returning to her home, and Sera was determined that she'd find some way to pay back the money she was using. That meant her meager belongings were going into her room or into storage in the attic.

Sera slurped the last of her coffee and put the mug in the sink. First order of business was to clear space in the attic. Jake and Ryan were probably at work like people who didn't have trust funds, so she had some time to focus on something that was going to scar her emotionally instead of physically.

It took her a couple of hours, but she finally got all her things out of the container and sorted into storage or keep piles. Bless her grandmother for being an organized magpie. There were trunks full of interesting things in the attic neatly placed under the eaves and labeled. Her storage boxes and the few pieces of furniture she'd kept would easily fit in the open space.

She'd decided to unpack the necessities in her room. Evie had kept the closet empty, and there was plenty of storage under the high wrought iron bed. By the time she'd finished putting everything away, the sun had shifted to the other side of the house, and she'd sweated through her tank top.

Evie's house had air conditioning, but Sera thought it was probably older than she was. It cooled the main room downstairs, but that was about it. Something else she'd have to look into once this mess with the Fae was over. Evie needed a respite from the Texas heat. Hell, Sera needed a respite.

A glance out the window showed Jake's truck back in his driveway. As tempting as it had been to use magic to help her, she'd sort of promised him she'd try not to play with it by herself. She fully intended to get him over for a little practice session, but in the meantime, it had been nice to finish something on her own. It reminded her she was stronger than she thought she was.

Sera flopped on the bed and picked up her phone where she'd abandoned it hours ago on her nightstand. Several new messages from Ryan and Jake that included increasingly disturbing insults to their respective manhoods. Probably best not to get Ryan involved in a practice session. She sent a private message to Jake.

Sera: Are you free tonight? I want to try to make some stuff glow.

Jake: No plans. Want me to bring dinner over?

Sera's stomach rumbled at the thought of dinner and she realized she'd skipped lunch.

Sera: Sure. No more pizza.

Jake: 15 minutes?

Sera: Make it 30, I need to shower.

Jake: Need any help with that?

Sera: You just couldn't resist, could you?

Jake didn't answer right away, and Sera was about to head to the bathroom when her phone chimed.

Jake: I'm glad you waited.

She didn't have a response for that, and the clock was ticking on her thirty minutes.

7

SERA

JAKE WAS true to his word. Sera was in the kitchen putting the dishes away thirty minutes later when he walked in without knocking. He set a paper bag on the table next to the bat that she still hadn't put away.

"I went to the Taco Stand. They said to tell you hi and they put your favorite in there." He dug through the bag and pulled out several items wrapped in wax paper and grease stains. Sera had never seen such a beautiful sight.

"They remembered me?"

"Everyone remembers you. It's not like we get a whole lot of new people in town. Besides, Evie talked about you all the time."

Sera sat down at the table and pointed to the closest bundle, trying not to let the choked emotions show in her voice. "This one for me?"

"Those two are both for you. It was my best hope to keep you away from my tacos."

She pulled one of the burritos toward her and

unwrapped it. Chorizo, potatoes, eggs, refried beans, zucchini, verde sauce, and nacho cheese. Perfect. The first bite made her moan, and Jake's eyes to heat, but she refused to be embarrassed because it was the best damn burrito in existence.

Jake joined her at the table and plowed through four tacos to her one burrito. "So how was your day? I saw the moving container thing was gone."

Sera chewed carefully and swallowed. "I don't want you to get any wrong ideas about this."

"We're friends, Sera. I'm curious about what you did while I was at work. I'm assuming there was some pining involved, maybe sighing of my name, but strictly platonic."

Sera rolled her eyes but smiled against her better judgement. "There was no pining. I'm not a Victorian spinster."

Jake's mouth was full of taco number five, but his face clearly asked if she was sure about that.

"You're not as funny as you think you are."

"Yes I am. So what'd you do today, Mistress Allen?"

"I unpacked. I also finally found the coffee. That's about all." There was no point in mentioning the text from her mom.

"Not even a little accidental magic today, huh? Good for you."

Sera remembered the dream and the golden dragon armor. "I guess there was one other thing."

"I knew there was pining."

Sera threw her wadded-up wrapper at him. "I had a dream with Zee."

"With Zee? That's a strange way to phrase it."

Sera shrugged. "It *was* strange. We walked through the woods, she answered questions with more cryptic answers, the wolf was there for a bit..." She took a deep breath and jumped in. "She taught me to make shields."

Jake set his taco down slowly. "She taught you, in a dream, how to do a magic thing?"

"It was real. I happened to be asleep."

"I wasn't questioning that. But, Sera, are you sure it was Zee?"

"Yes. Absolutely. She felt right. I can't explain it any more than that."

"I haven't heard of the Fae teaching humans anything that would help them use their power."

Sera's jaw clenched. "I guess I'm special then."

"That was never in doubt," Jake muttered.

She pushed the remaining burrito away and stood up to stretch. "Thanks for dinner, but that's not why I wanted you to come over."

"Is this the part where you want me to take my shirt off?"

Sera's traitorous inner hussy perked up with a *yes, please.* "No. All clothes will be staying on this time."

"Too bad."

"Jake, I know it's hard, but I need you to focus. I want to try a few things with my power and you insisted on being around for it."

He picked up his last taco and her burrito. When he moved to stick them in the fridge, she thought she heard him mutter, 'damn right it's hard,' but he turned to face her before she could voice her indignation. "Let's do it. One anchor, reporting for duty."

Sera took a moment to let go of what she *wanted* to say. Mostly because she wasn't sure where to start. The last few times, she'd gotten upset, her hands had started to glow, and something fantastic had happened. Zee had said magic was about intention and visualization. It was too bad all she could seem to visualize was Jake's naked chest. Thank goodness her hands remained their usual color. Jake would never let her hear the end of it if the first bit of intentional magic she did was to remove his shirt.

"Are we starting now or do you need a pep talk?"

"You are entirely unhelpful."

"Did Zee give you any pointers on how to do this?"

"Nope. She said we should work on it together and that..." Jake narrowed his eyes at her abrupt stop. She'd almost let it slip that Zee thought she needed Jake to not be sucked dry like a Capri Sun. "That I didn't make zombie bunnies."

Sera groaned inwardly. She'd planned to keep the rabbit thing to herself, especially the part where she'd slowly backed away from cute little rabbits in suspicion. Her stupid brain was refusing to focus.

Jake crossed his arms. "Zombie bunnies? I desperately want to hear this story."

"I desperately want to be able to control my power. Can we focus please?"

"I'm not letting this go, but in the interest of time and not getting exploded from the inside, okay. But we're *definitely* coming back to this. What do you want to try first?"

"I don't know. What's something that might come in useful in a fight against a super pissed powerful Fae?"

"Teleportation?"

He was probably joking, but Sera considered it. "Let's put it on the list, but we should probably start with something smaller."

"What about a shield?"

"I told you I already learned how to make those. It's pretty cool actually."

"Not for your mind, for your body. Make a shield to

protect against the tree that the super pissed powerful Fae is going to try to smash you with."

Sera cocked her head. "Do they have telekinesis or would he have to physically heft a tree and lob it at me?"

"Umm, I've never seen Zee move anything with her mind, but this falls into the area where she'd most likely keep it a secret. I've seen her change things and make things stop moving. And once she lifted a big ass rock like it was nothing."

Sera thought about Zee appearing as a built Amazon, and she wasn't surprised to find out she had super strength. An itemized list of Fae abilities would have been useful. Where was Ryan and his spreadsheets when they needed him? An external shield was a great idea, and she put it at the top of the list to try, but she wanted to go even smaller.

Sprites were gathering in the kitchen, and they made Sera think of Zee's tiny form. The Fae could change their appearances, maybe she could too. A glamour, then. Something simple. She'd change her hair color from brown to blonde. Dark to light. "Okay, hold on. I'm going to do...something."

She closed her eyes and dropped her head into her hands. Something told her it would be easier if she wasn't distracted by large attractive men smirking at her. It took a surprising amount of willpower to get the image of Jake out of her head.

Once clear, she imagined looking at herself in a mirror. Without meaning to, she was back in the powder room clad in her golden armor. It was still disconcerting that she'd become her dragon. She ran a finger along the scales at her collar bone. They were smooth and warm to the touch. Her whole body was warm, but not in an uncomfortable way.

It was like snuggling under a blanket on a snowy day.

Not that she knew much about snow, but her mom had taken her to the mountains for a weekend once. She'd gone skiing with a boyfriend and left Sera miraculously alone in the lodge to do as she pleased. It was one of the best weekends of her life until the boyfriend realized her mom had exaggerated her skiing skills.

Sera was distracting herself because she didn't know how to start the glamour. Even knowing that, she was tempted to keep walking through good memories. The gold rope flared as she was tempted with memories of her summer with Jake. She wondered if he'd like her as a blonde. A blush crept up her cheeks in the mirror, but her hair was still stubbornly brown.

At a loss, Sera ran her hand through it to pull it away from her face and saw a thin blonde streak form where she'd touched it. As she watched, it faded back to brown. Interesting. She'd pictured herself as a blonde and Jake reacting positively. When the hair had actually changed color, her focus had shifted, and she'd lost the vision.

In hindsight, it seemed obvious. She had to picture herself with blonde hair, and it would require continued concentration to maintain. Why would her armor stay up even when she wasn't thinking about it but a simple change in hair color took constant focus? She'd have to ask Zee if there was a way to apply the shield magic to the rest of it so that she could keep it going in a static state without having to focus on so much detail.

There was so much to learn and no way to know how any of it will come in handy against Torix.

"Sera?"

She opened her eyes to Jake lightly shaking her shoulders. "Sorry. I got distracted, then I figured something out, then I got distracted again."

"Uh huh. Do I want to know what you figured out?"

"It's not important right now. I'm going to try again."

"Sure. Anything I can do to help?"

"Say something if my hair changes color."

"That's all? I kind of thought I'd have to be more active in this process."

Sera shrugged. "I know as much as you do. Any ideas how you can be more active?"

He grinned. "Maybe if we held hands."

She narrowed her eyes. "Fine. Hands only. Don't get grabby."

"I'm never grabby."

Sera snorted and shut her eyes again, then felt Jake link their hands together. It was familiar and comforting. Back in the powder room, warmth flowed into her through the bond. This time the glow spread beyond her hands, her whole body was radiant. She ran both hands through her hair, imagining it blonde, and to her surprise, her hair changed from a dark chestnut to full Southern California gold. She tried her best to believe she was blonde, to fix the color in her mind. When she opened her eyes, Jake's grip on her hands was almost painful.

"Holy shit, Sera."

She grinned. "Do you like it? I was going for surfer meets pin-up model."

It took him a second to shift his eyes from her hair back to her face. "I didn't know Loreal offered that color."

"It's in the limited-edition section."

"Can you change it back?"

Sera pictured herself brunette again, to be safe, and let her focus go. She didn't need to see Jake's face to know her hair had changed back. Letting go of the magic was like taking her bra off at the end of a long day.

Jake released her to reach out and pull a lock of hair through his fingers. It was the least sexy thing she could think of, but she felt that slow glide all the way to her toes.

"I didn't really think it would work," he said softly.

Sera lifted a brow. "That's not what you told me."

He met her eyes. "I had every confidence you'd figure out how to use your power, but I've never seen a non-Fae do a glamour. Up until three minutes ago, I'd thought it was a species thing."

"Well, it was fun, but not exactly helpful against Torix. If you're ready to stop petting me, I'd like to try making a shield now that I have an idea of what I'm doing."

Jake dropped his hand. "Did the touching help?" He looked almost hopeful.

"I don't know. I wasn't quite doing the right thing last time, but I get it now. At least I think I do. Why don't we try it without touching to test it?"

He nodded and took a few steps back. The second time was much faster than the first, and the third time she was able to change the color several times without going to her special magical powder room. There was a spot in her mind that felt familiar, where she could press the image and it would hold and take shape. As long as she went back to that spot, the glamour worked.

"Guess that answers that question," he said.

Sera shook her head. "Not really. It did help the first time. Before when I...accessed it, I had a lake of power, but now it's a rusty faucet where I'm stuck with a trickle. I don't think it takes much to change my hair for ten seconds."

The bond seemed to give her greater access that she couldn't get to on her own. It was frustrating and reassuring at the same time. If she couldn't go big, she couldn't accidentally hurt anyone. On the other hand, she'd done some

pretty hefty magic without meaning to already, and the
faucet hadn't seemed to stop the flow at all.

There was a shivery part on the inside of her that was
freaking out over the whole thing. She was used to taking
information and running with it, but *magic is real* and *oh,
yeah, you have a lot of it* was still settling. Wizard boarding
school was definitely the better way to go when learning
how to use magic. But she'd never gotten her letter *dammit*
and now she had to figure out a way to not get anyone killed
all by herself.

Jake must have been waiting for a sign or something
because he stayed on his side of the kitchen all the way up
until Sera started taking deep breaths to ward off the panic.
He didn't move particularly fast, but Sera was caught off
guard when he pulled her against his chest and held her
tight. Her clenched back muscles relaxed, and her head
flopped down on his shoulder.

"I am not prepared for this. I didn't even go to college.
Why isn't there some kind of handbook?"

He was silent for a second. "Did you ask Zee if there was
one?"

She pulled back enough to smack him on the chest, then
slid her arms around his back. "I don't even know what I'm
supposed to do. What if I hurt someone?"

"There's always the chance people could be hurt. You've
got to decide if the risk is worth the payoff."

He was talking about more than her dubious magic
practice. Wrapped in his arms, everything seemed to
connect to their relationship, and the bond between them
wouldn't let her get some distance so she could find her
footing. Half the time she wasn't sure she wanted to find it.

Sera buried her nose in his shirt and took a deep breath.
Why did he always smell so good? Like tacos and dryer

sheets and home. Was the risk worth the payoff? Was Jake worth losing her independence?

At the first sign of difficulty, she'd let herself lean on him. Was she already losing it?

Sera shuddered and pulled back to stand on her own. "That took more out of me than I thought. I need to head to bed. Next time, I want to try doing it without any physical contact. I need to be able to control the power on my own."

Jake searched her face, but she wouldn't meet his eyes. "Okay. Same time tomorrow night?"

It was on the tip of her tongue to tell him no. That she'd do it on her own, but whether she liked it or not, he'd helped her pull that rusty faucet inside of her wide open. "Yeah, that should be fine."

"It's your turn to make dinner. I suggest steaks. Ribeye. Medium rare. And don't forget the potatoes."

Sera couldn't help her smile. "So bossy."

"Is that a yes?"

"Go home, Jake."

He went, but Sera knew she'd only bought herself time. Maybe if she was lucky, Torix would eat her and she wouldn't have to deal with complex emotions and human relationships.

THE NEXT WEEK went by faster than was comfortable. Sera spent her days wandering town, talking to people she hadn't seen in almost a decade. They greeted her as if she'd been gone for a long weekend. It was a lot of the same people she'd been afraid to interact with before. Some had moved away, some had died, but everyone who remained remembered her fondly. Sera was surprised to find that she remembered them fondly too.

She'd spent a lot of years feeling like an outsider in her own home, first with her mom, then with Will, but this town accepted her with no caveats. Plus, now that she was sure she wasn't crazy, her natural confidence wasn't buried under fears and pills. Too bad it took her grandmother becoming trapped and a dangerous Fae causing havoc to get her to this place.

And Torix *was* causing havoc.

The gossip tree was alive and well, so everyone was talking about the strange increase in vandalism and minor crimes. They mostly blamed teenagers or out-of-towners, but Sera knew better. One of the things she'd been working on was a way to detect the traces left behind when someone used magic. She'd gotten the idea from the way the sprites appeared each night at magic practice. They seemed attracted to the use of power.

She'd realized that if she shifted her focus when looking at something, like staring at a magic-eye picture, she could see tiny sparkly residue. Hers was usually gold, and she'd seen a variety of other colors, but she hadn't figured out their significance yet.

All the places that had been vandalized showed various traces of magic, some more obvious than others, but always in a dark blue, almost black. She'd been testing it with her own power, and the concentration seemed to be based on the amount of time that had passed since the magic was used.

Sera may have been a novice at using the power, but she'd had years of experience trying to figure out things no one else seemed to notice. Magic seemed to be following rules, different ones from the rest of the world, but still rules, and she was good at figuring out the subtleties.

Sera had settled into a routine of morning coffee at Java Junction. It was her second cup, since waking up demanded an immediate pod of liquid goodness, but who was counting. After that, she browsed the various antique stores in search of people to pump for information.

Jake came over every night. It wasn't getting easier. He must have picked up on more than she'd thought that first night because he was being careful to avoid unnecessary touches. The worst part was that she missed it. It was second nature to touch Jake, his body hadn't ever been off-limits to her, mostly because he was what Evie called touchy-feely. He craved contact. But for her, he'd pulled back without being asked.

She'd made the rules, but now she regretted the distance.

They took turns making dinner, or in Jake's case, ordering dinner. He helped her clean up, always left when she started yawning, and never let the conversation get too serious. If she didn't know him so well, she'd have thought he'd lost interest, but she could see it in his eyes sometimes. That look that said he had more to say but he was keeping it back for her sake. Not to mention there was that simmering connection between them that never went away.

However, even after all their work, she'd found that she could make a shield if she was touching Jake, but not without him. She'd concentrate, and he'd wait a minute then start flinging mini-marshmallows at her to test it. With her hand on his leg, a transparent shield appeared swirling with golden color. Any attempts on her own fizzled into failure and resulted in her getting pelted with marshmallows. They'd also gotten nowhere in trying to find Torix's helper monkey. There was a lot of failure going around.

On day six, Sera was in her usual spot at the coffee shop. She sipped her mocha and watched through the window as people walked by. It took a second for her to realize that someone was waving at her from the other side of the glass. The woman's face wasn't immediately familiar, but then the multiple layers of skirts and the trailing wool scarf in eighty-degree heat jogged her memory. Janet something-or-other was one of the few new people in town, having moved there several years before. She ran the boho shop where Maddie worked. It had to be her.

Sera wiggled her fingers back, and Janet pointed to the other chair at the table. Sera sighed, but smiled and nodded. It was prime wallowing time, but that wasn't a good reason to be rude. The smell of sandalwood wafted ahead of the woman as she sat at the table and started taking off layers.

"Whew, you can really feel Autumn coming in," Janet said.

Sera snuck a glance around the shop at the other patrons in shorts and tank tops. "Sure. Halloween is almost here."

"Halloween Eve. Or All Hallow's Eve... Eve. That one doesn't really roll off the tongue though." Janet placed both hands on the table, one on top of the other, and smiled.

Sera waited, then realized that the woman wasn't going to say anything else, like why she'd wanted to sit there. They'd met briefly once a few days before when Sera had checked out her shop. Maddie must have mentioned Sera to her because Janet had acted like they were friends. It had been an awkward conversation, but nowhere near as awkward as the current situation.

"So... how has your day been?" Sera winced inwardly at

the inane question. She was so bad at small talk. It was another of Will's complaints. He'd felt he had to do all the talking at the prestigious social events he dragged her to, but he also never let her speak, so now that she thought about it, what the hell was he complaining about? Regardless, when one is basically a social outcast, there are some skills that get rusty. Case in point, she hadn't been paying attention to Janet's answer. She'd been staring at the rows of silver hoops that climbed all the way up her ears.

"—but Henry always gets cranky when his chi is unbalanced."

"Sorry, who's Henry again?"

"Oh, you remember Henry, my iguana? His tank is in the back of the store behind the sacred crystals. He likes the prisms they make when the sun sets."

"Right. Of course."

"But when I let him out to stretch, he hid under the local honey display. It was terrible. He simply refused to come out. You know Maddie is the only one he listens to."

Sera didn't know that. She took a big sip of her coffee and nodded to avoid answering.

"It's too bad Maddie's been absent the last few days. Our schedule is fluid, but it would be nice if she showed up to a few of her shifts at least."

"Maddie hasn't shown up to work?"

Janet tsked. "I don't like to think of it as work so much as spreading positivity through material goods."

"That's very... open of you."

Janet beamed. "What a wonderful thing to say. I can see why Maddie likes you. Be a dear and tell her there's no hurry but I could use her help if she has the time."

"I—" Janet was up and gone before Sera could explain that she'd seen Maddie once since she'd moved back. That was one strange woman. Janet offered a hearty wave as she passed the window outside.

Sera took a deep drink of her coffee and considered her options. Janet clearly expected her to see Maddie soon, and Jake *had* mentioned where Maddie was living. Jake had also mentioned that Maddie was becoming increasingly flaky and he was worried about her. Missing shifts at work, even a workplace as forgiving as Janet's shop, seemed exceptionally irresponsible. Even for Maddie.

Maybe she was sick. Or worse. It wouldn't take long to check on her.

8

SERA

Mind made up, Sera finished her coffee and gathered her things. Maddie's place was on the edge of town, like hers, but on the other end. She needed to have a conversation with Maddie anyway. It was past time that they talked about the incident from seven years ago.

Sera didn't pass anyone going up Maddie's street, and she could see why when she parked. There were three properties on the road that jutted into the woods. One was at the turn off, then Maddie's, and Sera could see another place through the trees a ways.

The driveway was all dirt and empty. The house looked like frat boys had vacationed there. This must have been one of the rental properties the town had tried to set up. Turned out no one wanted to vacation in a little town in the middle of the woods in east Texas. Jake had told her they'd sold them off to residents, most of whom still use them as short-term transitional rentals.

The porch leaned heavily to one side, and Sera seriously

doubted if it would hold her weight. Rusty cans littered the yard taken over by weeds and dead grass. The window to the left of the door was boarded up, but the window to the right was open. She could hear beads inside clacking together in the breeze. Weirdly enough, the ever-present crickets were silent.

The town was pretty safe, but most people didn't leave their windows open during the day if they weren't home. Maybe Maddie parked behind the house and went in the back door. If there was a back door. The whole place looked like it was at most two rooms.

Sera slammed her car door and followed the dirt trail around the house. Instead of turning toward the back, it continued on in a straight line to the woods. The trees rustled and something made a chittering noise, but the house was silent. She tore her gaze away from the pines and confirmed that there was indeed no back door.

To her surprise, the steps were solid and the porch barely squeaked. Sera couldn't believe Jake let Maddie live out here. Why wasn't she in the house with him? The beads clacked again and the curtain drifted to the side enough for Sera to peek inside.

After the brightness on the porch, the dimly lit room was hard to make out. She got a glimpse before the curtain fell back into place, but it was mostly large shadows. Sera was uncomfortable sneaking around and looking in windows. It was ridiculous, but it felt like someone was watching her from the woods. Her shields were solidly in place and nothing else felt off. Just in case, she pulled her cell phone out of her bag and pulled up Jake's speed dial.

The planks groaned when she stepped up to the door and knocked. There was no sound inside, but Sera knocked again, to be sure. The beads clanked, but it was clear no one was home. Sera turned around to leave and saw the wolf sitting at the edge of the trees, tongue lolling out. He could have passed for a big dog, but she knew what those teeth looked like when he snarled.

The wolf yawned wide and cocked his head to the side like he'd done in her dream; he was definitely watching her. Slowly, she reached back for the doorknob and prayed that Maddie was as complacent as the rest of the town. The moment she came in contact with the knob, she felt a static shock. She kept the wolf in her sights in front of her, and tried to open the door behind her back. The knob turned easily under her hand, but the door seemed to be stuck on something. Sera took a step back and shoved. The door opened, but a hard wall stopped her backward momentum.

It felt smooth, like river rock, and completely solid to her hands, but she could feel the breeze coming out the door now that it was open. Sera glanced behind her briefly, then back to the wolf, who hadn't moved. Whatever it was, she couldn't see it. She reached out behind her with her power. It was flat and almost even, with a slight depression in the center of the doorframe. All at once, she knew what it was.

A shield.

What was Maddie doing with a shield around her house? Sera slapped a hand against the invisible force, and the wolf perked his ears up. She needed to get inside. The depression was probably where Maddie went in and out, so Sera visualized it opening like a zipper up from the ground.

The shield collapsed, and Sera fell into the house. She scooted back far enough to kick the door closed, then tried to calm her racing heart. Unless the wolf had suddenly grown opposable thumbs, he'd be stuck outside. By the time her eyes adjusted to the dark, her pulse had returned to normal.

Sera had expected a lot of Ikea furniture and hand-me-downs, but Maddie was full of surprises. The inside was meticulously clean, and the furniture looked new, what little of it there was. She'd been right, two rooms. A kitchen-living room combo and a doorway that probably led to the bedroom. The entire room was filled with sprites.

There was a round kitchen table in the middle of the space with two chairs. No couch, no tv, not even a throw pillow, but there were bookshelves everywhere covered in stuff. Sera stepped gingerly around the table and approached the closest bookshelf to get a better view. There were books on witchcraft, paganism, mythology, even the Fae. Some of them weren't labeled and looked really old. Around the books, Maddie had put trinkets with bits of feathers or dried plants. A necklace on a leather cord caught her attention on the bottom shelf.

Sera stopped short of touching it. Even from a few inches away, she could feel waves of magic emanating from it. Her hand glowed as she ran it over the bookshelf, brighter over some objects, dimmer over others. The bright objects were filled to the brim with unused magic, like batteries. Sera returned to the necklace.

This one felt different. With her sight, she could see the traces of the magic on the items, all different colors, from different sources, but this one was familiar. The magic was turquoise, a swirling mix of blues and greens, and the pendant was silver shaped into a swirl around a blue stone. Real silver, she'd bet. It had a distinct feel, and somewhere in her reading the last week, she'd seen something about conduit metals, including silver.

Beyond all that, she'd seen it somewhere before.

Sera stroked one finger down the stone and a vision slammed into her. Evie, bent in the garden behind her house, her fingers deep in the earth with the necklace swinging free from her loose top. She snatched her finger back and realized what she was seeing. Objects from other people with power who didn't know better. She'd been right; Maddie had collected a house full of magical batteries. But why?

Sera searched with her power, but she didn't sense any other magic beyond the items and the shield. Her eyes lingered on the closed door to Maddie's bedroom. She'd already come this far, what was the harm in going a little further?

It was the picture of Maddie and Jake, laughing and mugging for the camera that stopped her. She hadn't noticed it until she'd come around the table, but Maddie had put it right next to the bedroom door on a small folding tray. It was a scene she recognized; Jake had the same picture at his place. The white frame showed signs of wear, like it had been placed face down more than once.

They looked so happy, and Sera knew it had been taken the summer before she'd met them. What was she doing, snooping on Maddie? This wasn't who she was. Maddie had been her friend once, and Sera intended to honor that. She looked around one more time and backed toward the door. So what if Maddie collected magical trinkets? Maybe they were gifts. The shield was certainly weird, but Maddie might not even be aware of it.

Sera's inner realist snorted and questioned her judgement, but this was Maddie. Maddie, who didn't have any power, and could barely hold a job. Who regularly mooched off her brother, and with whom Sera had spent a night that changed her life. Everyone deserved their privacy, and Sera owed Maddie more than most.

She shifted the curtain and looked out for the wolf. The

tree line was empty. It didn't mean the wolf was gone, but out of sight made the run to her car a lot more appealing. She opened the door and stepped through the shield with no effort. It seemed to be meant to keep people out instead of in.

Her senses and power stretched wide to search for the wolf, but either he was gone or she wasn't very good at that particular skill yet. It could be both. She took the chance and sprinted to her car.

With the doors locked and the car started, Sera pulled out her phone and called Jake. She probably should have done that in the first place, less possible felonies that way, but she was getting restless. The phone rang four times then his voicemail picked up. She ended the call without leaving a message. There was no point in worrying him. She was safe, the wolf was gone, but Maddie was definitely hiding something.

Sera drove slowly through town, expecting to be pulled over any second for breaking and entering. Technically, she hadn't broken anything, only entered, but it seemed like that might be a flimsy excuse if faced with handcuffs and prison food. Logically, she knew no one would notice her trespassing, but her hackles were raised and she still felt like she was being watched. It was strong enough that she bypassed her own driveway to pull into Jake's. Sera felt like the car offered some measure of protection, and she didn't want to go back to sitting in her house alone twiddling her thumbs. Much better to do it at Jake's house.

When all this was over and Evie was back home, she'd have to start deciding what to do with her time. She needed a job. Even if Evie offered, she couldn't live off her grandmother's generosity forever. The street was deserted, but Sera reached out with her power to check anyway. A couple of angry squirrels in the trees between their houses, but no people in the vicinity. As she closed down the net, several sprites floated out of the woods toward her car.

For some reason, she'd assumed they simply appeared when magic was nearby, but they were definitely moving in a straight line toward her. She hoped she never had to secretly use her power in public or those little buggers would give her away.

Jake's truck was gone, but it was mid-day. She hadn't expected him to be home. Why had it seemed better to wait at Jake's house than her own? She'd be alone either way. The sprites had passed her car by that point and started drifting up to his door. Okay, decision made. The sprites wanted Jake's house, so Jake's house it would be.

Sera yawned and wished she'd grabbed a second coffee from the shop before she'd rushed out. Late nights and a lot of power expenditure was taking its toll on her beauty rest. Feeling silly, she eased open the car door and pre-locked it before slamming it and dashing up the steps into Jake's house.

It would have been really awkward if he'd locked his door, but like his sister and most of the town, he'd left it open. With the solid wood behind her and the cheerful glimmering of the sprites in front of her, Sera was able to relax for the first time since Janet had waved at her through the coffee house glass. She had so many questions, and every time she answered one, six more popped up.

Would Maddie know she'd been at her house? Why was she collecting magical objects? Who'd put up the shield? Sera listened to the house settle and let that last question come to the front of her mind. What kind of person would it make her if she planned to snoop through Jake's house like she'd done his sister's?

A prudent one, she decided.

She was still leaning against the inside of the door when a shuffling sound from the front porch broke through her attempts to rationalize her poor decision-making. Her first thought was the zombie bunnies had found her. The image wouldn't leave her alone, even after a week.

A brisk knock vibrated the wood next to her head. Sera weighed the consequences of answering Jake's door when he wasn't around. In a town that size, news would spread like wildfire that she was making herself at home. She was ninety-eight percent sure that Jake would be cool with it, but that last two percent kept her still and silent huddled against the door.

Another knock, followed by the last voice she expected.

"Hello? I know Sera's here. Her car is in the driveway." It was Will. A quiet curse then the doorbell chimed in the hallway. "Sera. It's inappropriate to hide in another man's house."

He was so far out of line she was surprised he was still in the state. On the one hand, it was a little humiliating to be hiding in Jake's house, she could take care of herself, but on the other, it was entirely none of Will's business what she did or who she did it with. If she decided to have crazy monkey sex with Jake in the town square, she'd damn well do it. And after a week of hands off, the idea wasn't as far-fetched as it probably should have been.

Will's footsteps went to the edge of the porch, paused, then came back to the door. He was muttering, but she couldn't make out the words. Maybe if she showed him in no uncertain terms that he was out of her life... she'd bet Jake could help her with that. He paced back and forth again. Sera sighed and eased over to the window. She needed to make sure he wasn't doing something dumb.

The first thing she noticed was the bottom of Will's pants. He was standing in front of the window with his back to the house. The second thing was his stupid fancy car parked in the street. The third thing was the wolf in the woods, his teeth bared.

Her breath came in a quick gasp, and for a moment, she desperately wished Jake was there. *No! I can do this.* She had to fight down a surprising amount of panic though. Not for her, but for Will. There was a solid door between her and the wolf, but Will was outside with it, and he was stubborn enough to stand on the porch yelling for her while the wolf chewed off his leg. She didn't need a stubby, legless Will on her conscience.

She needed a solid distraction that would work on someone completely obsessed with himself. Her gaze flashed to his fancy car again for a second before fixing back on the wolf. It was staying under the trees for now, but the fur on its back was spiked up. The distraction would have to be the car.

It was something she hadn't tried in her short experience with magic, but she was pretty sure she could nudge the car hard enough to set off the alarm. Against her better judgement, she stopped watching the wolf and focused all her attention on the car. Sprites drifted in front of her as she opened herself up to the power and visualized a glowing ball in the yard. It took a second, and was so bright she worried Will might see it, but it was there.

Sera drew in a breath and pushed the ball with all her power as she exhaled. It slammed into the passenger door, and the car shook a little with the force. The alarm immediately started blaring, and Will cursed again before heading down the path to his car.

To her great relief, the wolf slunk back into the trees

instead of charging across the street. Two birds with one magic ball. *Score.* Her muscles were screaming from the awkward position, so she finally slid to the floor. *What a day.*

Some small part of her was disappointed that she hadn't just let the wolf eat Will. It would have solved a few of her problems at least, but that kind of disregard for human life wasn't in her. Sera sat on the floor, her back to the door, and watched her hands fade back to their usual color. If everyone who used magic started glowing like a night light, why hadn't they found Torix's servant yet? Zee hadn't glowed. Also, Will hadn't seen the magic ball. Jake could see it though, and he didn't have any magic. *This isn't making a lot of sense.*

Her phone buzzed next to her on the tile floor, and Sera nearly smacked her head jumping away from it. It buzzed again, and she considered not answering. If it was her mom, she was going to say some very bad things about her taste in men. Will's reaction to their divorce was not rational.

A rising sense of anxiety that made no sense whatsoever made her pick up the phone. It was Jake.

"What's wrong?" He asked as soon as she hit answer.

"Why would you think there was something wrong?" It was habit to deflect. Why ask for help when she'd already taken care of the problem?

"I felt it. The bond damn near yanked me off my feet in the middle of a conversation with one of my crew leads. What's wrong?"

Sera ran her hand along the grout lines in the floor. The tile was different from when she'd been there as a teenager. He'd probably done the work himself.

"Sera, talk to me. Let's start with where are you?"

She was sitting in his foyer, hiding from a lot of things. "Your house. Will was here... and the wolf."

"Are you okay?"

The anxiety ratcheted up as she hesitated, and Sera realized it wasn't her anxiety. It was Jake's. *That's new.* "I'm fine. I had the pleasure of hitting Will's car with a magic ball, and the wolf left me alone."

"I'll be there in five minutes, don't move."

Relief flooded her, but it wasn't hers. Like the anxiety hadn't been hers. She checked her shields, but they were intact and strong. It must be the bond. She'd reached for him when she'd seen Will and the wolf outside. *Great.* Her moment of weakness must have snapped something into place and now they had a shiny new set of weirdness to contend with.

Sera checked outside again, but the wolf was nowhere to be seen. She told herself to get up and go into the kitchen or sit on the couch, anywhere except splayed on the floor in front of the door. It was bad enough she'd come to his house, she didn't need him convinced she needed rescuing. She wanted him to see her as strong and in control. Cowering in fear kind of gave the opposite impression.

JAKE WAS true to his word. He was home in less than five minutes. Sera was in the kitchen making tea when he burst through the front door. Another good reason to not be sitting there.

"Sera?"

"In here." She set two cups down on the kitchen table. "I'm fine, or at least I would be if you'd calm down. I have enough of my own anxiety, thank you."

He stopped in the doorway, and Sera was struck again by how much he'd filled out. He was wearing a grey Henley with the sleeves pushed up to his elbows, low slung jeans, and the same work boots she'd seen the first night she'd been back. His shoulder to waist ratio put Chris Evans to shame. Aaand... she was distracting herself from the jumbled emotions she'd been feeling through the bond.

"Did you see the wolf outside?" she asked.

"No." He walked to the table, but instead of sitting down, he pulled her into his arms.

"Jake? Are you okay?"

"I felt you panic. I thought you were in danger, and I was too far away to do anything about it. I ran all three stop signs."

She let him hold her. Who was she kidding? This was why she'd come to his place instead of hers. "You rebel. Next thing I know you'll be jaywalking with abandon." He was warm, and he smelled wild. She rested her head on his chest and breathed him in. Right now it was pine and mint and something spicy.

"Are you sure you're okay?"

Sera pushed down irritation along with the tingles that spread with his touch because she could sense that he was still freaked out about the situation, not questioning her ability to take care of herself. "I swear I'm fine. Will never got confirmation I was here, and the wolf never approached either of us." Sera frowned. "But it looked like he was going to attack Will."

Jake snorted. "Good for him. Maybe I'll get him a treat next time."

Sera pulled back to look him in the face. "And how do you think Zee would respond to a stranger being mauled by the demon wolf running around in the woods? Or the people in town who are aware that there's more here than small-town charm?"

"Those are good points, but I still say he deserves a bite in the ass." He brushed a kiss against her temple, then released her to sit at the table. "Not that I mind, you're always welcome, but what are you doing here?"

"I..." Sera could feel herself blushing. There was no way she was going to tell him that she'd gotten spooked by an invisible watcher, followed some sprites, and come running. "I went by Maddie's place."

"And..."

Sera sat opposite him and picked up her tea. "And have you been inside her place?"

He shrugged. "Once, right after she moved in. I helped her put together a bunch of bookshelves."

"Has she ever shown any signs of power?"

Jake's face closed down. "No. Why? What happened at Maddie's?"

"First of all, don't give me that look. I went because I was worried about her. Janet cornered me at the coffee shop and mentioned that she'd missed a bunch of shifts."

Jake sighed. "Dammit. Does Janet plan to fire her? She's barely scraping by as it is, and I can't get her to understand that she can't keep using this place as a safety net."

"No, actually. Weirdly enough, Janet was fine with the missed shifts. She just wanted me to ask Maddie to come in when she has the chance because she needed some help with something. Apparently, Maddie gave her the impression we were friends."

"Aren't you?"

"I mean, we were, but not for a while now, and I got a little bit of a hostile vibe the last time I saw her."

Jake grinned. "When I had you under me on the couch."

There went the blush again. Sera wasn't normally a blusher, so this was obviously somehow Jake's fault. "Yeah.

Anyway, Janet happened, Maddie and I are apparently besties again, and I've had no luck lurking around town looking for random signs that someone is using their power for evil."

"So you went for coffee?"

"Coffee always comes first, don't be stupid. After coffee and Janet, I went to Maddie's." This was the part she was unsure about. Jake was protective of his sister, and she didn't want to get him all agitated. Talk about hostile vibes. "There was a shield around her house."

Jake leaned forward. "A shield? Like the one in your head or the one you can't do?"

"The one I can't do. I bounced off of it when I saw the wolf and tried to go through the door."

He held up a hand. "Back up. The wolf was there?"

Sera fiddled with the mug. "I was on her porch. She didn't seem to be home, when I turned around the wolf was watching me from the edge of the woods. The strange part is he was sitting there like he was waiting to be pet. It wasn't aggressive."

"Sera, that wolf is not a dog. Do not try to pet him."

"I know. That's why I tried to go into Maddie's house. It was closer than my car, and I didn't want to take any chances. No one around here locks their doors, but I hit a solid wall of invisible power."

"I'm glad the wolf left you alone long enough for you to get to your car. Next time call me and I'll go with you. Who do you think did the shield?"

Sera was tempted to take the out he was unwittingly offering. He assumed she hadn't been able to get in, not a bad assumption considering her luck with shields thus far, but she wasn't going to get any answers keeping everything to herself. Even if Jake shut down, he deserved to know what

Maddie was doing. "I don't know who made the shield, and also we sort of skipped a part."

"What part?"

"The part where I figured out how to get past the shield and invaded Maddie's privacy."

9

SERA

SHE WAITED for the cold anger, but none came. Jake crossed his arms and leaned back.

"You were trying to get away from the wolf. Not exactly nefarious motives."

His belief in her better side warmed her, but he hadn't heard the rest of it yet. "Yeah, but I wasn't hiding once I got inside. There's magic all over Maddie's place, not only the shield. Those bookshelves are full of books on magic and the Fae and one on orienteering that doesn't seem like her, but whatever. And stuff. Magical stuff."

"What does that mean?"

"Other people's magic imbued into items that Maddie seems to be collecting in her house. Does Maddie know about Zee?"

He ran his hand through his hair. "I didn't think so, but she's also never shown much interest in anything magical. The Fae keep a pretty low profile, so unless you're looking for magic, you usually can't find it."

"Well, Maddie found it all right. That shield was strong."
Sera didn't know what to think, but she was glad Jake hadn't
immediately discounted her.

"There's something else bothering you."

Sera stared down at her hands. "She had one of Evie's
pendants, one I know Evie loved. It was full to the brim with
her magic."

"After you left, Evie was pretty down. Maddie started
spending a lot of time over there. I thought she was being
nice, but it was also around that time that she started strut-
ting around all confident, like she had a secret."

Sera sat back. "You think Evie was training her? But you
said Maddie doesn't have any power."

"I don't think she does, but that doesn't mean she can't
learn. Maddie can be cunning and resourceful when she
wants something, but she's got a good heart. If Evie was
teaching her, she had to have seen that."

Sera reached over and put her hand on Jake's. "Don't get
upset, but should we look at her more closely."

"No." Jake shook her off. "No. Torix needs someone with
power, and Maddie doesn't have it. Did you sense any of her
own magic anywhere in her house?"

"No... but—"

"You'd know. You'd know if it was her magic."

Sera blew out a breath. She could feel him getting
worked up again through the bond. "I'd know, and there
wasn't any of Maddie's there. What's bothering me is how
did the wolf know where I'd be?"

"Was he there when you got there?"

"Not that I noticed, but I wasn't looking toward the
woods. I was trying to see if Maddie was home."

"You think Torix is tracking you somehow?"

"Maybe? The wolf was at Maddie's damn near the same

time I arrived, then he was here a few minutes after I got into the house."

"It's not far from Maddie's to here if you cut through the woods. A wolf could run it easily. I have no idea if a demon wolf is faster than a normal wolf. Honestly, I'm making some assumptions here about how fast a normal wolf is."

"You mean you admit you don't know everything?"

"I admit no such thing. Since we're in a sharing mood, I have some questions about Will."

Sera groaned. "Not this again. He's a terrible person, and I'm doing my best to cut him out of my life."

"I'm glad to hear that. Did you ever talk to him about your grandmother's house?"

The question made her pause. Had she mentioned Evie to Will? She remembered a couple of occasions, but there were always more pressing things happening. Like a critique of how she chewed or a demand for a different color scheme in the sitting room.

"Sera?"

"Yeah, sometimes, but he mostly didn't listen when I talked. It seemed like I was meant to be an easily controlled trophy wife, and trophy wives aren't supposed to have personalities or thoughts, just a large collection of designer heels."

Jake blinked at her a few times. "There's a lot to unpack there, and I'm looking forward to you telling me all about how much of an asshole your ex is, but is it possible he knew about this place? That maybe he's been here before?" He looked distinctly cagey. *What does he know?*

"Here in Mulligan? No way. He'd eat his favorite golf shoes before he'd come here without an ulterior motive."

"What if he had an ulterior motive?"

"Like what? Stealing Evie's secret sugar cookie recipe?

Trust me, there's nothing here that would tempt him to leave his cushy nest in California." Jake was silent, and Sera started to get suspicious. "Why do you ask?"

"He stopped by the site today."

That got her attention. "He did what now?"

"He came to my newest jobsite on Magnolia Street, the one where we had the problems last week, and got in my face about you."

Sera gritted her teeth. She'd divorced his ass and moved halfway across the country. What else did she have to do to be free of him? She kept her voice and her face calm, but inside she was seething. "What did you do?"

Jake smiled. "I told him he'd lost his chance and that he was trespassing. He could leave on his own or I'd call the police."

She highly doubted that was all Jake had said. "I assume he blustered around until you pulled out your phone."

"Yep. Then he turned tail and ran like a gazelle. He's surprisingly graceful."

That surprised a laugh out of her. "Yeah, like a praying mantis."

"The interesting part came after he peeled out of the dirt in his little car. Rodriguez recognized him."

Sera deflated a little. "That's not unusual. He's a news anchor for a big station in California. Sometimes his broadcasts are shown nationwide."

"Nope. I asked about that. Rodriguez saw him in town. He's lived here his whole life and knows everyone. A stranger stands out. He said Will was skulking around about two and a half years ago. There was some tussle over a parking spot in front of the courthouse. Different car, same attitude."

"You're telling me Will was in Mulligan right before our wedding?"

Sera had thought Will couldn't surprise her any more with his lies, but she'd been wrong. They'd gotten married a little over two years ago. He'd been a paragon of support and caring then. Her first inkling that things weren't what they seemed was when he insisted they get married right away. Even her mom had balked at that one, but in the end, he'd gotten his way. They'd gone to the JP and signed the papers, then a few months later they'd had the lavish wedding her mom had wanted.

With all the bullshit that had followed, she'd forgotten about the rush. In hindsight, Will had always had a selfish reason for his unreasonable demands. How did that connect to her grandmother and Mulligan?

Jake looked smug. "Yes, and I found out what he wanted at the courthouse. Evie is worth a hell of a lot more than the trust she left you."

"What? How much more?"

"She owned the land adjacent to town where the developers keep wanting to build."

Sera's brow furrowed. "That swampy area?"

"No, the pastures on the other side."

"I thought those were part of a ranch or something."

"They were, but the ranch went under and Evie was able to buy a bunch of their land."

"Who owns it now?"

"You."

It was news to her. Her mom had acted as Evie's lawyer, and Sera had trusted that she'd been honest. She may have been misguided when it came to Sera, but her mom lived and breathed the law. She was absolute in her devotion, more so than in her devotion to her daughter. Maybe Jake was wrong? "How'd you get this information?"

"I went to the courthouse and asked."

"And they told you?"

"I know the county clerk. She used to tutor me in English sophomore year."

Sera shook her head. "Right. I keep forgetting about the small-town thing."

"You didn't live here long enough for it to affect you. Everyone knows everything, but when you need help you can get it. You take the good with the bad."

"So you sauntered into the courthouse, smiled at the clerk, and talked about the good old days two years ago when a stranger came in asking questions."

"I don't know that sauntered is the right word."

"Will's digging led to you digging, and now I have the potential to be filthy rich but no one bothered to inform me."

"Will knew about Evie and the land when he left town."

It would really be great if Sera could stop finding ways that people had betrayed her. She got up from the table to pace. "Okay, if this is all true—"

"If?"

She sent him an icy look. "I just found out my ex-husband most likely married me, and subsequently made my life hell, because he was hoping to get to my grand-mother, the land baron, which I also didn't know about because reasons. Can I have a few minutes to process before I jump in with both feet?"

He held up both palms and leaned back.

"Will never showed any signs of power. Not that I knew what to look for, but I wasn't drugged out of my mind the whole time. When weird stuff happened, his go to was to get another pill to calm me down." Her fists clenched, and she was quickly approaching the part where she thought violence sounded like a delightful answer. Her therapist would be thrilled. "He certainly had the motive, working with an evil force of nature sounds right up his alley, and apparently the opportunity, but I think he would have used that power on me if he'd had any. He spent over a year trying to convince me I was unstable. A little glamour would have gone a long way to sell that."

When she looked over at Jake, he was leaning back in the chair with his arms behind his head, but his jaw was twitching. Probably not the best time to go into that. She approached him and squatted next to his chair. "There is definitely something fishy going on with Will, but I still don't think it's him. I'll keep him on the list though, okay?"

"Don't do me any favors. By all means, keep protecting your ex. It's not like I'll be much help. Let me know when you need me to stand around being useless, oh powerful one."

Her anger rushed up out of nowhere at the stubborn, pig-headed, and annoyingly calm man in front of her. "I'm not protecting him. Does it bother you, me being powerful? Men can't stand a woman they can't control, after all."

She spit out the words still crouched next to his chair, so she had to look up to meet his eyes, which pissed her off a little more. Thunder crashed in the distance, and she realized the kitchen was getting progressively darker. A storm must be rolling in.

Jake took his time and leaned down close to her face. "Don't put that on me. I don't want to see you get hurt. You could pull gold bars out of your ass for all I care. Everyone has power in some form. There's even power in this." And he kissed her.

The bond roared to life, and her anger drained out of her. Unlike the previous times, his lips weren't gentle. This was staking a claim, a possession. He cupped her cheek, holding her head in place, but she had no intention of pulling away after a week of deprivation.

Sera kissed him back, putting her own claim on him. In one movement, she rose from her crouch and straddled him in the chair without breaking contact. He leaned back to give her space, but she followed, flattening herself against him.

His other hand tangled in her hair while his mouth demanded a response. She opened for him and couldn't help a moan when his tongue swept inside. All the little touches, the smiles, the brushes and the breaths had built up inside her. In her mind, the bond pulsed with golden light. He was right. There was power in their connection. She could sense his need, it flooded her system and flowed back into him.

She ran her hands under his shirt, desperate to feel his skin against her palms. Delighted at the sharp intake of breath when her fingers splayed across his chest. He ran his hands down her sides and around her back, pushing her shirt out of the way. The fabric stopped him halfway up, and he laughed against her mouth at the tangled mess they were making with their clothes.

She arched into him and his laugh cut off with a groan. His tongue found her collarbone, and he left open-mouthed kisses up her neck until he nipped at the sensitive skin under her ear. It was a spot she'd forgotten, but he'd remembered. The last of her reservations fell away. This was her Jake, and she was done waiting. He was hard under his jeans, and Sera wanted them off. Her fingers slipped under his waistband, but he grabbed her wrists.

"Wait—" He closed his eyes and sucked in another breath when she wiggled against him. A pause, then he met her eyes. "Wait. I want you naked more than I want air, but this chair won't work for what I've got in mind."

Sera raised a brow. "What've you got in mind?"

He released her wrists and suddenly stood with his hands on her butt to hold her against him. She wrapped her legs around his waist and marveled at how they always seemed to end up in the same position.

"We're going upstairs where I can lock the door and take my time with no interruptions. Last chance to back out," he said.

She'd already made her decision. Sera slid down his body real slow until she was standing in front of him. He released her with a pained look on his face. She smiled.

"Good idea. Race you to the top," she said and took off running.

Sera laughed all the way up the stairs with Jake at her heels. She edged him out coming around the corner at the landing, but he caught up to her at the bedroom door. His arms came around her from behind, and she squealed as he lifted her off her feet and spun her around.

Somewhere in that maneuver he kicked the door closed, and Sera ended up with her back against it and Jake pressed against her where she wanted him. Her body was on fire with need. She was breathing hard, and it was from more than the mad dash up the stairs.

She couldn't help one more comment. "I won, what's my prize?"

The lock clicked behind her. "Me," Jake growled just before he took her mouth.

Sera broke the kiss for a second to pull her top over her head, then shoved frantically at Jake's until he yanked it off.

His chest really was impressive. She ran her hands down toned muscles and warm skin to his waistband and nipped at his bottom lip.

The bond pulsed with feeling, almost more than Sera could decipher, but the predominant one was the fierce need to protect. It was intertwined with triumph and admiration and joy, and a strong desire to see her naked.

She wanted him naked too.

His hand on her lower back kept them in delicious contact, as he trailed soft kisses down her neck that nearly buckled her knees. When she unbuttoned his jeans, he grabbed both her wrists and pinned them above her head with one hand. The other popped her bra open with a snap. She thanked the lingerie gods that she'd chosen the cute bra with the front clasp that morning, easier to get out of the way. Jake took his time kissing his way down her neck, repaying her with little bites that shot right to her center. She rolled her hips against him, and they both groaned. He held her there for a moment, pressing her back against the door, but his mouth wouldn't be rushed.

He teased the sensitive skin of her breasts, circling with his tongue but never reaching the center where she wanted him. When he finally, finally, closed his lips around her nipple she let loose a guttural moan and tugged hard on the hand holding hers captive. He sucked hard and she arched her back, demanding more.

"Jake, please." She panted, yanking again, desperate to touch him.

One more long pull, and Jake obliged, dropping his hand to unbutton her jeans. Sera didn't waste her chance.

She shoved his chest and he stumbled back a few steps. A gentler push had him backed against the bed where he sat down hard. Her bra flew over her shoulder, and her pants thumped against the door as she kicked them off. She could feel through the bond how much he was enjoying her enthusiasm, but he was wearing way too many clothes still.

"Your turn," she said and waited with her hands on her hips.

It was dim in the room thanks to the storm, but she could easily make out his shape. He shucked his pants in one quick move and leaned back on the bed with a grin. Rain pelted against the window, and Sera's pulse beat with it. There was no hesitation this time, need drove her.

She made it two steps before he reached out and hauled her against him. He rolled them until she was under him in the center of the bed, and Sera welcomed his weight. It had been a long time since she'd enjoyed a man's body, and the bond between them created an additional layer of gratification she hadn't expected. Every touch sent a zing of electricity through her and the bond bounced it back to him.

Through a haze of pleasure, she noticed that his shields were partially up. He must have been practicing, and normally Sera would've been impressed and appreciated it. Maintaining shields between them at all times to keep the influx of Jake to a dull roar was exhausting. Even with the connection shuttered, his pleasure sang through her. But right now? She wanted all of him.

Sera pressed up against him, hitting just the right spot and moaning. Jake shuddered and pushed himself up on his arms. The air was chilly compared to his warmth, and Sera was about to pull him back down when she realized he was reaching for the bedside table.

Jake dropped a kiss against her temple and muttered, "This drawer is further away than I remember it being."

Sera laughed and nipped his shoulder, then soothed it with her tongue. A quick slide later and he was back against her, but instead of rushing forward, he stilled. His breath was as ragged as hers, but she could tell he wanted a moment to remember. Sera felt his need to make her see the way they fit together, and she did. She really did. His unruly hair tickled her face as he leaned down to kiss her.

This one was different than the other kisses. Softer, but no less intense. This was a joyous reunion, a coming home. Sera framed his face with her hands and deepened the kiss. He eased into her, and it *was* joyous.

This was what she'd missed the most. Not the physical sensations, though that was fantastic, but the rightness. The knowing. Jake began to move and she sighed.

The beat of the rain and the rhythm of their bodies built her up and up until she lost herself and opened for him. They released their shields in unison, and the bond pulled taut. Sera distantly registered golden light flashing across the room, but she couldn't do anything other than cling to Jake and ride out the storm.

***

SOMETIME LATER, Sera woke from a dream where she was being chased by the zombie bunnies again. Those fuzzy monsters wouldn't leave her alone. She'd kicked off the sheets that she vaguely remembered Jake throwing over them earlier. The room was completely dark, but she knew Jake was lying next to her. The same way she knew the instant he woke up.

She was still for a moment, listening to him breathing, until he rolled over and pulled her against him. It had been a long time since she'd been the little spoon. Dried sweat on her skin made her feel sticky, and she had delicious aches in places she hadn't used in years. It would probably be prudent to stretch the next time. Habit had her itching to jump up and take a shower, but for the first time in forever, she didn't want to.

Jake was warm and the contented feelings coming through the bond encouraged her to snuggle in and go back to sleep. She wiggled closer and discovered that Jake was more than contented. Then there were the other things she could feel. Happiness at the forefront. Jake was happy she was there.

Even more surprising, Sera was happy she was there. Jake yawned in her ear and chuckled when she playfully elbowed him in the stomach. His hand traced her hip then dug in to tickle her. Sera shrieked and grabbed at him, but he was too fast. He rolled her under him, arms above their heads where her elbows couldn't reach him.

"Guess we're both awake," he said.

"I never meant to fall asleep."

"We used up a lot of energy earlier, it makes sense we'd pass out."

Sera slid her hands out from under his and popped up on one elbow. "Did you see it too? The flashes?"

Jake nodded slowly. "I saw something flash, but it could have been a bunch of pervert sprites getting off on all the magic being tossed around."

Her excitement dimmed. "Yeah, I guess. I thought maybe we'd tapped into something new."

"Oh we definitely tapped something new." He grinned suggestively. Sera rolled her eyes, but her smile was back. Jake trailed a finger down her cheek and lifted her chin until she met his eyes. "It could have been sprites or it could have been some kickass power you harnessed on accident or it could have been a lightning strike near the house. I'm no expert on magic, especially magical humans. As far as I know, I've never been with anyone with power, though it could've been buried deep down. I suppose you count in both cases."

A flare of jealousy at the thought of Jake with anyone else made Sera take a concentrated breath. She had no reason to be jealous. Hell, she'd been married. His hand continued down her neck, over her shoulder, and settled at the small of her back. A trail of warmth followed where he touched. It would be easy to reach up and pull him back down to her, but the flare of light weighed on her mind. Something had happened between them and manifested physically.

They'd been fully connected, no shields, no hiding, and it felt like they hadn't come all the way back from that. She sensed him, even though his shields were back up. He was keeping his attitude light, but she knew what she'd felt earlier. It scared her because she wasn't ready for it. She wasn't sure that she'd ever be ready for it.

It wasn't fair to keep quiet.

"Jake, we need to talk."

He flopped back against the pillows and blew out a breath. "I hate that phrase. It never comes before anything good. You're not about to tell me you're secretly a werewolf or something, are you? Because I'm pretty sure I would have noticed."

Sera smiled. "Not a werewolf, as far as I know. And this was one of the most enjoyable afternoons I think I've ever had."

"We're well into evening now."

"I noticed. Just in case I'm giving mixed signals or the bond is making things confusing, I need to be clear that I'm not interested in marriage and babies and a picket fence."

"I'm going to point out that you actually own a picket

fence around your garden. I helped Evie build it. And I don't remember proposing. We're good together, and I have a lot of jumbled feelings about you, for you, but I'm not looking for a wife and babies yet. I like you, more than I probably should considering our history, and I really like seeing you naked." He twined their fingers together and kissed her knuckles. "Be with me now and we can take the future as it comes, okay?"

She'd started this conversation expecting it to end with hurt feelings and an unfortunate walk of shame, but Jake surprised her. He seemed to know exactly how far to go before she started wanting to run the other direction.

Sera rolled into him and pressed her face into his shoulder. "Okay," she whispered. A moment passed before she pulled back a little and spoke more firmly, "Okay, as long as you're not seeing anyone else naked in the meantime." She hadn't meant to say the last bit, but it made sense. No need for miscommunications or extra complications. *Sure, keep telling yourself that's the reason.*

"As long as that goes both ways," Jake added.

She nodded. "Okay." And strangely it was okay. Her traitorous heart was appeased by the stipulation, and the rest of her wasn't freaking out about the perils of commitment. Nothing was going to convince her that marriage led anywhere other than anger and disappointment, but she could enjoy Jake as long as they were both willing.

"Well that wasn't too bad." Jake shifted so he settled between her thighs again, hard and ready. "Want to go for round two?" He ran his nose gently up her neck to that spot she liked behind her ear.

Yes. Yes, she did.

10

SERA

SOMEONE WAS BEING RICK-ROLLED. "Never Gonna Give You Up" blared from somewhere in the bedroom, and Sera was ready to kill whoever it was. She kept her eyes closed and listened to Jake sit up and answer his phone. Who in their right mind used Rick Astley as their ringtone?

The sun shone through the window and birds were chirping outside. It was a cheerful morning, but Sera still wanted to pull the blanket over her head so she could sleep for another full day. The bed bounced as Jake got up, and memories of the reason she was tired surfaced. She cracked one eye to watch his fine ass disappear into the bathroom.

Giddiness came over her at the thought that, at least for the moment, he was all hers. She could join him in the shower, or position herself seductively for his return. A couple of practice poses made it clear that she'd never be a pin-up girl.

Indecision made the choice for her. The shower turned

off and Jake emerged in a cloud of steam with a towel wrapped around his waist. Sera pulled the sheet up over her boobs and sat up.

"Rick Astley? Seriously? Is there something wrong with you I don't know about?" Without coffee, her morning filter was non-existent. Mocking his choice of ringtones would probably not get him back in bed with her.

"You don't like Rick Astley?" He took off the towel to rub his hair, humming the chorus, and Sera couldn't decide if she wanted to jump him or strangle him. She'd bet either one would shut him up.

"Why are you up so early?" she asked instead.

He looked pointedly at the window. "It's not early."

Sera groaned. "Oh man, you're one of those morning people I want to beat to death with my coffee cup, aren't you? Why, god, why must you test me so?" She considered raising a fist to the heavens, but it seemed like a lot of work when she'd already sat up and had part of a conversation this morning.

"Maddie called. She needs me to come help her move some stuff."

A warning pinged against Sera's senses. "What stuff?"

"I don't know. Boxes or something. She woke me up and I wasn't really listening. She wanted to borrow the truck, again. I love my sister, but she's clumsy and my truck is worth more than her."

It all sounded completely normal, but Sera had a bad feeling. "Be careful, okay?"

Jake collected his wallet and keys and sat on the bed next to her. "I shouldn't be gone long. Will you please stay here?"

"You want me to throw my agenda for today out the

window in favor of keeping your bed warm?" Actually, it didn't sound like that bad of a plan.

"Do you know what today is?"

Sera squinted at her phone. "Tuesday?"

"Halloween."

"Right..." Sera frowned. For the last twelve hours, she'd completely forgotten about Torix and his threat. One she hadn't told Jake about. They had only today left to find his follower, but now Jake needed to deal with Maddie first. Something weird was going on with her, and he'd be the best person to figure out what it was. As much as she wanted to pull him down for a repeat of last night's fun, they were basically out of time. She really needed to be out looking for the minion.

Jake lifted her hand to his lips and brushed a kiss over her knuckles. "I promise to be as fast as possible, then we can figure out a way to lure the bad guys into the open. Promise me you'll stay safe."

"That's mighty optimistic of you."

Jake glared at her meaningfully.

"Fine." Sera rolled her eyes. "I promise to stay safe." Jake might not know it, but that was a huge concession from her. She was used to handling things on her own.

Jake kissed her hand again, then her lips, sending tingles through her. Sera deepened the kiss, and for a second, she thought Jake might stay after all. One swipe of his tongue against hers, then he pulled back with a groan,

"Ugh, Maddie ruins everything." A chaste peck on the cheek, and he got up to leave.

Sera stayed in bed for all of two minutes. She needed a shower, and it was tempting to go next door to her own stuff, but it wouldn't hurt to indulge Jake's worries. Besides, his shower was way nicer than hers.

Twenty minutes later, Sera was clean, her clothes were in the dryer, and she was ready for coffee. Heading down the stairs in one of Jake's shirts, she balked at sitting around brainstorming when she could be doing something instead. She kept expecting a panic attack to sneak up on her. Things were going too well, so her mind had to freak out about something insignificant. To her great relief however, since she'd picked up the shields, she hadn't felt any panic. It made sense in a twisted way. She had faith that the shields would protect her, and her newfound power made it hard for anyone to force her into anything.

She sat down at the table with a cup of coffee and a bowl of generic Frosted Flakes before she saw the note.

I mean it. Don't go anywhere without me. I took your keys just in case.

The memory slammed into her before she had a chance to react. A sunny morning at their house in Irvine. She'd woken up with a stomach ache, but Will had been gone. She'd stumbled down the stairs in search of her purse only to find that her keys were missing. Hunched over, trying to alleviate the shooting pains, she searched the house, but couldn't find them anywhere.

Will had insisted that all the locks on their house be key access only, and all the doors were locked. None of their windows opened, again because Will wanted fixed picture windows. He had a thing for large swaths of glass. Without her keys, she was trapped inside. She spent the day in the bathroom by herself, puking and writhing in pain from food poisoning.

When Will came home, he'd berated her for not getting dressed or cleaning the house. He'd called her lazy and useless, and when she'd dared to ask him about her keys, he'd scoffed at her. *What do you need to leave the house for? Everything you should be concerned with is right here.* He'd claimed she was overreacting and given her a pill to calm her down, then left again for a last-minute dinner appointment.

She'd promptly thrown up the pill, along with everything else, and it had been the first time in months that she'd felt clear-headed for more than a few minutes. When he came home from dinner, he'd smelled like perfume, and he'd watched her closely. It took three days of healing and pretending to be drugged, before he gave her keys back. Each day, she spit out the pills after he left and felt stronger. The day he returned them, arrogant and doting, she packed up her stuff and moved out.

Her keys were her freedom.

Outwardly, she knew she looked calm. It was a useful skill she'd developed while married to Will. Inwardly, she was fighting the urge to set the note on fire, along with the table, and probably the kitchen too. She'd wondered where she'd left her keys, but it had never occurred to her that Jake would abscond with them.

Who does he think he is? He didn't have the right to decide her actions, and she'd damn well go gallivanting off if she wanted to. Her heartbeat throbbed in her ears, and she tried to keep her breathing even. She wasn't trapped. Her house was right next door, and it was easy enough to walk into town if she needed to. She wasn't locked in. It took a minute to realize she wasn't feeling panic. It was rage. Hot, powerful, justified rage. Plain and simple. She let it roll through her, feeling it fully and acknowledging its validity.

After letting herself process for a minute, it was time to reign it in, decide what she wanted to do and fucking do it.

She still didn't trust herself not to destroy something if she got up though, so she didn't stomp directly back to her place for a change of clothes. She stayed seated and ate her cereal, and imagined what kind of pain she could inflict with the spoon. Jake was great in bed, but she was done letting anyone else control her. If Jake didn't understand that, and she highly doubted it because her keys really were gone, then he could fuck off.

The more she thought about breaking away from Jake, the better it sounded. Zee wasn't omniscient or they wouldn't be in this mess, so leaving Jake behind was suddenly back on the table. Her magic would suffer, sure, but she'd gotten through twenty-five years without magic, and she'd get through this. She had to unclench her jaw to eat the next spoonful.

She'd take care of Torix on her own. Thus far, they'd gotten diddly squat anyway, and she knew Zee hadn't told them everything. Hell, everyone knew that. She could go grab some clothes more appropriate for tramping through the woods and pay Zee a visit. She didn't need keys for that since she'd left the door unlocked, and she didn't need Jake or any other controlling asshole with a hero complex holding her back.

The front door opened, and Sera prepared for battle. With Jake and with herself, because a large part of her still wanted to drag him and his stupid hero complex back upstairs for round three. Except it wasn't Jake that appeared in the doorway.

Ryan pulled up short at the sight of Sera in one of Jake's shirts eating cereal at the table. "Well this is going to complicate things."

Sera decided to be polite, even though she could feel a

breeze all the way up her thighs. There was no reason to take her anger out on him. Yet. "Want some breakfast?"

"Is Jake making it?"

"He's not here. He had to run off to save the world all by his lonesome."

Ryan raised both brows. "Then no." He hesitated. "You seem upset. Everything okay?"

Sera swallowed another spoonful of soggy flakes. She must have been out of practice with her poker face. *Something to work on.*

"What is wrong with men that they think I'm incapable of making smart decisions on my own? They're possessive and stupid and so sure they're right all the time. Yeah, it was amazing sex, but that doesn't mean he gets to trap me here. And what makes him so convinced he can protect me? I'm the one with the power. What's he going to do, punch Torix? One night of mind-blowing orgasms and suddenly he's invulnerable?"

Ryan looked askance at her, then pointed to his face. "This is my 'I immediately regret my decision to be polite' face. Please stop talking."

"You should be taking notes, maybe you'll learn something."

"Mm-hmm, like I should stop coming over uninvited."

Despite his words, he sat down at the table with her. Sera knew she was cranky, partly because the coffee hadn't kicked in yet, but mostly because it was taking time for her to work through her anger with Jake. Taking her keys didn't really stop her from doing anything. All she had to do was walk across the street to go into the magical forest. He was trying to exert control, and she was going to make sure he understood the consequences.

Her stomach cramped at the thought that she'd been

about to follow him blindly. She'd certainly learned her lesson there. Again. Jake's actions had made her doubt herself. Again. Tears formed in her eyes, but she'd be damned if she'd let them fall in front of Ryan. The last thing she needed was him telling Jake all about how she'd cried into her cereal.

Sera didn't take orders well on the best of days, so she was definitely going to be gone by the time Jake got back. She was half-worried seeing him might weaken her resolve to stay away from him, so she needed to be strong. Her chest got tight imagining living next to Jake for the foreseeable future, and she considered leaving for a while after everything was over. Jake could do as he pleased.

Ryan had waited patiently while her relationship silently imploded, surprisingly nice for a snarky dude, but Sera wasn't feeling very charitable.

"What are you doing here, anyway?" she grumbled.

"It's Halloween, and I don't want to be sucked dry and left as a shriveled-up husk. It's not a good look for me. I'm here to strategize. As a side note, Jake makes amazing pancakes, and I was hoping to score some."

Her heart squeezed painfully at the mention of Jake's pancakes. "Priorities."

He hesitated. "There was one other thing. There was another break-in at school."

Sera winced. She was pissed and hurting, but not enough to welcome another set of zombie bunnies to distract her. "Not more dead animals?"

"Dead? As far as I know those rabbits are still categorized as missing."

"Right. That's what I meant."

He watched her, and she fought the urge to fidget. "No, not animals this time. It sounds like it was part of a series of break-ins yesterday in town. The sheriff is blaming teenagers causing trouble before Halloween, but the missing items rang some bells for me."

"You think it was Torix's minion?"

"I think it's likely."

"Okay, what was missing?"

"Candles, a cauldron, matches, a *lot* of salt, beakers, two filet knives, a couple of cubic feet of garden dirt, and three packages of gummy dinosaurs."

Sera blinked at him a few times. "I know I should be concerned, and we're going to circle back to where one might swipe an actual cauldron, but all I can think about is what does an evil minion need with gummy dinosaurs? And what exactly are gummy dinosaurs again?"

"Well, my best guess is that even evil minions probably need tasty snacks. Gummy dinos are the local version of gummy bears, and thievery, if done right, can really work up a good appetite, so our intrepid evil-doer snagged some treats." Ryan shot her an adorable grin, but then sobered. "One of the grannies in town makes and sells them at the student store. Everyone loves them, so it doesn't narrow much down. The rest of the stuff is all pretty useful for a summoning circle."

Sera shook her head at him and went to take a drink of her coffee but found her cup empty. She wanted to get a refill, but the shirt was downright indecent when she was standing, at least she wouldn't have this problem any more once she gathered her things and left. There would be no more surprise overnights at Jake's house. "Would you like some coffee?"

He grinned. "Need a refill?"

She crossed her hands primly in front of her. "Yes, thank you."

Ryan grabbed her cup and didn't have to rummage through the cabinets looking for another one. He knew right where they were. Sera wondered how often Ryan popped in for breakfast, and how often he became an awkward third wheel during a morning after. Judging by his surprise when he came in, not often. *No warm fuzzy feelings, we're still mad. Yeah, mad!*

He brought her newly filled cup and his own and sat down across from her at the table. "We need a plan."

Sera pulled her thoughts away from Jake's dating habits. "What happens if we leave. Let Torix have his moment. We go to California or Tahiti or something and let the Fae handle their own problems."

Ryan scrubbed his hand down his face. "Oh, how I'd love that, but if there's one thing I've learned since moving here, it's that the Fae don't solve their own problems. Torix would get free, he'd eat your grandmother and his minion and any other humans stupid enough to be in the Wood on Halloween at midnight. So, a large population of the high school probably. Zee would try to stop him, but he never agreed to be bound like the rest of them, so he could leave the woods and rampage through town. The more power he eats, the more powerful he becomes. Eventually he'd finish with Mulligan and move on to another place. By the time he hit Tahiti, he'd be a god and we'd be doomed."

Sera blinked. "That was surprisingly detailed, and with some new information in there, so good to know. Not that I could do that anyway, leave someone else to deal with this mess. It would piss me off to no end if I died because someone else screwed it up. Also, how do you know all that?"

"One of the first things they had me do was upload all

their texts into a database in case of disaster. I'm still an admin, so I have access. It's searchable."

"Does Zee know you still have access?"

"We haven't discussed it, but I think she does. And Tahiti won't be that great if I'm being tortured by Torix. Did I mention that part? The more intense the emotion, the more he likes it. It's unclear if it gives him more power or if it tastes better, but he was very into the torture scene during his last rampage."

"Why didn't you bring this up the last time?"

"I wasn't sure there would be much useful information in there. Some of the Fae were crap at note-taking."

"Is there information about humans with power? Maybe a guidebook on how to use it?"

Ryan cocked his head. "Probably, but I thought you'd already figured it out. Wasn't that what you and Jake have been doing all week?"

"Seriously? All this would have been very useful a week ago." She tried to push away the frustration and anger at stupid, closed-mouthed, controlling men, not to mention the painful memories of laughing with Jake, and focus on the problem at hand. Based on the alarmed look Ryan was giving her, Sera wasn't sure she was doing a very good job. *Deep breaths. In and out. In... and out.*

Ryan hurried on. "Zee believes you learn more by figuring it out yourself. I tried to tell her the same thing about how to work her smartphone, but she wasn't amused."

Sera almost growled, but she really wanted access to that database. Maybe there was something in there about how to defeat Torix for good. The Fae may have trapped themselves in their little area, but she could roam freely, as could the other people in town with power. Her mind was racing with possibilities, but Ryan interrupted her by tapping her hand.

"Nothing it could teach you would help with Torix," he said.

"But what if the others and I worked together—"

"Even if that was possible, in the time we have, you wouldn't be able to master it. And what about all the people who've never used their power or use it passively? They'd show up and get eaten, and we'd have to deal with a more powerful Torix."

"Well if I'd know all this a week ago, we could have been practicing this whole time and wouldn't be completely unprepared now would we?" The rage still simmering under the surface began to bubble up again.

Ryan wouldn't meet her eyes. He just stared at the table and mumbled, "Nothing we can do about it now."

Sera slumped back in her chair. He was right. "So what do we do? Samhain is tonight, we have no idea who's helping Torix, and weird shit is happening all over the place."

Ryan's head snapped up. "What weird shit?"

"I went by Maddie's yesterday and it was shielded. The wolf was there but he didn't attack me. He followed me back here and looked like he was going to attack Will until I got rid of him. Will, not the wolf, though they both went away at the same time. And I slept with Jake. More than once."

"Maddie's was shielded? How?"

"I don't know. That's why it's weird. I figured out how to get through the shields, and there's all this magical stuff in her place, but Jake swears she's powerless."

"You broke into Maddie's magically warded house?"

"Yes. I'm a badass. Keep up. The wolf was watching me,

but he didn't move, even after I had to run through the open to get to my car."

Ryan's eyebrows came together. "That doesn't make any sense."

"I know. Again, that's why it's weird."

"Are you sure the magic you felt in Maddie's wasn't you doing something on accident?"

Sera held up a finger. "I'll let that one pass because it's a valid concern, but I'm getting better at keeping the power controlled. It was magic from people all over town."

He nodded. "Okay, we'll shelve that for now. The wolf followed you here? Why did you come here instead of your place? What was Will doing here?"

"Yes. None of your business. I don't know." Sera hesitated then continued. "He was looking for me, I think. The wolf looked pissed. All spiky along his back, and he was slinking forward out of the woods."

"What did you do?"

"I blasted Will's fancy car with magic until the alarm went off and he left. The wolf retreated back into the trees once Will was in his car."

"I assume Jake wasn't here?"

"Why would you assume that?"

"Because Will was still in one piece on the front porch."

Sera raised a brow. "He was at work. He came home right after that."

"We can skip the nookie. I don't want to know why it was weird."

Sera tugged at the shirt not quite covering her thighs. "Now that you're all caught up, can you turn around or get out or something so I can change?"

"Why don't you glamour it?"

"Because I'll look clothed, but still feel mostly naked. Turn around."

Ryan turned his chair with a loud scrape, and Sera ran back upstairs to retrieve her clothes from the dryer. She'd explained the day twice now, and she wasn't any closer to answers. Time was ticking by, and she had to find some way to stop the servant or Torix or both, ideally both, and rescue Evie. Oh, and keep herself from running back to Jake's bed at the first opportunity. That ship had sailed.

Nervous energy had her itching to make a list, but she wasn't feeling the telltale signs of panic. Another weird development, shouldn't she be panicking at the thought of failing and dooming the town, maybe the world, to being tortured and eaten by an evil fairy?

The laundry room was really more of a laundry nook, so Sera took her clothes back into the bedroom to change. The rumpled bed brought back memories of Jake, not only last night, but years ago.

She'd been so happy to feel normal for the first time in her life. Jake had made her feel wanted, and she'd been planning to stay with Evie permanently. The summer was coming to a close, and she'd looked forward to starting school in an entirely new place. It was a chance to reinvent herself. Evie had hinted heavily that she wanted Sera to start training in the family business. At the time, she'd assumed that meant working at the antique shop Evie had owned, but in hindsight, she'd probably meant the magic.

If she'd stayed, would she have been properly trained? Could she have stopped Evie from going against Torix in the end? Or would they both be trapped in Fae limbo?

Sera shook off the feeling of foreboding. She quickly made the bed and found a picture of Jake's parents under one of the pillows on the floor. They must have knocked it off the nightstand at some point. She said a silent thanks that they hadn't broken anything, and picked it up to get a closer look. His dad had his arm around his mom, and she was giving him a smacking kiss on the cheek.

She set the picture down. As far as she knew, there were no pictures of her parents together. Her mom refused to tell her anything about her father. She wouldn't even acknowledge that there'd been another person involved in making Sera. Evie had commented once that her mom had been hurt badly and wanted to forget everything. Sera had been hurt at first because she felt like she was part of the everything, but her mom never made her feel like she regretted having a daughter. This specific daughter, yes. She was pretty sure her mom had cursed the gods for the daughter she got, but she'd never tried to ignore her.

The summer she was with Evie, her mom had called every day, and though she'd wanted so badly to stay, she'd hesitated because it would mean hurting her mom. After she returned home, she'd wondered why both Evie and her mom went to such great lengths to avoid each other. They wouldn't even say the other woman's name if they could avoid it. What kind of rift could split a mother and daughter so severely? Her own relationship with her mom wasn't exactly healthy, and Will made it way worse, but she still picked up the phone most of the time when her mom called.

The room was clean, Jake's bed was piled high with bedding once more, for a guy, he was really into pillows, and she was running out of ways to procrastinate. Once she left, there would be no going back. Her eyes returned to the picture of Jake's parents. They looked normal, and she knew Jake didn't have any magic. She'd have felt it. It was clear she'd gotten her magic from Evie, but what about her mom?

Sera was one hundred percent convinced her mom didn't know. Something they were going to have a long discussion about once Evie was free. What else had Evie kept secret?

Looking back, Sera was pretty sure Evie'd been hiding something that last night before Sera left. She'd been distracted and more accommodating than usual. Evie had trusted her, but she'd always required that Sera be home by eleven. When Sera had asked if she could go out with Jake then stay the night with Maddie, Evie had given in without a fuss. Jake had planned to take her out to a fancy dinner, but his parents had decided to go away for the weekend at the last minute and left him to watch Maddie. They'd ended up eating Rosie's on the back patio.

Sera sank down on the bed and let the memories take her for once. She hadn't meant to lie to Evie, but Maddie had decided to go off to a friend's house. Sera had stayed the night with Jake instead. The next morning Maddie had called, and Jake had rushed off to help her. Sera hadn't realized it until just now, but that last disastrous day and night were turning out to be very similar to this one. He'd even left a stupid note the last time too.

I love you. See you soon.

She'd thought that had meant he'd be back soon. Except he wasn't. After an hour, she'd gone home to find Evie already at the shop. She hadn't seen him again and he hadn't called, but Maddie had come over later that evening. She wanted to go to a bonfire at a friend's house on the other side of the woods, but she didn't want to go alone. Her parents would never have let her go, but Sera was feeling abandoned by Jake and rebellious.

Evie had asked that she take a flashlight, and Sera had left with her blessing. The rest of the night was fuzzy. When Maddie'd turned to cut through the woods, Sera had followed her down a path she'd never noticed before. Minutes later, Sera's head was swimming and she was gliding through tiny golden glimmers. *Sprites.* She didn't remember drinking anything, but she'd felt drunk. The trees loomed above them, and Maddie danced and laughed ahead of her.

They never made it to the bonfire.

The last thing Sera remembered about that night was a horned black shadow figure chasing them through the brush. She'd looked back and been slapped by a sharp branch that'd left a series of small cuts across her cheek. Everything after that was dark. She'd woken several hours later on Evie's back patio, curled up under a blanket on the swing.

Evie had been waiting inside with tea. Sera hadn't known where Maddie was, and every time she'd tried to bring up any memories, she'd been drenched in fear. Even now, in the relative safety of Jake's bedroom, her heart sped up and her breath came short. After a lifetime of being told she was mentally ill, Sera had been convinced that she'd snapped and done something to Maddie. Sometime later, Maddie showed up at home, seemingly drunk, covered in twigs, and with a broken wrist. The guilt and fear made Sera pack up and leave that night.

Sera was gone before morning. Evie tried to stay in contact, but Sera couldn't face her. Her mom was willing to pass a few messages along. Maddie was fine, but she didn't remember anything either, Evie missed her... nothing about Jake. That lasted a few weeks, then silence. Sera wasn't sure if her mom stopped passing the messages, or if Evie stopped trying; at the time, she hadn't wanted to know which it was.

The truth was still a mystery to her, but recent developments had her questioning things she'd taken as fact.

They'd been on a fairy trod, she'd been under the influence of something, and Maddie may not have been an innocent casualty. Overshadowing everything else was the knowledge that Evie knew what had happened that night. The things Sera had told her, and the things she couldn't remember.

The sun streamed through Jake's windows, and Sera picked at a snag on his bedspread. She was back where she'd started all those years ago. Fresh from Jake's bed but without Jake, unable to talk to Evie, and feeling rebellious.

There was one big difference though. Sera wasn't running away this time.

11

SERA

RYAN WAS EXACTLY where she'd left him, facing the wall in the kitchen. "Did you have to weave the pants yourself?"

"I'm dressed. I think Evie was going to train me."

Ryan turned and raised his eyebrows. "Okay, I'll go along with it. That makes sense. You're her granddaughter, you obviously have power, and you were living here."

"She was going to train me, but she kept things from me and I left before she could even tell me about any of this. She had power, and I spent most of my life thinking I was crazy because no one bothered to tell me about mine." Her voice was approaching hysterical at the end there. She tried to calm down enough to get through one last conversation with Ryan before she went searching for trouble.

"If you're trying to make Evie into the bad guy here, you're wasting your breath. That woman was amazing and if I'd been a couple decades older, you'd be calling me grandpa."

"*Is* amazing, and gross. But she did let me leave *and* let me live for seven more years believing I was crazy. That's not right, but it's also not relevant right now. My point is that Evie wanted to pass along her knowledge, and I took away the easy answer. I think she started training Maddie instead."

"How could she if Maddie didn't have any power?"

Sera shrugged. "It's all knowledge, right? It's just the amount of power behind the knowledge that's variable? Anyway, that's not the important part. I think Evie was hiding some things from me. More than that. When I lived here before, she kept talking about the family business. I thought she meant the antique shop, but I never got the feeling she saw that shop as a family legacy thing. The magic and her relationship with the Fae, that seems like something she'd pass on."

"You said all this already. We've established that she wanted to train you."

"I think it was more than training, and I'm thinking she started with my mom."

Ryan's smile fell away. "What are you getting at?"

"My mom left when I was a baby and refused to come back. I ran away screaming when I was seventeen with my powers sealed inside me. Could Evie have done that?"

"You need to be very careful about what you're saying here."

Sera's hackles rose. "Am I supposed to be afraid of my grandmother who's incapable of affecting this realm right now?"

"No, you're supposed to be careful because I can only answer carefully phrased questions."

Sera's brows shot up. "Holy crap, you know. You know the truth, and Zee stopped you from talking about it."

Ryan didn't respond. He didn't even blink.

"Why would the Fae get involved?" She shook her head. "No, wrong question. Why did my mother leave?"

Respect shone in Ryan's eyes. "Good question. Your grandmother, with some help, softened her memories, but even so she was afraid to live here."

"Evie could do that? Take away someone's memories?"

Ryan paused, then continued. "I guess I'm allowed to talk about this. It's possible to take away the trauma of an event, but not the actual memories. I'm told it's about speeding the healing process by making the memories seem like they're farther away than they are."

"That sounds like a Fae thing."

"Magic is magic. It's limited by the practitioner."

"Do you know why my mom was afraid?"

"I know very little about your mom personally, only stuff that's been told to me secondhand or that I overheard when they thought I wasn't listening."

"They? Who was talking about my mom when they thought you weren't listening?"

Ryan grinned. "Evie and Zee."

Sera stared at the shadows on the wall and tried to come up with a way to ask the next question that would get her an answer. It was clear he couldn't give her direct information and that the Fae were involved somehow, but he wanted to help. Evie wasn't a bad person, and Sera believed she loved her daughter. The magic must have been meant to protect and heal, but from what?

"What else was happening around town during the time Zee and Evie were talking about?"

"The 32nd Annual Strawberry Festival was kicking off with a pie-eating contest."

A quick Google search and some basic math told Sera the 32nd Annual Strawberry Festival happened in May twenty-seven years ago, six months before she was born. Whatever happened, her mom had been three months pregnant.

Sera let her phone thunk to the table and stared at Ryan. The process of prying information out of him was exhausting. Why would the Fae care about her pregnant mother? If she asked Zee, would she get a straight answer? Probably not, unless Zee thought it would benefit her or her people in some way. The whole thing was probably not important anyway.

"Did Evie make the seal?"

No response from Ryan.

"Did Zee?"

Nothing. Maybe something crazy.

"Did Jake?"

"No."

Sera sucked in a breath. "You'd have said no, that means yes. Evie and Zee made the seal? How did Zee lie about it when I first met her then?"

Ryan got up to refill his coffee. "Fae can't lie, remember."

Sera shifted around in her seat. "Then Zee didn't make the seal, but you're not allowed to talk about something involved with Zee and the seal. And you overheard Zee and Evie talking about something that happened to my mother when she was pregnant with me. Evie was insistent that she train me, probably because I had no experience thanks to her seal. It's not like my parents were around to teach me about magic. Mom is completely powerless anyway, and my dad..."

The idea dawned slowly, and she almost dismissed it because it was utterly insane. Ryan leaned against the counter and waited. She wasn't sure how she could tell, but he seemed eager. If she was right, there was a lot more that Zee owed her than a quick lesson on shields.

"Do you know who my father is?"

Ryan raised his cup and took a sip without breaking eye contact.

"You can't answer that. You fucking can't answer that." Sera felt like someone was sitting on her chest. She couldn't get a full breath, and it took her a second to realize it was the beginning of a panic attack. Her stupid lungs weren't working, so Sera closed her eyes and reached for her shields. To her surprise, she grabbed the bond instead.

Jake's energy flowed into her, and she was able to take a deep breath. It wasn't like before, when they'd been intimately connected. She couldn't feel him personally, but she could sense his presence in the bond. A second breath, and she let go much calmer. It was a useful tool, but it bothered her on a lot of levels that it was Jake that calmed her instead of something in herself. Especially now that she'd decided to distance herself from him. That couldn't happen again.

She almost expected Jake to call, like he had the day before when she'd freaked out about Will and the wolf. Her eyes opened, but her phone stayed silent. It was for the best. She told herself what she was feeling was relief, but it was suspiciously close to disappointment. Either way, she had other things to deal with at the moment.

Ryan was watching her, but he hadn't moved from his spot by the coffee maker. If she could read his mind it would make things so much easier.

"I'm going to squash Zee the next time I see her. This is stupid. I can only think of one reason that Zee would care who my father is... he's Fae."

Sera wasn't sure what she was expecting with that declaration. Fireworks, a sudden influx of knowledge, maybe an admission that she was right. She didn't get any of that. Instead, Ryan put his cup down and started a slow clap.

"I think I hate you, this whole stupid situation, definitely all the Fae, and possibly Jake, though the jury is still out on that last one," she said.

"I just felt the spell release, so ask me your questions, bridge keeper, I am not afraid."

Sera narrowed her eyes. The phrase sounded familiar, but she couldn't place it. He was probably making fun of her somehow, but she'd gotten what she wanted. "Is my father Torix?"

Ryan started laughing and kept going until he was bent over wheezing for breath. It was both annoying and a welcome relief. Torix was the only male Fae she knew of, the only Fae she knew at all outside of Zee, and she'd wanted to be absolutely sure. It would have explained the memory wipe, but not how he'd managed to impregnate a human female from inside a tree. Sera shuddered and tried to imagine something small and cute. Of course, zombie bunnies popped up instead.

She'd take it. Anything to distract from thinking about her mother having sex with a tree.

Ryan straightened up and wiped tears from the corners of his eyes. "I was really convinced up until now that you were some kind of master detective, but wow, that was super off. Your father's name was Richard, and he was summoned back to the homeland after it came out that he'd knocked up a human."

"Did my mom know he was Fae?"

"The consensus is no. Evie thought she had suspicions, but messing with her memories took care of that. As far as your mom knew, he simply up and left her one day, pregnant and unloved."

"That was harsh, but it's almost verbatim what my mom always told me." The shock was wearing off a little. "How is it possible? How am I possible? I thought the Fae and humans were completely different species or whatever."

"I'm no expert on biology, but both groups seem to have the appropriate parts, and you're evidence that it's possible. Evie and Zee were talking about Evie messing with your mom's memories and whether or not it was a good idea to leave you under your mom's influence. Evie was confident the seal would hold your magic in place. She wanted you to come back on your own, because it made you happy not because you needed help." He slurped up the rest of his coffee and set the cup in the sink. "Guess that plan backfired."

She could believe that about Evie. "What did Zee think?"

"That your magic would keep building until you exploded. Metaphorically. She was pretty sure you weren't going to be raining down like confetti, but the magic would find a way to burst free even if it injured you in the process. I know they mentioned a promise too, but they didn't go into detail about that one."

Sera rubbed her temples. "I can't believe they kept all of this from me. I'm not even human." Tears threatened, but she willed them away with brute force.

"You're half-human. And if Evie was even slightly right, that half was pretty powerful to begin with, add in a whopping shot of Fae magic to anchor you and you're a superhero. Yeah, secrets suck and your life was probably a mess, but if you tried hard enough, I'll bet you could fly."

Ryan looked pissed, but Sera wasn't interested in sparring with him when they still had Torix to deal with. They'd wasted a long time excavating all this information. She strongly suspected she was compartmentalizing, but the thing with her father was important because it might give her more of an edge.

"We were talking about Maddie before we dredged up all this insanity. I was with her the night Evie sealed my magic, could it be possible that they did the same to her?"

Ryan shook his head and walked aimlessly around the kitchen, picking things up, examining them, and putting them back down. "Maddie doesn't have power."

"Everyone's so sure, but—"

He set an empty vase back down with a thunk. "You need to learn to trust the people around you."

"Yeah, because everyone has been so honest and forth-coming thus far. Every person in my life who I trusted has lied to me about who I am and what is going on. I trust myself, period. End of list."

"What about Jake?"

The bond flared to life inside her, filling her with warmth. "Did he know?"

"No, and if he had, I think he'd have moved heaven and earth to tell you somehow."

Sera nodded. "I believe you, but it doesn't matter."

"You don't trust him?"

"I know I'm really mad at him right now, but I don't know if I trust him." It was the unvarnished truth. She'd spent a long time questioning herself. But once she'd devel-oped the confidence to believe in herself, she'd had to start questioning everyone else. She couldn't handle being in a relationship with him, but maybe with time they could be friends again. "Jake thinks it might be Will."

Ryan laughed. "Because he wants a good reason to beat Will's ass. Honestly, I'd join him, and I've never met the guy."

"He had some compelling evidence that Will at least had the opportunity to be in Torix's service."

"What do you think?"

"I think it's too easy. Will is a narcissist, so he's sneaky and cunning, but he'd have used the threat of Torix to try to bring me back under his control. It could be a stranger, but why keep breaking into the high school to steal stuff? I've talked to most of the people on the list in the last week, and as far as I can tell, they don't even know they have power. They all just think they're lucky." She couldn't contain her nervous energy any longer, so she nudged Ryan out of the way to wash the dishes. "It's impossible to deductively figure out who it is. We have to find some other way."

Sera washed, and Ryan dried, both lost in thought. It was kind of nice to be able to exist with someone in silence that she didn't need to fill, though Jake seemed to have an unending number of dirty dishes.

"Can you keep an eye on Maddie and Will at the same time?" Sera asked eventually.

"I can't be in two places at once. Give me twenty minutes and a laptop, some duct tape, a paper clip... maybe."

The idea struck her hard enough that she stopped mid-scrub and speared Ryan with a look. "Two places at once. The servant has to be present to summon the circle, right?" He nodded, and she turned her focus back to the suds, triumphant. "We don't know who's helping Torix, but we know where they'll be at sundown."

Ryan slapped his forehead. "I'm stupid, and I retract my previous statement. You *are* a master detective."

They were almost done, Sera figured they might as well finish the dishes. "The hard part is going to be finding the right trod to take us to Torix's tree."

"You can do that. The trods come when the Fae call, and I saw you do it that first day."

"I didn't have access to my power the first day."

Ryan dried the last dish and tossed the towel onto the counter. "You had access to more than you thought. We should call Jake."

"He claims he won't be long, and I don't want to involve him."

"Well then, want to take a walk in the woods?"

"I believe I would."

He made an after-you gesture, and Sera grabbed a small pack sitting by the door. "What's that?"

"A little something I started carrying around after all this started."

"That's vague and somewhat alarming. It's not TNT, right? Wile E. Coyote seems smart, but he's always blowing himself up."

Sera snorted out a laugh. "It's not explosives. C'mon, I want to be in and out of the woods before it gets dark on this side."

They walked out of Jake's house and into a beautiful fall day. The temperature was hovering around seventy, but when the sun went down, she'd need a sweater. There was one in a box somewhere in the attic next door. She glanced at her house, Evie's house, but decided it wasn't worth another long detour. They'd be fast.

Across the street, a trod was clearly visible between the trees, sprites floating around happily. The time difference worried her. She had no intention of confronting Torix and his helper without backup, preferably a Fae army, but she wanted to see if she could figure out who it was. The list Ryan had compiled of stolen stuff was extensive, and she was betting it would take some time to set everything up for the ritual.

She didn't try to do anything magical when they left the street. The image of Torix's tree was firmly in her mind, but the path seemed darker than usual. Ryan followed her lead then moved up to walk beside her.

"I texted Jake."

Sera glanced at him out of the corner of her eye, not surprised. "Fine. He was going to follow me anyway. I'm not clear on why you're here though. I thought you hated Fae stuff, and yet here you are throwing yourself into the fray."

He raised a brow. "If there's a fray, I fully plan to throw myself out of it. I'm here so you can keep your promise to Jake."

"How do you know about the promise to stay safe?"

"I am the great and powerful Ryan, I know all."

"Jake texted you to come over."

"Forgot you were a master detective. Yeah, he thought you might want some company. In my defense, I thought the note was a terrible idea and advised him strongly against the keys."

That made Sera smile a little because she agreed with him. She was still pissed at Jake, but summoning Ryan, whatever his reasons, had proved useful.

THE TROD CARRIED them further into the woods than Sera thought it would. They'd gone into the trees at mid-day, and it appeared to be dusk in the fairylands. She wondered if the ritual was supposed to be completed in Fae time or in human time.

Sera stopped and looked up at the darkening sky, considering. It would make sense for the two times to converge at points of power, like midnight on Samhain. She'd bet it would be both.

Ryan nudged her. "Staring at the trees isn't going to make the time difference make sense."

She stepped past a bush thick with brambles and glanced back at him. "Actually, I think Samhain will be the same here and outside the woods."

This time Ryan stopped. "If that's true then—"

He was cut off by the sound of growling to their left. Ryan immediately pushed Sera behind him, much to her chagrin. They'd come past the brambles into a wider part of the path, but she could feel that they weren't at the end yet.

Sera couldn't find the wolf at first, but as she shifted out from behind Ryan, it appeared a few feet off the path. The sprites were still dancing around them in the weakening sunlight, and Sera remembered the last time they'd faced the wolf on one of the trods.

He'd been unable to approach them as long as they stayed within the boundaries of the path.

Sera had no idea if Ryan knew that, but when she tried to tell him, he shushed her. Zee was right, it was a miracle her species survived. She caught sight of her glowing hands and corrected herself. Her human side anyway.

The wolf was staring at Ryan, and Ryan was watching the wolf, both of them appeared on the verge of violence. In that matchup, she'd bet on the wolf, so it was a good thing they were protected. She tugged on his sleeve, and when he ignored her, she huffed, then resumed following the path without him. Let him continue the stand-off until midnight, she had shit to do.

Sera hadn't taken more than a few steps when a yelp of pain had her spinning around.

Ryan had a long scratch in his forearm that was dripping blood, and the wolf had maneuvered between them on the path.

"Go, Sera. I'll keep him busy."

The wolf lunged at him, and to her shock, narrowly missed his leg. They were supposed to be protected. Chills shot up her back as she realized that the sprites were few and far between now, most of them congregated around her. When she'd walked away, she'd taken the sprites with her.

It wasn't the trod that protected them, it was the sprites. Which was exactly what Zee had told her in the beginning.

Sera wanted to smack herself, but the wolf was inching closer to Ryan. He'd managed to back Ryan away from her, and no matter how hard she'd tried she couldn't make shields appear outside of herself. She'd have to go past the wolf to bring the sprites back to Ryan.

"Sera, stop standing around and go. I can handle this."

He dodged another lunge, and Sera made up her mind. She was sick of people, men especially, trying to protect her. *She* could handle this.

She relaxed her sight and caught her breath at the beauty of the magic all around her. The forest breathed with it. Streaks of colors blended into one another. If she'd had more time, she could have stood there for hours gazing at the movement, but Ryan was still dripping blood.

The wolf was encased in a shimmering dark blue field shot through with black. It looked like oil, and she recoiled at the thought of touching it. He was still ignoring her in favor of Ryan, probably went for the weakest first she thought with irritation. Her magic flared, and the number of sprites doubled. She'd intended to use her magic to knock the wolf to the side, then rush past him with her army of sprites. Her plan didn't extend beyond covering

Ryan in sprites, but she was confident something would come to her.

Before she had a chance to do much more than rev her power, the wolf made his move. The oily covering pulsed, and the wolf jumped at Ryan's throat. It was clear he wasn't dodging this one, and Sera's magic sputtered as she gasped in fear.

Ryan said something low and flung his injured hand out. A spattering of blood shimmered and flew, striking the wolf across the nose before he slammed into Ryan's chest. They both went down with the force of the leap, but the wolf whined instead of tearing out his throat.

Sera took a step forward, not sure what she planned to do, but the wolf shook himself and jumped away from Ryan. The fur along his back was still stiff, but he wasn't baring his teeth, only growling low in this throat. Ryan hopped to his feet, and the wolf positioned himself solidly between them with his back to Sera. If she'd had any kind of offensive magic, she'd be able to use it on him with ease, but all her magic wanted to do was protect. Too bad they hadn't taken a look at that handbook.

To her amazement, sprites began pouring out of the trees by Ryan's side. He ignored them, but she heard the muttered curse. The oily magic covering the wolf shifted and gathered around his mouth. Sera couldn't get a good look at what happened because she wasn't keen on approaching the pointy part of the dangerous demon animal, but solid bits of crimson dropped to the ground as the wolf shook his head again. The magic returned to normal, and he lunged forward and snapped at Ryan.

Sera crept closer to the stand-off to get a better look at the red bits on the ground and realized that it wasn't blood, it was magic. Ryan had used magic, and it appeared dark red. The wolf had moved Ryan at least another ten yards by the time she looked up again. She watched as he tried to juke the wolf and dart around him, but Ryan wasn't fast enough. Whatever the reason, the wolf wanted Ryan and Sera separated.

She glanced at the blood drops on the ground then back to Ryan's arm, which had stopped dripping at some point. He'd done something magical to the wolf to defend himself, but it hadn't lasted long. Behind her, the trod wound through the woods, leading to the clearing around Torix's tree. If she left Ryan and ran, would he follow?

Ryan had lied to her. Just like everyone else. He seemed capable of protecting himself, and the sprites were gathering, which would hopefully give him an advantage. She couldn't trust him, but she didn't want him to die.

He'd even told her to go, but it went against her morals to leave someone in danger. A small part whispered *what if Ryan is part of the danger?* At least, he and the wolf seemed to be opposing forces. She could use that.

She opened her mouth to shout a warning to Ryan, but with an overpowering jolt, something knocked all the air out of her. She sank to her knees and dropped her head. It was like the time she'd almost hyperventilated and fallen hard on her back, but this time she was conscious and trying to suck in air. She pressed hard on her abdomen and forced in oxygen. Her shields were still in place and the wolf was dancing Ryan further and further from her. This wasn't from them; it had come from the bond.

Jake had taken her power, and it had hollowed her out.

12

_____

JAKE

An hour earlier, Jake had parked his truck next to his Corolla in front of Maddie's place. It had deteriorated since the last time he'd been there, admittedly several years ago. He'd tried to stay away out of respect for Maddie having her own space. Sera hadn't mentioned how much work the house needed, but he guessed she'd been preoccupied.

He was preoccupied now, but thinking about Sera naked in his bed wasn't going to make things go any quicker. Halloween night was only hours away, and they desperately needed a better plan than run away and hope for the best. Speaking of Halloween, it wasn't like Maddie to not decorate. She'd always loved Halloween, but there wasn't a single skeleton or pumpkin near her house.

What was going on with her? Maybe Mom was right and she needed some time away. It didn't feel right to reward her for skipping out on work and being generally irresponsible with a European vacation, but nothing he did seemed to be working.

He remembered Sera's insistence that Maddie's house was shielded, but he wouldn't have been able to tell unless it physically knocked him back. The only magic he had was the bond with Sera, and that was more like borrowing her magic. Jake sighed. Time to get the whining over with. The porch shuddered suspiciously when he walked across it, but nothing stopped him from knocking and then opening the door.

Maddie was in the kitchenette stirring something on the stove. It smelled like old gym socks, but she was always trying new disgusting foods. "Hey, that was a pathetic excuse for a knock."

Jake winced, both from the smell and the comment. "You're right. I'm always getting on your case for doing that to me. I'll try to remember next time."

She didn't answer, and he tried not to get irritated that she'd called him out of bed for an imaginary emergency. How self-centered could she be? He missed his nice little sister, but this selfish one was the version he was dealing with most of the time lately.

"Maddie, I have stuff to do today. What was so important that I had to come over right away?"

She looked up and smiled through the steam. "I need to use your truck."

He wandered around the living room looking at the items she'd put on the shelves he'd built. "We already covered this. You can't use my truck. Is there anything else?"

"How about... I'm your favorite sister, and if you let me use the truck, I'll stop harassing you about Sera."

"This feels an awful lot like blackmail." A wooden duck got his attention on the top shelf. He remembered seeing it in Rosie's, in the kitchen. He searched his memory, but all he could recall was that it had been a gift to Mr. Hogan.

"Eh, I'm not particular about the label."

Jake glanced up when something in the pot sizzled. The room was starting to smell like bacon, which was a welcome relief. Maddie bent to pick up a towel she'd dropped, and a heavy necklace swung out from inside her shirt. The duck bothered him, but the pendant around Maddie's neck pissed him off.

It was a family heirloom Evie was saving for Sera. She'd shown him several times. There was no way Evie would have given that to Maddie, no matter how much she liked his sister.

She'd gone back to adding things to her pot. Jake left her collection of potentially stolen things, and joined her in the tiny kitchen. "What are you doing, Maddie?"

"I thought Sera might have gotten to you, so I took a precaution." She looked up and smiled at him again, but there was something wrong with her eyes. "You know Evie always liked me better."

The room was getting a little fuzzy, but Jake blinked it away. "Mad, I don't know crap about crap, but you can't take stuff from Evie's house."

The smile faded and her jaw clenched. "It was rightfully mine. I listened to her talk for hours, *days*, about Sera's legacy and the Fae and wasted time. I was right there in front of her, and she went on and on about how sad she was that she'd have to wait to pass on her knowledge."

Jake was wary about the way Maddie phrased that, but he pressed on. "I'm glad she had you to talk to, but that doesn't automatically mean you get her stuff. The pendant is a family heirloom. It belongs to Sera."

"Always Sera, isn't it, big brother? Well, she's not here now, is she?" Maddie flung her arms out wide. "But I am. I always am." She sighed and scraped her hair back from her face with both hands. "Ugh, this glamour is distracting. I hate having to hide myself, especially when I'm hanging out with my favorite brother. You don't mind if I drop it, do you?"

He was having trouble focusing his thoughts. "A glamour? You look the same."

"It's to hide magic, not an ugly haircut. I don't know why I even bother with you. You're about as magical as a box of hair. It's too bad you didn't bring Ryan, that would have been a fun test. Eh, I'll keep it up for now."

He did *not* like the way she'd said Ryan's name. It was likely he'd have to punch his friend later, but it was getting more difficult to follow the conversation. His head felt like it was full of cotton.

The steam wafting gently from the kitchen was slowly filling the top part of the room. That had to be it. It wasn't affecting Maddie, but he felt like he'd had one too many six packs.

"We have to get out of here. That steam is making me loopy." He stumbled over to the door, but the handle wouldn't turn.

"Oh, I locked that. It was one of the first spells Evie taught me."

Jake's brain finally caught up to his ears as he slumped to the floor. "Spells? You have magic? Since when?"

She shook her head at him, but there was glee in her eyes. "Since Torix. We had to keep it a secret though, so he taught me the glamour to hide my power."

Jake closed his eyes for a second to stop the room from spinning. He was in trouble. Sera had been right, and he'd dismissed her. Hell, he'd taken her keys. It seemed like there was something significant about that, but he couldn't pinpoint what it might be right now. He needed to focus, but

Maddie? His little sister? Jake just couldn't bring himself to believe that she was one of the bad guys. For the first time in his life, he sincerely hoped he was hallucinating.

When he opened them again, she had moved the table out of the way to draw a complicated circle on the floor. She was almost finished. How long had his eyes been closed? His limbs felt like spaghetti, but with effort he could flop them around. One of Maddie's little treasures sat on the bottom shelf next to his hand. A ceramic bird's nest of all things.

She was humming as she drew intricate symbols around a multi-layered circle on the wood floor. He slid his hand over and was able to close his fingers around the nest. It was light, but he didn't have many options. There wasn't much of a plan involved, but he figured he could probably heave it through the window behind him and get some fresh air.

Jake hadn't done much more than shift around when Maddie flicked her hand at him. He drooped back against the wall and the nest rolled out of his hand. This time he couldn't move at all.

"Oh no you don't. Can't have you mucking around in here causing problems." She dusted her hands on her pants and stood. "Tim will be here any minute, and I need you still."

He wanted to ask who Tim was, but he couldn't get his mouth to move. It was a spell he recognized because Zee had used it on him before. He could still breathe and think, but that was all. Maddie kept talking though.

"Tim is one of the high school jocks. Plays football, big into 4-H. Poor guy lost his prize rabbit recently. Really a shame how irresponsible kids are these days." She tsked, but her smile widened. "I've been tutoring him in English.

He's supposed to come over today for a session, but I have a better idea."

A dawning sense of horror washed over Jake. She was all the way a bad guy, and he couldn't do a damn thing to stop her. Maddie crouched in front of him and patted his cheek.

"Don't worry, he won't feel anything. I'm not a monster." She raised a brow. "Stop looking at me like that. I'm not. The way to get Torix through the shields is to replace him with someone else. No one is going to miss a whiny kicker who's failing English."

Jake hoped she didn't mean that. That was some serious dark-side shit, and he wanted to believe his baby sister was acting out instead of evil.

"It's not like I'm killing him, just trapping his essence in a tree for all eternity. Torix is going to need a body after all, and he swears the kid won't feel anything. Unlike what those douchey Fae did to him, Tim won't be conscious for his imprisonment."

Maddie rolled her eyes and pouted as if Jake had said something, and he desperately wished he could. At least if he could talk, there was a chance he could reason with her. She flounced back to the circle on the floor and gestured at a symbol that looked like gibberish to him.

"See, this is so he'll sleep." She pointed to another. "This is so he won't feel anything." The third was almost at his feet. "This is to convince the shields that he's Torix. The tricky part is the timing. They have to pass at the exact same moment."

She flipped her long hair behind her shoulder. "I've been practicing this for years. Evie was the hardest, and I was worried she'd counter it for a second, but it worked in the end. It was tough getting the circle done before she wandered into the clearing, but we need it to prep the body. Humans don't pass easily through Fae shields."

It was like she'd never seen a superhero movie. She was honest-to-god monologuing. Jake wasn't sure who she was trying to convince more that she wasn't a bad person, him or herself. He clung to the hope that she wasn't a lost cause.

The fog in his brain was receding, probably because his face was so close to the ground, and if he quieted himself, he could feel the warmth of the bond inside him. When they'd been together yesterday, he and Sera had been able to share emotions, and he'd felt her panic once before that. The bond flared to life when he nudged it with his mind, and he could feel Sera's power trickling into him, barely more than a whisper. It gave him an idea. He couldn't stop Maddie on his own, but he hoped he could at least do something to help the kid.

Right on time, what sounded like a truck engine cut out in front of the house. Maddie nudged him to the side so she could look out the crack in the curtains above him. He collapsed to the floor completely, but that was fine with him. The circle was inches from his face, and he needed to be as close as possible in case his crazy plan worked.

"Guess I didn't need your truck after all. Tim brought his own." Maddie stepped back and surveyed the living room. Jake could barely see her out of the corner of his eye. He didn't think Tim would see him until he was fully into the room, and by that point it was probably too late.

Thanks to his week of practice with Sera, and a lifetime of listening to Ryan bitch about the Fae, he had a basic idea of how magic worked. There had to be a catalyst for Maddie to trigger the circle. She'd probably do to Tim what she'd done to him. Get him loopy on the steam, walk him where she wanted him, and finish the spell. Except it had taken him a while to get loopy. More likely, the steam was meant for him, and she was going for speed instead of security.

Jake couldn't tell if she'd put her glamour back on, but she was more confident and bitchy than usual. It felt disloyal to think that, but she'd also used hidden magic to freeze him in place so he didn't interfere with her evil plot, so he rolled with it. Tim knocked, and Maddie opened the door with a big smile.

"Tim, you're right on time, as usual. And did you get a new truck? It looks fancy."

"Yes, ma'am. My parents gave it to me for my sixteenth birthday," Tim said from the porch. Jake willed him to stay out there, or better yet, turn around and go back to his family, but he wasn't that lucky. He bet Maddie hated being called ma'am.

"It's a beaut. Maybe you could take me for a ride later."

"I'm not supposed to be driving around with girls, but you'd probably be fine." Jake could hear the kid blushing. It was almost painful to listen to.

"Well c'mon in, that essay won't fix itself."

Maddie was all Southern charm, and Jake knew it was almost time. He opened himself to the bond, dropping the shields he'd been shoring up. Sera would feel this, but he hoped she was still relaxing at his house and would be fine. Heavy footsteps vibrated his head on the floor as Tim walked into the room. He visualized tangling his fingers in the heavy rope of the bond. Warmth flowed up his arms, over his shoulders, and into his chest. It was more than Sera's power; it was their shared emotions and memories and strength, and he needed it to break Maddie's spell.

Tim stepped into Jake's line of sight, a frown across his face. He'd said something low, but Jake had missed it. Maddie's smile had slipped as she motioned him further into the room. She'd put the table on the far side against the wall to make space for the circle, so Tim would have to walk across it to get to his normal study space.

He stumbled, and Maddie put her hand on his arm to steady him. The steam must have been for both of them after all. Tim was twice her size, but she had no trouble maneuvering him to the edge of the circle. Behind his back, Maddie made a motion with her hand, and with his mind firmly locked in the bond, he could faintly see the circle change. The white chalk glowed blue like a glow stick left out in the daylight. It was time; he hoped his belief that his little sister was still in there somewhere wasn't misplaced.

Jake pulled hard on the bond, absorbing as much of Sera's power as he could get, and it was a lot more than he was expecting. Suddenly, he could see the stillness spell on him. The circle blazed with dark blue light, shimmery and sliding over itself like an oil slick. He could see the glow of other magic around the room, different colors and sheens, translucent over the objects on her shelves. It was breathtaking. This must be what Sera saw when she opened her mind, and he had the sudden need to see her like this, ablaze with magic and light.

He hoped he'd get the chance.

With a punch of Sera's power, the spell dissolved around him and he could move again. He popped up on his feet and raised a hand to Maddie and Tim. He wanted them to stop moving forward, but not be trapped, so he used the shield imagery he and Sera had been working on. The air in front of them became solid, and Tim bounced off of it, knocking Maddie back as well.

Jake could see the golden magic shimmering in the air. He'd done it. He'd made a shield. Holy shit, Sera was going to be so proud. Her power was still filling him up, and he felt a little light-headed from the sheer magnitude of it. Maddie snapped her head to him and raised her hand. Time for part two of the plan.

Jake lunged past the golden shield and into the circle himself. It was like diving into a freezing lake. His body seized up, and he fell to the floor. Through a haze of pain, he thought he was spending a lot of time face down on Maddie's floor today. He grimaced and tried to move the arm he was laying on, but he was motionless again. This time all his muscles ached.

He probably should have released Sera's magic first. The bond was still there, but it was sluggish, and he could feel her exhaustion. All the awesome power he'd borrowed was gone. He'd hoped it would go back to Sera, but she definitely felt drained.

Behind him, Maddie was shrieking something about fools, but he didn't care much. His eyelids were getting heavy, and his aching muscles were begging him to go to sleep. Tim was suspiciously silent. Jake forced his drooping eyes open when Maddie nudged him with her foot.

"You ruin everything," she seethed. Behind her, he could see Tim's legs on the floor. Maddie followed his gaze and narrowed her eyes. "I put him to sleep. It'll wear off in a couple of hours, and he'll think this was all a dream." She walked over to the stove and clicked it off, then walked back.

"Why would you do this to me? I only needed to borrow your truck to move Tim to the clearing. Okay, and I wanted you to know the truth about me. About my power. But I didn't want to hurt you." She raised a fist like she was going to punch him then let it fall. "I'm so much stronger than you, and you still can't help trying to be the hero. Now look what you've done. Torix is going to have to use your body instead, and you're going to be lost forever. What would

Mom and Dad say?" She leaned down into his face, angry and defiant. "What would Sera say?"

Jake knew what Sera would say. So many 'I told you so's, for the rest of his life, which he hoped would include her and wouldn't include being stuck in a tree. Now he needed her to save them both. With the last of his energy, he tried to reach her through the bond, to tell her he was sorry about the key thing and he loved her. He wanted her to know, even if as an adult he'd been too chicken-shit to admit it to her face.

13

SERA

SERA's eyes met Ryan's from the forest floor. The sprites were slowly drifting away from her, back into the trees or closer to Ryan. She knew her hands had lost their glow, and she could see the moment that Ryan realized her magic had deserted her. His eyes got wide, and he threw another bit of magic at the wolf. This time it slid off the oily coat like water.

She tried to stand, but her knees gave out again. They might be in more trouble than she thought. Her body was exhausted, even though she'd felt fine a minute ago. Whatever Jake had done had sapped all her energy as well as her magic.

The bond was still there, but the glow was much fainter than before. What the hell had he done? Was this his way of making sure she didn't go off without him? Without warning, a bit of her power slammed back into her. Not enough to make her feel confident, but she was able to stand effectively. It felt like a rubber band had snapped along the bond.

Along with her power came a burst of emotion from Jake. She'd been unsure if they could do that if they weren't physically touching and vulnerable.

Warmth and confidence washed over her, along with a whopping sense that he was in danger. He hadn't been trying to stop her, he'd been trying to save himself. The threat faded and left remorse and need in its wake.

She wanted to ignore the woods and the wolf and Ryan and focus on Jake, but she couldn't afford any more mistakes. The wolf looked back at her over his shoulder as if he'd sensed her distraction, but he didn't make a move. Standing on the trod, with the sprites floating around like confused dust mites, he took stock of her position then turned and growled at Ryan.

The pieces finally clicked for Sera. The wolf wasn't threatening her, he was protecting her from Ryan. He hadn't been aggressive at Maddie's place or at Jake's until Will showed up. Not even in her dream. She'd felt threatened by him that first day when they'd met with Zee, but the wolf had chased all three of them out of the clearing. When she'd broken off, he'd kept chasing Ryan.

The one who had hidden magic and knew how to use it. It was time to reassess her allies.

The trod stretched out behind her, and this time she didn't hesitate when she turned to run. Her body protested, but she didn't trust Ryan not to catch her if she took off at a slow shamble. She heard him curse behind her then the snap of teeth coming together. A quick glance back showed Ryan watching her and trying to get past the wolf. True to form, the growling animal kept himself between them.

"Sera, don't go against Torix on your own." He sounded like he was struggling, but she refused to turn around again to find out. It was obvious he could take care of himself.

The path turned, and Sera lost even the sounds of their stand-off. Sprites drifted out of the trees ahead of her, as the dusk deepened. A split in the path appeared, and Sera slowed to a walk. The rightmost path was filled with sprites lighting the way. Her senses told her that way led to town, with kids running around in costume and Halloween festivities starting. That way was promised safety, but it was temporary. She'd be going back on her promise to the Fae to help deal with Torix, that in itself was probably dangerous, but she'd also be risking all those people to save herself and only temporarily at that.

It wasn't even close to a fair trade.

The leftmost path was dim, and the sprites there looked like they were low on batteries. Every horror movie she'd ever watched told the monster was that way. With the knowledge that Ryan might be right behind her, she took a deep breath and felt for the bond. It was steadier than before, but nowhere near back to full strength. A sense of urgency tugged her to the left, and the choice became obvious.

Jake was down the monster path. So was Torix, and the fate of the world most likely depended on her fledgling magic skills. Sera wasn't sure why the trod offered her a choice when she'd been focused on reaching Torix's clearing, but it wasn't much of an option anyway. She thanked the Wood for the out, then turned left and walked into the dimness with no Ryan in sight.

The sprites wafted ahead of her, providing a little more light now that full darkness was falling. Not for the first time, she wished she wore a watch so she could see how close the time was getting. Every few steps, she probed the bond, and it told her Jake was somewhere in front of her.

Sera wasn't sure how she felt about that. There was still

residual warmth from whatever he'd done to her, but her power level was dangerously low when approaching a confrontation with a super powerful Fae. Then there was the matter of him taking her keys. She had large confusing feelings for him, and there was a good chance she'd fallen back on her past and seen Jake through the lens of her relationship with Will. He'd taken her keys, yes, but he'd sent Ryan so she wouldn't be stuck by herself. And now he was probably in trouble.

What had happened to him? A big part of her was glad she wouldn't be facing Torix alone, but she was equally worried and pissed at Jake. He'd told her not to go alone, and yet here he was without her.

They'd shared an amazing night together, and she'd responded by throwing logic out the window in favor of assumptions and panic. She could admit she might have overreacted... a little, but the truth was the truth. Relationships were limiting. They required compromise, and she wasn't interested in compromising herself any more. Will had demanded she shed more and more of herself the longer they were together. Her mom hoped every day that Sera would turn into a normal woman who had a 401K, shopped at the Gap, and didn't see little people hiding in the garden. Granted, that only happened once, but it'd made an impression.

Evie had wanted her to embrace her magical heritage, but hadn't trusted her enough to talk to her about it openly.

That one probably hurt the most. Evie was supposed to be her stalwart defender, on her side no matter what. Why was the truth so hard for people to speak? Why did everyone feel like they knew better than her how to run her life? The bond pulsed inside her, and she had to admit that Jake had never really treated her like that before today. Even though he didn't listen to her and didn't trust her to take care of herself, he was upfront about what he wanted, even if it made her angry at him. She wondered what had prompted him to take that path with her today.

Sera's legs were dragging, and she swore the next time there was an epic battle she'd do more cardio to prepare. Night had fallen completely, but it was peaceful walking along the path with the sprites to light the way. She hadn't seen or heard another creature since she'd left Ryan and the wolf, and she wondered if anything lived in the in-between along the trods. Zee's warning to stay on the path echoed through her head, and she looked nervously into the darkness to her right. There were no sprites out there, and the moon didn't penetrate past the tree canopy to reach the forest floor.

It was completely black and still. She could hear her labored breathing and the crunch of dead leaves under her feet, but nothing else. If something was out there stalking her, it was silent. It would also have to get in line behind Torix and his servant if it wanted to suck the life out of her.

With that cheerful thought, several of the sprites in front of her blinked out. She stopped walking and cast out her senses. At the very least, she'd know if something magical was approaching.

Several seconds ticked by, and nothing moved. The remaining sprites lingered anemically, but they provided enough light for her to see. The path continued to stretch forward, and she was hesitant to create a brighter light and make a better target. One day, she'd learn not to spook herself, but today was not that day.

The bond hadn't changed. It urged her forward with a mild urgency, but told her nothing about her current level of danger. Sprites were fickle things, maybe they got bored or found something more interesting. More likely, considering her drained state, they sensed a stronger magic and abandoned her. That didn't bode well for where she was heading, but at least they weren't hovering around some nightmare creature off the path.

Her feet wanted to keep moving even though the rest of her wanted a quick nap. The bond and her own sense of resolve spurred her into moving again. Realistically, there was no reason to hurry. Running down the path would get her there as fast as a leisurely stroll, but she couldn't shake the feeling that something was wrong and she was woefully unprepared.

SERA DIDN'T KNOW what she'd expected when the trod finally deigned to spit her out, but Maddie struggling to shove tiki torches into the ground was not it. She looked around, but they weren't in Torix's clearing. A clearing, yes, but it was missing the giant dead tree. The Fae were messing with her once again.

The morning at Maddie's hadn't slipped her mind, but she was plagued with doubt about her people judging skills. There were no filet knives or gummy candies in sight. Unless Maddie did something threatening, Sera was going to treat her like the girl she remembered.

"Hey Maddie."

She jumped and spun around. "Sera?" A look of panic flitted across her face, then she pasted a smile on. "Sera. It took you long enough."

"Excuse me?"

"I've been trying to get this party organized for hours and this is all I've done so far." She gestured around the break in the trees that contained a lit camping lantern, several more tiki torches scattered haphazardly about, and a bulging grocery bag. "I could really use your help, so thanks for coming early to set up."

Sera felt like she'd stepped into an alternate universe. "I'm sorry, Maddie, I don't know what's happening. I'm sort of here by accident."

Maddie visibly deflated. "Oh, of course. I thought when Jake showed up that he'd talked to you."

That confirmed Jake was in the Wood, explicitly where he'd told her not to be, but it didn't feel right. If he'd had to track down Maddie, it would explain why he'd been gone so long, but not why he'd need to defend himself.

"Where *is* Jake?"

Maddie went back to her torch and spoke over her shoulder. "Oh, he's around here somewhere. You know how he is, can't let us weak little women take care of anything ourselves."

Her comment rang very close to what she'd been telling herself all day, that Jake saw women, and Sera in particular as weak. When Maddie said it, though, everything in her revolted. Jake didn't see her as weak. Even if she didn't have the bond to confirm it, every time she'd asked him to back off he'd listened. He was definitely overprotective, but he'd only plowed past her objections once, and that had been this morning. She had to admit it was possible he'd made a mistake while grappling with the change in their relationship.

Either way, Jake had never come off as condescending. He interfered, a lot, but his intentions were always to help or protect, not to take over. He protected out of love. Maddie should know that.

"What's going on, Maddie?"

She finished with the torch and moved on to the next one. "A party for some of my friends. I really thought Jake told you about it. You should hang out. It'll be like old times. We don't start for a while, but it should be a lot of... fun."

The way Maddie said fun didn't sit right with Sera. The bond was clear that Jake was very close, but he hadn't shown up yet. The sprites had disappeared when she'd emerged from the path, and their absence told her there was no active magic happening. Sera was hesitant to relax her guard enough to look for a more insidious reason. In her current state, it wouldn't take much to work her over. There was no point in wasting the energy she had with potentially unhelpful magic, but she didn't need magic to tromp through the woods looking for a grown-ass man.

Maddie didn't seem to care one way or the other what Sera was doing. It went a long way toward convincing her that she'd told the truth. If she was helping Torix, wouldn't she care that someone had shown up to stop her? She had a momentary twinge for not helping when Maddie was so clearly struggling, but she needed to find Jake and regroup.

She'd taken two steps past Maddie when a rustling came from outside the clearing behind her.

She tensed and turned, ready for a new threat, but it was Ryan that stumbled out of the woods. He had twigs in his hair and his cargo pants were ripped across one knee, but the blood on his forearm had stopped flowing freely. As far as she could see, he hadn't come off a trod.

He wiped his hands on his pants and stared past Sera. "Maddie?"

"Ryan." Her whole face lit up when she noticed him. "I'm so glad you're here." She dropped the torch and ran past Sera to fling herself into his arms. Ryan looked as surprised as Sera felt. "I knew you'd change your mind."

"That's not what you said before, Mad."

Sera took small steps backward toward the opposite trees. Jake trusted Ryan, but she couldn't afford that luxury now that she knew he'd been hiding his magic this whole time. He knew she was weak, and she'd feel a whole lot better if she could get behind some cover.

She'd also feel better if she could get a read on Jake. The bond told her he was alive and approximately close by, but she couldn't get anything else from it. The frustrating lack of emotion was making her anxious.

Ryan's hands rested on Maddie's hips with a familiarity that made Sera increasingly uncomfortable. It looked like there were more secrets Ryan was keeping. She wasn't really surprised when Maddie lifted her face for a kiss, but she'd hoped she was wrong. Jake was going to be so pissed.

Sera expected Ryan to bend down and kiss her, but he didn't. He didn't push her away either. She took advantage of their preoccupation with each other and crossed further into the trees. Ryan was speaking too quietly to Maddie for her to hear, but the responses were loud and clear.

"I'm perfectly safe. Besides, it's almost time. We're waiting on one more and we can get the party started." She did an awkward little shimmy, and Ryan finally released her.

"Mad, I'm trying to do the right thing here," Ryan pleaded. Then he said something Sera didn't catch, but Maddie shook her head and walked away.

"I need to get the rest of this stuff set up. Help or get out of the way."

Ryan dragged a hand through his hair as Maddie picked up the third torch. She positioned it across from the first one, and Sera finally picked out the pattern from the torches on the ground. Five on the inside, nine outside.

Two concentric circles. It was time to get Jake before whoever she was waiting for arrived.

The bond said she should be right on top of him, but the undergrowth was heavy and dark. Sera stepped past an overgrown berry bush and tripped over something solid. She landed on her knees, but her hand ended up on something warm. A tiny buzz of magic gave her enough light to see by, so she could pull back the brush someone had placed over Jake.

This was definitely something suspicious, and Sera was kicking herself for letting Jake sway her. Sprites flitted over his face as she checked to be sure he was breathing, even though the bond told her he was alive. He didn't appear injured, and with her magic revved, she could see he was covered with the same oily magic as the wolf.

They were inside the tree line, but the glow from her hands made them targets against the dark underbrush. Sera willed her magic to calm down, and the light faded away. A glance told her that Maddie was on the fifth torch, completing the inside circle. She didn't seem to notice that Sera had disappeared, and Ryan had moved close enough to their side of the clearing for her to hear him this time.

"You broke up with me, Mad. I agreed it was for the best, but you can't keep trying to booty call me." Sera thought it was probably for the best that Jake was unconscious for this part.

"It was important that I not be distracted, but I always enjoyed our time together. No harm in that." Maddie gave him a come-hither look over her shoulder, but Ryan didn't take the bait. The smile slid off her face and revealed her contempt. "Whatever, I don't need you anymore anyway."

As if he was waiting for Maddie to stop messing around, the wolf skulked out of the trees. Ryan saw him immediately and backed closer to Sera and Jake. The wolf growled at him then went to sit at Maddie's feet. She looked down and giggled, then reached down to run her hand along his head between his ears.

"Oh, Mad, what did you do?" Ryan's voice was choked.

Maddie looked up and directly at Sera. "I did what I had to."

A chill went down her spine.

She had to give Ryan credit; he didn't hesitate. While Maddie was focused on Sera, he rushed forward. She didn't know why he didn't use magic, but it was a poor choice. Maddie lifted an arm, and Ryan stopped moving so suddenly that he toppled forward and slid several feet on his face. The wolf didn't even have a chance to show his teeth. *Dammit. He* was *a good guy after all.*

"A pity. Ryan was always fun. Great in the sack and had killer abs hidden under all those geeky t-shirts. It's a shame really. Remind me to thank Evie for teaching me that spell. She called it 'Still', but I like 'Paralyze' better. Her version was more complicated, of course, but I found that a well-drawn circle can fix a lot of problems." She gestured at her feet, and Sera could see where Maddie had drawn in the dirt below the fallen leaves. "I think it's time we dropped the façade, don't you?"

Maddie didn't do anything outwardly, but Sera could suddenly sense the magic all around her. Under her hand, Jake's chest lifted and fell in rhythm, but he didn't respond when she shook him. Maddie danced a circle around the wolf and giggled again. Now that her glamour had lifted, Sera could see the oily magic oozing over her. There was a good chance that even if she could figure out how to throw a spell at her, it would slide right off like Ryan's did with the wolf. That didn't leave her a lot of options.

To make matters worse, the clearing itself changed. The placement of the tree line was about the same, but a large, twisted pine suddenly became visible near the middle of Maddie's circle. They'd been in Torix's clearing the whole time.

Maddie resumed placing the torches, and Sera tried not to draw the attention of the wolf. She'd already been wrong once about his abilities. "Torix will be so pleased that the plan is working. I was upset when I thought I had to use Jake as the double, but Ryan will be much better."

It was tempting to stay silent, but Sera needed to keep her talking and not tossing around spells. It's not like she was hiding all that well anyway. "What double?"

"That's the brilliant part. We can't get the Fae shields down, even when they're weak, but we can replace Torix with someone else. It fools the shields into thinking they're doing their job, and Torix is free to reward his favorite acolyte."

"What's your reward?"

"Magic, of course. When Torix is free, this magic is permanent. I'll be more powerful than anyone else. And I earned it. The wolf may have killed the rabbits, but I had to spread them around on your porch." She shuddered.

Well that answered the question of what Maddie got out of it. Sera didn't remember her being quite so ambitious, but she'd been able to fool her brother and her boyfriend, so what hope did Sera have of knowing the real Maddie.

"Where is Torix anyway?"

"He's resting. It's a big night for him, and he needs to conserve his strength. Now I need to finish this. It's almost midnight."

That was a relief at least. She wasn't ready to tangle with the evil fairy yet. Maddie was strangely not concerned about

Sera. It was disconcerting, being considered no threat at all. Was she so sure of her abilities that she didn't care that Sera was crouched over Jake? Or was there some other terrible surprise in store? Probably both.

Sera couldn't let Maddie use Ryan, or anyone else for that matter, to free Torix. At the very least, she needed to apologize for thinking him a bad guy before they were all horribly killed. She had practically no magic, and she needed Jake to wake up, if for nothing else than to carry Ryan out of there physically.

Maddie seemed to be done talking, but Sera kept an eye on her while she examined Jake. The magic coating depressed wherever her hand touched, but bounced back when she moved it. Maddie had finished lighting the torches and pulled a chalice and sharp-looking knife from the grocery bag. Sera didn't know the first thing about how to help Jake, and she had to fight off the panic looming in the back of her mind. She was on her own, like she'd wanted, but everyone was in danger anyway.

Jake was breathing, ostensibly asleep, and covered in a layer of magic. It stood to reason that he'd been forced into that state with a spell, so if she could remove the spell, she could wake him up. Maddie's nonchalance meant that anything magical she did would probably not work, but she had a secret weapon. The bond that Zee had given them worked inside her shields, so it probably worked inside that magic shell.

Her hand over Jake's heart, she opened herself up to the bond. Instead of the warmth she usually felt, a cold sensation tickled her palm. She opened her eyes to see the oily magic disappearing into her hand. The coldness was the blue magic, and she was absorbing it. Maddie was preoccupied with getting the placement of a bowl of feathers right, so Sera tried something crazy.

She dropped her shields and pulled the magic into herself.

A rush of chilly energy burst through her. Her exhaustion disappeared. The magic mingled with her own and settled as it warmed. In an instant, the oily coating was gone, and Sera was back to feeling like she wouldn't blow over in a strong wind.

Jake still had a blue tinge about him, and he still didn't wake up. She wasn't sure what that spell had been intended to do, but it had been a doozy. The last bit of magic lingering on him felt familiar to her. Like it was one of the spells she'd practiced, but never managed to make work. Maddie was busy maneuvering Ryan into the circle, and the wolf was watching her instead of Sera.

Once more into the breach then. Sera pulled and the vestiges of the spell sank into her. She'd sucked in all the magic and added it to her own. No wonder her spells never worked; she was eating the magic on accident.

As a plan unfolded in Sera's mind, Jake sat up with a giant breath and almost collided with her. She put her hand over his mouth to keep him quiet, and leaned down to whisper in his ear.

"I have an idea."

14

SERA

JAKE PRESSED a gentle kiss to her palm then moved her hand. "What do you need from me?"

Sera could hardly see him in the firelight from the torches, but she could feel him again, joy and confidence and other warm fuzzy stuff. He was completely open to her, and the magic was flowing freely between them. It seemed like a lifetime ago that he'd left her that note, and she could feel him questioning the distance she was forcing between them. In the last few hours, she'd decided not to write him off, but that didn't mean they had a future. It meant she was entertaining the possibility. There was no time to discuss it, but if they survived, they were going to have a long talk about boundaries.

Zee had been right in the beginning, she needed Jake, but not to stop Torix. Her shields were up because she didn't want him to feel the guilt she had over what she was about to do.

"I need you to distract her without getting frozen by her."

Jake narrowed his eyes. "What are you going to do?"

"What I do best. Break stuff."

Sera went to move past him along the tree line, but he stopped her with a hand on her arm. "Be safe."

"You too. By the way, you and I are going to have a serious discussion about warning people before using all their magic."

Jake leaned forward and kissed her. All his fear and hope and strength poured into her with the kiss. She could feel his regret over this morning, and his desperate need to keep her safe. Despite that last one, he was following her lead into danger. He trusted she would find a way to keep herself safe. The bond couldn't lie, and Sera realized she trusted him, at least this far, so she forgave him. She leaned into him and gave as much back as she could with her shields mostly intact. The tension that had been spiraling inside her released, and she found herself wishing it was all over for a much different reason than just survival.

Maddie chose that moment to focus on her again. "What are you doing over there?"

Jake pushed himself to his feet and strode out of the woods. "Maddie, I'm disappointed in you."

It was perfect. He struck the exact right tone between upset parent and annoyed big brother. Maddie frowned and looked past Jake into the trees, but Sera had already moved. She scanned the trees, but for once the sprites were helping by grouping up at random points well away from Sera's location. She needed to get close enough to touch the shields without Maddie noticing, and the best way to do that was to come up behind Torix's tree.

Jake was doing a great job scolding her, but Sera could see her scanning the woods looking for a sign. She'd made it about halfway around the circle when Maddie interrupted Jake.

"Go get her. Bring her back here. I don't care if you have to hurt her."

It took Sera a moment to figure out Maddie was talking to the wolf. He'd been so quiet and still that she'd forgotten he was there. Unlike Maddie, the wolf knew right where Sera was. He bolted before she'd even finished her last sentence.

Four long strides took him to her position, and Sera barely had time to brace herself for his leap. Instead of solidifying her shields and pushing back, she opened and let him come. The moment Sera made contact with the coarse fur, she pulled. The wolf yelped as they tumbled down into the pine straw, even though Sera took the brunt of the fall.

He stood up, shook his head, and whined as he backed away from her. Sera got slowly to her feet. The oily magic was gone, and she had a weird churning sensation inside her like she'd eaten sushi that was still flopping around. By the time the magic settled, the wolf had faded into the trees. She was almost giddy with power. It explained a lot about Maddie's excitement.

Sera didn't feel tired at all anymore, but she could tell there was still space for more. How much power could she hold? She'd bet her limit was somewhere below the full weight of the shields holding Torix in place, and that didn't factor in Torix himself. As if sensing someone saying his name, Sera felt another presence in her mind. Torix had arrived.

Hello again, my dear. It's so nice of you to welcome my return by presenting yourself so conveniently. I fear it won't merit any mercy though.

Sera had partially shielded herself after the wolf had run away, and she knew she could raise them again to lock him out. It was one of the few things she'd excelled at in all her practice, but she needed Torix distracted as much as Maddie. She wasn't close enough to the tree yet.

Big words from a Fae in a tree, thought Sera. She knew she could respond out loud, but she didn't want Maddie to hear as she crept around the circle. If he needed to, Jake could find her with the bond.

I'm afraid I'm going to have to retract my previous offer of a trade. I do wonder what your mate would offer for your life. If it would be worth all that delicious power you have swirling inside you.

Sera scoffed. *He wouldn't offer anything, and he's not my mate.*

A slow chuckle rolled over her. *In that you are mistaken.*

She wondered which part he was talking about, but she didn't ask. She'd reached the tree, but instead of touching rough bark, her hand slid off smooth magic. The barriers. It took a little more concentration to see them, but eventually she could make out a light silver glimmer etched with symbols that looked like the ones in the stone circle.

Torix tried to probe further into her mind, but her shields kept him firmly locked on the surface. He was sneaky, looking for weaknesses, but Sera had complete faith in her dragon armor. From the side of the tree, she could hear Maddie and Jake again, but she didn't like the way he'd positioned himself. He was between Maddie and the tree, and it meant his back was exposed to at least one bad guy at all times. She wanted to yank him back to safety, but there was no safety. Her emotions must have agitated the bond because Jake looked back over his shoulder, finding her immediately.

Maddie followed his gaze, then smiled as she raised her hand. Jake turned back in time to throw his own hands up. Sera's mouth dropped open at what appeared in front of him. A large, translucent bubble stretched several feet past them, both to the left and right, and well over their heads. It was almost the same color as the sprites, if someone were to blow them up like a balloon. She'd felt the pull from her center immediately, and the longer he held it, the more power trickled out of her. Last time, he'd taken way too much, but this time he was being careful to only take what he thought he'd need.

It was amazing. Jake had made a shield.

Maddie was not pleased. "You can't do that. I'm the one with power. He promised." She tried another spell, and Sera could see it this time as it fizzled against the golden bubble.

"Sera, do what you're going to do." Jake didn't dare turn around.

"You know what, it doesn't matter. It's almost midnight, and everything is in place. As soon as the barriers weaken, Torix will take care of Sera himself."

Maddie's words were eerily similar to what Torix had told her, so she wondered if he was speaking to her now. She could still feel him poking at her mind, but his words had gone silent. Either way, Maddie was right. They needed to move Ryan out of that circle to buy time. Jake's shield didn't reach him, and she could feel him concentrating on holding it in place. Maddie checked her watch and threw another spell, ostensibly to keep Jake occupied.

Sera could feel a shift coming in the woods around her, a build-up of power. She guessed she had less than a minute. Ryan was a few feet in front of her on the other side of the tree. Sera didn't see any other way than physically pulling him.

"Jake, I need you to make the shield bigger, further right." She spoke as softly as she could, almost a whisper, and Jake nodded subtly. The pull from her increased, and a wave of weariness washed over her. And the shield expanded enough to slip between Ryan and Maddie.

Sera didn't wait, she shot into the circle, grabbed one of Ryan's arms, and braced herself to move his dead weight. Her magic flared, and Ryan's weight suddenly disappeared. One heave, and she was able to move him through the dirt to the other side of the tree. *Super strength! Finally an ability that's useful.* She let her triumph flow through the bond, and Jake's lips tipped up in a smile.

Torix must have been paying attention after all because Maddie's gaze shifted to the circle and she shrieked. She abandoned toying with Jake and ran to the circle herself, as far as Jake's shields would let her go. It was far enough. Sera could feel the power building and Jake's panic mixed together. He wanted to save his sister, but he didn't drop the shields protecting them, and he didn't risk Sera by taking more power.

What have you done, little half-breed? Torix had lost his sheen of smug civility.

I took away one of your toys. You're going to have to find someone else to play body-snatcher with.

His amusement washed over her. *I have one toy left.*

If you take Maddie, who will help you? Sera was starting to feel panic of her own. She couldn't afford to jump into the circle again. Maddie would for sure attack her, and she'd waste precious time defending herself. Not to mention making Jake choose which of them to protect.

Who said I would take her? She offers herself freely. A pity, really, I was hoping to save her sacrifice for another time. Sera was treated to a vision of the stone circle littered with bodies of the Fae, Maddie prominently displayed in the middle. *My release is certain. What could you possibly do to stop me?*

Whatever I have to.

Sera couldn't let Maddie sacrifice herself. Their conversation had taken seconds, but she could feel the power seeping into her from the woods. The smooth Fae barrier began to warp and weaken, and Sera knew it was time.

Her plan involved sucking in potentially lethal amounts of magic, so she needed to break the bond between her and Jake before she did it. It was an acceptable danger to herself as far as she was concerned, but that amount of magic would kill him if she screwed it up. Zee's warning echoed in her mind, but she wasn't willing to risk Jake. She put one hand on her chest and one on Torix's tree. It had to be one right after the other.

"Sorry, Jake," Sera whispered. She felt for the bond between them, bright with power and coated with a very thin layer of Zee's magic holding it in place. He turned at her voice, and she met his eyes as she pulled all of the magic back into herself, hers and Zee's.

It snapped into her like the last time, but she was prepared for that. The look of confusion and pain on Jake's face etched itself in her memory. His shields disappeared with no power to hold them up, and Jake collapsed to the ground. She knew what it felt like to have someone empty her out. He'd be unable to move for a bit, and she had every intention of keeping Torix and Maddie focused on her.

Immediately after breaking the bond, the magic under her peaked. It was amazing, and in any other circumstance, she'd love to bask in the waves of power. The circle roared to life, and Maddie screamed from inside it. The Fae barriers became so thin she could no longer see them, but she could feel them.

Sera sank her fingers into the silver symbols and dropped her shields all the way. She absorbed the magic like a sponge. There was so much of it, and it was spread out over vast distances, much larger than she'd thought. A shot of cold made her shiver, and Maddie stopped screaming abruptly. Sera hoped she'd taken the magic from the circle before Torix had taken Maddie's body.

The power filled her completely, and Sera let her head fall back as it surged through her. When the barriers had shrunk to the area around her fingers, Sera pulled her hands back and they winked out. Torix's tree crumbled into ash, and a gale gusted out of where it had been. The force of it knocked Sera back several steps and extinguished the torches. She'd lost feeling in her fingers, but everything else was hyper focused. Her whole body was glowing. A whirl-wind of leaves and small sticks circled the clearing as the power under her feet eased back to normal. Samhain had peaked.

When the wind cleared, the twisted oak was replaced with a man in a simple brown cloak. He was classically handsome, chiseled features, blonde hair that reached past his collar adorned with small braids, broad shoulders under the cloak, and eyes that glowed like emeralds in the dim light. Behind him, a figure lay crumpled on the ground, and Sera breathed a sigh of relief. The barriers were gone, and they'd released both Torix and Evie. It was unclear if Evie was alive, but at least she was physically there.

Torix's eerie green gaze took in the clearing and landed on Sera. He smiled, and Sera felt truly afraid for the first time that night. She didn't miss the disdain in his look or the way his lip curled in disgust when he looked past her at Jake. She knew it was Jake because somehow, even with her shields most of the way back up, she could still sense him behind her. Only faintly, a general sense of warmth and direction, but it was there. Maddie got unsteadily to her feet in her half-erased circle, but Sera knew that because she could see her. The sense of knowing applied solely to Jake. She'd broken the bond, it shouldn't be possible.

She wasn't sure if it was a benefit or not, since at this point her plan veered off into wishful thinking.

"Well this was unexpected. What a treasure you are, my little half-breed," said Torix. His voice sounded like he looked, traditional bad guy, deep, with a slight British accent. Totally unbidden, an image of him dressed as Loki from the Avengers movie popped into her head. A moment later, he laughed and his form changed. The brown cloak became black and green leather over pants and a tunic with gold highlights and enormous shoulder pads. Full Loki armor without the silly helmet. "Is this how you prefer me?"

"I preferred you as a tree." Sera raised her shields the rest of the way. A movement at her legs had her glance down, and to her surprise, golden dragon scales replaced her clothing, locking into place up to her neck.

"Strange, since you're the one who released me." He took a step toward her, and Sera stepped back. At some point while she was armoring herself, she'd lost track of Jake. He wasn't behind her anymore, but somewhere in the woods to her left getting further away.

Sera took a second step back, and Torix's smile widened. "Afraid? I do love the taste of fear."

"Cautious and prudent." She tilted her head to the side. "What does that taste like?"

He shrugged nonchalantly, and raised his hand, but not

at her. She hadn't noticed he'd moved within reach of Maddie until his arm wrapped around her waist.

"Sorry, dear, I'll be needing this back." He pulled her against him and took her mouth in a surprisingly chaste kiss. Maddie didn't move, but her skin paled in the few seconds they had contact. Sera shifted to stop him, but he'd already drawn back. The oily blue sheen that had coated Maddie was nowhere to be seen, and as she watched, Maddie's eyes rolled back and her knees gave out. Torix caught her weight, then tossed her into the trees like she was an apple core.

Sera heard a thud as Maddie's body hit the ground, but she didn't dare take her eyes off of Torix. They were alone in the clearing lit only by her power. She couldn't see Evie, Jake was gone, and even the sprites had abandoned her. "Everyone was right. Maddie didn't have any power."

Torix dropped his chin in a single nod. "I allowed her the use of my power to work in my interests. Why do you lock yourself away from me?"

It took her a moment to figure out he meant the shields. "I'm particular about who I let into my mind. Can't have any old riff raff bumbling around in there."

He lifted a hand to his heart and mocked being affronted. "And here I thought we had something special, but I suppose it's busy in there sharing it with your mate."

The words hit her hard. She'd lost the chance to share herself with Jake. Removing the bond had left an empty spot inside her, a space her superficial sense of Jake couldn't replace. He'd held the shields, and she'd been the one to break everything. No wonder he'd left her to deal with Torix herself.

"No answer for that?" Torix picked up the knife that Maddie had placed near the inner torches and examined it.

"No denials or excuses? Ah, but I can feel your pain. Let's explore that, shall we?"

He whipped the knife at her, so fast it was a blur. Sera jerked to the side, but it still slammed into her left shoulder. She stumbled back with a grunt, but it didn't penetrate her scales. Her armor protected from punctures, but not blunt force. *Good to know.* Pain blossomed down her arm as if she'd been punched. Torix licked his lips like he could taste it.

"Tell me, which hurts more, your shoulder or knowing your mate has left you?"

Sera bent down and picked up the knife at her feet. She didn't know how to throw it, but she knew the pointy end went in the bad guy. "Have you always been this weak?"

The insult must have hit its mark because Torix lost his lazy grin and a flick of his wrist shot out a stream of iridescent blue magic. Sera ducked as it streaked past her face. He pulled the magic toward him, and she quickly looked over her shoulder. A rustle and crash preceded a large log, about half her size, flying through the air in her direction. She threw herself sideways, narrowly avoiding it. Torix released his magic and tossed it in the same direction as Maddie. It looked like all her shielding concerns about blocking trees were spot on.

She jumped up and blew her hair out of her face. "You missed."

"Perhaps, but I'm not ready to kill you yet, that would ruin all the fun. Incapacitating you and toying with your prone body will be much better."

"I've had worse first dates." Sera barely dodged the small boulder he tossed at her, again wrapped in dark blue magic. At least he didn't have telekinetic abilities.

Where the crap were the Fae? Wasn't this part of their

forest? She was defending it all alone, and it was going about as well as she'd thought it might. Her shoulder throbbed, she'd finally pushed Jake all the way away, Torix was playing a one-sided version of dodgeball, which was terrifying, and her plan for winning involved draining herself or possibly exploding. The end result was unclear. She desperately wished Jake was there, but in the end, she was glad he'd left. Him dying at the hands of Torix was worse than anything that could happen to her.

Torix began to circle, and Sera moved with him. The amount of power pulsing through her made her nervous. She needed to release it somehow, so why not try some of Torix's moves. Her pack was lying practically at his feet, and she could see a wooden handle sticking out of the top of it.

Sera started by using what she knew. She shifted the knife into her left hand and flexed her fingers a few times to be sure they'd work when she needed them, then she squeezed her eyes closed. A giant ball of golden light blazed into existence; she could see the flash behind her lids. If it was enough to rock Will's car, it might at least knock Torix around a little. She shoved the magic at him as she opened her eyes, careful to keep her gaze averted.

She closed the distance to Torix behind the magic ball. It slammed into him, and he didn't budge. Before the light had faded, Sera sliced at his abdomen with the knife. Like she'd thought, he didn't block the knife. Like she'd feared, it bounced off a thin blue shield. Torix grabbed her wrist above the knife and squeezed. Pain shot up her arm in the opposite direction from earlier, and she cried out. She dropped the knife. Torix watched it fall, and Sera grabbed the bat out of her pack with her free hand. The knife embedded itself in the ground point first, and Sera swung at his face as hard as she could.

Without looking, he blocked with his arm and yanked her forward. Sera fell against him, off balance. The bat joined the knife on the ground. Torix snaked an arm around her waist, holding her upright, and the other clenched around her wrist painfully. Cold radiated from every place he touched her, freezing down her fingers and up her back. Sera tightened her shields, and the cold retreated a bit.

Torix raised his head and met her eyes. "Interesting choice, but useless, I'm afraid." A lustrous blue coating began covering her wrist where they touched, oozing toward the rest of her. "Perhaps this will be more effective."

Sera called on her power to give her a boost. She shoved him hard enough to break his hold and force him back a few steps, but his blue goo kept creeping up her arm. It was cold, like all his magic had been, and she wasn't willing to find out what it was supposed to do. She flexed her fingers again, and relaxed her shields enough to pull the magic inside of her. The blue soaked into her armor and disappeared.

Sera rubbed her shoulder, then her arm. Her left side was really taking a beating. Getting within physical distance of Torix was proving problematic. She'd used as much power as she could, and it had barely phased him.

Torix raised a brow. "Interesting skill you have there. It appears I chose the wrong child all those years ago."

"What do you mean years ago?"

"Surely you don't think this was a recent development. I've had centuries, what's a few more years to mold a creature to my will."

"That night in the woods…"

"It was unfortunate that your grandmother found you when she did. Your mind was already half twisted. I would have had to do little work. The other was adequate, but always held back by her kind heart." He spit the last two words as if they were poison. "I had to take more and more control over her as the years passed."

"Jake knew it wasn't her." Sera's triumph was short-lived.

"Ah, but you. You would have provided me with such power. You had so much darkness in you already, a simple nudge, and you would have been mine."

A ghostly touch flitted across her lips, much like the first time they'd spoken, and Sera shivered. He was right. She'd been in a dark place when she'd first come to Mulligan as a teen, and it wouldn't have taken much for her to follow a path that gave her gobs of power. But he was wrong too. She'd met Jake, and spent time with Evie, and even Maddie pushed past her defenses. That kind heart again. They'd helped her find joy and lightness, and even though she'd run, that light had always been there.

It still burned in her, and no matter how hard she'd tried to break that bond with Jake, it endured. Torix was going to have to find someone else to manipulate.

"Yeah, that's a no from me."

"A pity you don't have a choice."

One second they were circling each other in the clearing, the next he was in front of her. Sera tried to back away, but he grabbed both arms and wrenched them behind her back. He held her with one hand, despite her attempts to break free with her super strength. She brought a knee up, but he side-stepped then pulled her fully against him. It was like falling into snow.

With all her power, she couldn't get him to let go, and the terror started to rise as her body temperature dropped.

"Ah, there's the fear I wanted."

Sera's panicked brain told her to tighten her shields, to force him away, to throw all her power at him even if it drained her completely. She bucked and writhed, but his hold on her never wavered. His hand was a vice on her jaw as he lifted her face to his. He leaned down, and Sera could feel his cold breath across her lips.

A pulse of warmth from the connection with Jake, closer than she expected, spread out from her center. It reminded her that it wasn't her power she had to use. It was Torix's.

She stopped trying to pull away, and instead dug her fingers into his hand behind her back. "No means no, asshole."

Sera dropped her shields and yanked at his magic with all her might. Pain and surprise flashed across his face. Her scale armor disappeared, and her body recoiled from the drenching cold, but she didn't let go.

Torix clawed at her face with his other hand then pushed her head back, but his magic flowed into her. Swirling and churning in her belly, fighting for space in a place already full. Her mouth fell open as she gulped in air. In her mind, his strength shrank with every heartbeat. Collapsing in on itself and rushing into her.

Sera was full to bursting with contentious power, but Torix retained too much still. He sank to his knees, but he continued to fight her, picking at her mind, futilely trying to pull his hand away.

Her stomach cramped, and sprites floated off her bare arms as if she was coated in them. The clearing was bright as day with her light, and Sera forced herself to take more. For Maddie. Her hand seized, but she didn't let go. For Zee and all the Fae. Tiny blue cracks began to form on her fingers, then her hands. Torix's magic trying to escape one way or another. For Ryan. Her breath emerged in frozen clouds. For Evie. Her legs shook until they were on the verge of giving out, and Sera tightened her grasp on Torix. If she was going down, he was coming with her. It looked like her plan was going to end the way she'd expected, and her big regret was that she wouldn't get the chance to make a future worth of stupid mistakes with Jake.

Instead of falling to the forest floor, Sera was caught by a furnace of heat. Arms came around her, holding her tight and letting warmth seep into her from behind. A familiar strength circled her, offering support however she needed it. Their bond settled into place, stronger than before. Even with all her power, she hadn't been able to sever it completely. Sera heard a voice in her mind.

Let me help you.

Relief filled her, and she knew what to do. For Jake.

She opened the floodgates and the excess magic rushed out of her and into him. His arms tightened, but didn't pull her away. The membrane of her power kept the flow coming out of Torix and into Jake. Magical osmosis. The cracks in her hands closed, and the heat from their bond melted the ice in her body. Jake was open to her, and she could feel it all. His sadness, his pain, his fear, but also his hope, his trust, and his rock-solid faith in her ability to handle it. Underneath it all, she ultimately recognized the warmth for what it was... love.

Between them, they drained Torix until his power was barely a trickle. He lost his glamour and collapsed into the pine needles as a man in a tattered brown robe. His face was white, and his eyes were a boring green with no other-worldly glow.

Sera looked, but she could see no more magic in him. It was then she let Jake take her weight and finally let go.

15

SERA

SERA COULD HAVE SWORN she'd closed her eyes for only a second, but when she opened them, her face was tucked into Jake's neck. He was sitting on the forest floor, with her curled up in his lap. She lifted her head, and Jake looked down at her. He wasn't smiling, but the bond was going strong, and she could sense his relief mixing with hers.

"You're not getting rid of me that easily," she said.

Jake laughed and dropped his forehead to hers. "I'm sorry about your keys. I had a stupid moment and thought that taking away your choice meant you were safer. I promise never to do that again. I'll make entirely new mistakes in the future."

Sera sighed. "I'm sorry too. I didn't give you a choice either when I tried to break the bond to protect you."

"You scared the shit out of me. Next time we fight a super villain, maybe give me a heads up when you're about to do something crazy."

"Do you get a lot of super villains in Mulligan?"

"Only since you moved back."

He hugged her, and she winced when he hit the sore spot on her left arm. She really wanted a long soak in the tub and three days of sleep, but it wasn't even dawn yet, and they had bad guys to take care of.

When she lifted her head, the clearing was full to bursting with sprites. Sera caught her breath. It was beautiful, like a magical snow globe. The torches had been blown down and scattered, the small cauldron was on its side, the grocery bag's contents were spilled out and scattered on the ground, and the goblet of water was broken and empty. Best of all, the area felt fresh. Even the air smelled a little different, a subtle rotting smell that she hadn't noticed before was gone. Now it was all pine and sweat and dryer sheets.

Her magic had returned to normal levels, and the bond she'd broken had reformed. When she examined it with her senses, it felt different than before. Last time, Zee's magic had formed a channel. This time, it was her and Jake alone. The magic wove through them both in complicated knots, and when she touched it, it welcomed her but didn't bend. She couldn't influence this one. It was already made of her magic, so she couldn't absorb or break it. Even when she lifted all her shields, it was safe and snug inside.

Jake waited patiently while she explored, but when she raised her shields, he poked her side. "We have a lot to talk about, but there's something more pressing you should probably know."

Sera dropped the shields again and straightened so she was sitting in his lap instead of curled up in it. "What's that?"

He nodded toward where the circle had been. "Torix is gone."

Her head whipped around. Sure enough, the clearing

was empty of Fae, evil or otherwise. "How is that possible? He should be a husk."

Jake shrugged. "I may have been distracted trying to settle the last dregs of magic once you passed out."

"I didn't pass out. I was resting my eyes."

"Uh huh. He must have crawled away while you were resting your eyes."

Sera stood and groaned. "Physical battle sucks. He was empty. I'm sure of it. I checked."

"Well then, I'm not sure there's much we can do about it anyway." Jake joined her on his feet and stretched his arms above his head. Sera watched his shirt ride up and remembered gliding her mouth down tight abs. A hot flush raced through her, and Jake grinned. "I'm liking this new bond. It's a lot more responsive."

Sera felt his amusement and his answering heat. She met his eyes and closed the distance between them. He didn't move, but his pulse picked up. She wanted to touch him, and through the bond, he urged her on. Her hand flattened along his stomach and slid up his chest. The bond did interesting things when they touched. She could feel the trail of heat left behind by her hand and how much he enjoyed it. His eyes flashed, and he covered her hand over his heart.

For the first time, Sera wasn't terrified by the prospect of sharing herself with him. She knew he could block her with shields, like she could, but he was choosing not to. He wanted her to see him. After everything they'd been through, everything they'd both done, his faith in her remained. To him, she was a superhero, and she was starting to believe aspects of that herself.

"Sorry to interrupt, but I think there are better places to

make googly eyes at each other, and I, for one, would very much like to get out of the woods," said Evie.

Sera squealed and ran at the slim older woman picking her way across the debris. They collided in a tangle of limbs, and Sera sniffled into Evie's dusty shoulder. She'd tried to be confident that she'd rescue Evie, but there'd been chasms of doubt deep down. After a long squeeze, Sera pulled back and ran her hands over Evie to be sure she wasn't injured.

Evie chuckled and patted the back of her hand. "I love a good hug, but save the hanky-panky for your man over there."

The word *mate* floated across her mind, and she wasn't sure if it was from her or Jake, who was standing back to give her a moment. She refused to think Torix still had enough power to get into her head, wherever he was.

"I missed you." Satisfied that Evie was in one dirty piece, she stepped back and propped her fists on her hips. "You and I are going to have words about all the meddling you did and all the information you kept from me."

Evie sighed. "I suppose Zee spilled the beans."

"I got most of it out of Ryan."

Evie raised a brow. "Now that *is* interesting. I'm sorry, Sera. I never wanted you involved in all of this, but I had to try to help."

Help always comes at a price... "Why didn't you just tell me? Why did you let Mom try to convince me I was crazy?"

She winced. "I made an agreement with Zee. I wouldn't tell you unless you agreed to stay in Mulligan. She wanted to train you herself. You're half-Fae, and she wanted you here within her sphere of influence. One doesn't break promises to the Fae, and I don't have any control or influence with your mother. Things got out of hand." She tucked Sera's hair behind her ear. "I wanted to tell you so many times. Especially once you married that super-douche."

Sera believed her, but it also still stung that so much had been kept from her about her own life. She nodded, unsure of what to say. Evie gave her one more squeeze then walked past her to Jake, who was just standing there, eating something out of a little cellophane bag and watching avidly.

"Ooo, yummy. Gummy dinos." Evie stole a few from the bag. "So do I have you to thank for being me again?"

Jake shook his head. "No, ma'am. Sera did all the heavy lifting. I was here for support."

"Good boy." She patted his cheek, popped a few candies in her mouth, and walked past him to a path lit by sprites that hadn't been there moments ago. "You're going to want to retrieve Maddie. She's still back in the hidey hole. Torix did a number on her, but she's a good girl. She'll heal." She waved without looking back as she crossed into the trod.

Sera watched her go, then turned to Jake. "Hidey hole? Why do I think you know what she's talking about, and what are you eating?"

Jake reached for her and linked their fingers. "Gummy dinos. I found an unopened pack by the grocery bag." He offered her the open bag. "Want some?"

"Evil minion snacks? No thanks. What hidey hole?"

Jake shrugged. "Your loss. When you broke the bond, it knocked the air out of me—"

"I might know a little about that."

He kissed her fingers and continued. "But I knew you'd have a good reason. I hoped you'd have a plan, but figured that was probably wishful thinking so I got the girls out of the danger zone. You'd already flung Ryan off into the woods somewhere."

Sera gasped. "Ryan. I forgot about him." She dragged

Jake past the remaining ashes of the oak and a few steps into the trees. There, under a thin layer of dead leaves and pine needles, lay Ryan, still coated in oily blue magic. It was almost pretty, but as much as she'd love to leave Ryan in a state where he couldn't speak, she had a strong feeling they'd need him in the future.

It took a second to absorb the magic and break the spell. She was getting used to the momentary queasy feeling when the magics mixed, and it was passing faster each time. Ryan shook his head and glared at them.

"You guys suck as backup," he said.

Jake scoffed. "Man, you were the backup. Sera kicked their collective asses all on her own. Gummy dino?" Jake held the bag out to Ryan.

Sera smiled at Jake over her shoulder. "I had a little help."

Ryan rolled his eyes at them. "Yeah, okay." He got up and tried in vain to brush off several layers of dirt, then went over and grabbed a little handful of candy. "Whatever. Next time Zee orders me to summon someone, I'm going to knock myself out until she finds someone else."

Sera looked up at him. "Why didn't you tell me you had magic?"

He stopped straightening his clothes, swept tousled black hair off his forehead, and stared back at her. "Why didn't you tell us about that night with Maddie?"

She stood slowly, neither willing to break eye contact nor back down. "Fair enough." He still had a subtle red glow, especially around his eyes, but Sera didn't think he was consciously channeling magic. More like he was repressing it.

There was a lot more to that story, but she could sense

Jake's mounting impatience. "Are you coming with us to get Maddie or heading home?"

Ryan winced. "Probably best if Maddie doesn't see me right now."

"Afraid she'll try to get back in your pants again?" asked Sera. She knew how Jake would react, but Ryan deserved a little payback.

Right on cue, Jake swung around from scanning the trees. "Say what now?"

Ryan held up both hands. "It's not like that. It was a while ago, we were interested in each other, and we wanted to see where it would go. Completely respectful."

Jake's hands clenched into fists. "Did you sleep with my sister?"

"Yes, but—" Jake's fist crashed into Ryan's face before he had a chance to finish. It knocked him back a few steps, and Ryan rubbed his jaw as he straightened up to his full height, meeting Jake's eyes. Jake took a step forward, and Ryan held up a hand palm out, but it was crackling with red magic. Sera stopped Jake with a hand on his arm.

Ryan looked at his hand in disgust, then lowered it. "You get one because I deserved it for not being up front about our relationship at the time, but I had feelings for your sister. *Had.* It didn't work out between us, but I respected her and her wishes when she ended it. You'll have to get used to that."

Jake nodded stiffly, and Ryan walked away from them through the trees. He didn't call a trod, but she had a feeling he'd be fine getting back.

Sera ran a hand through her hair. "Two down, one to go. Let's go rescue your sister."

Jake's shoulders relaxed, and he led the way back across the clearing. "It wasn't her."

"I know. Torix said as much."

"I wish I'd seen it. How did I not notice her changing the last couple of weeks?"

"Because he'd had her for a lot longer than that. The night after you and I were together the first time, Maddie and I went into the woods. Remember when she broke her wrist? Well, it was then, but I don't remember what happened. I know at some point, we encountered Torix, Evie found me, brought me home, and sealed my magic. When I woke up, I had these visions of demons and monsters, and the thought of going into the woods caused my first panic attack. That's when the nightmares started and they all ended with you dead. I tried to be strong, and Evie insisted I was better off here, but I took the easy way out and ran away."

Jake had stopped walking at some point, but Sera couldn't meet his eyes. She didn't have to. She could feel his sorrow for what they'd lost and his hurt that she hadn't even tried to contact him. They were old feelings though, muted with time, and massively overshadowed by the need to comfort her.

She held up a hand when he would have come closer. "Let me finish. I believe Torix has had control over Maddie since then. You'll have to ask her what went down because I still don't remember it, but it also might not be a good idea to bring it up. It's not about you and what you missed. She was basically enslaved for almost a decade."

Jake ignored her hand and gathered her close, then tilted her face up for a soft kiss. "I get it. We'll find a way to help her heal."

Sera kissed him back, relieved that he knew what she was trying to say. "We will. Together."

Jake's joy washed over her. "Ha, so you finally admit that you love me."

Sera rolled her eyes. "Yes. I love you."

"And you know I love you too."

"Yes."

"And one day I'm going to marry you and we'll make gorgeous grandbabies for my mom."

Sera rolled her eyes. "About that... turns out I'm half-Fae."

Jake blinked. "Okay then. Gorgeous, magical, trouble-making grandbabies."

"That sounds a lot more accurate, not to mention something that would actually thrill your mom." They laughed, and Sera pulled him down for a long, slow kiss that she ended way before she wanted to. "Let's go be heroes."

EPILOGUE

SERA

Two weeks after nearly killing herself with magic, Sera was able to successfully put a candle out under Evie's watchful eye, but that was about it. Her magic continued to refuse to do much more than eat other magic and be shiny. Jake, on the other hand, was getting pretty good at using it to get himself a beer from the kitchen, much to Evie's disdain.

Turned out, Evie being legally dead also made things complicated. No one could find Zee, or knew what had happened to Torix. Sera didn't know how to even begin to explain to the authorities that the body of Evelyn Allen they'd buried was actually a magical double meant to hide the fact that she'd essentially been kidnapped by Jake's possessed little sister. Sera had spent most of her life trying to convince people, including herself, that she wasn't crazy, and announcing that Evie wasn't dead and magic was real didn't seem like the best way to start fresh in a new town.

They'd agreed that, for the time being, Evie would have to stay in the house until they could find Zee to fix the mess.

Ryan made himself scarce for a little bit, but when he did start coming around again, even he thought it was weird that Zee hadn't responded to any of them. Especially when she'd been the one who demanded that Ryan figure out how to make Wi-Fi happen in the middle of the woods. Ryan only showed up after Maddie left to visit her parents in Europe. Jake thought it would do her good to get away for a while, and Ryan was glad to not have to tiptoe into the house.

Sera tried to reach the stone circle through the trods, but ever since Samhain, they'd led her in circles then spit her back out where she'd started. Evie said to give it time, but Sera didn't want to wait. She loved her grandmother, but having two stubborn Allen women in the same house was a lot harder than she remembered from her teenage years. When Jake suggested Sera stay with him, Evie had nearly packed Sera's bags herself.

Will drove by at least once a day. Sera didn't know what he hoped to achieve, but he never got out of his car. Every time they'd caught him, he'd slowed down to stare at the houses, then sped off. Her mom said Will was hoping she'd come to her senses, but Sera knew better.

Eventually, they were going to have to deal with him.

In the meantime, every night, she and Jake went to bed wrapped around each other, and every night, she was glad she'd come back to Mulligan.

Now if only Zee would answer her damn phone.

Continue the adventure with Zee and Ryan in Insidious Magic!

If you loved Accidental Magic, please take a moment to leave a review on Amazon, Goodreads, or Bookbub.

Can't get enough of snarky magical heroines? Get a fun short story with all new characters set in the Modern Magic world when you sign up for my newsletter, Muse Interrupted!

A Note from Nicole

This book wouldn't have been possible without some amazing people. In no particular order: my amazing editor, Karen Thurrell Gledhill. I'm so grateful to you for taking a chance on me. Can't wait to make more awesome books together. Jesse, Nicole, Liz, Evelyn, and Beth, thank you for reading for me. Amy and Kelly, you are the rock-solid foundation upon which my confidence is built. Three girls with the brain of one. Eli, it's your turn to make dinner. I love all of you.

To my readers, I do it all for you. Thank you from the bottom of my heart for taking your precious time to read Accidental Magic. I hope you had a satisfactory amount of sass, magic, and romance. I had so much fun writing Sera and Jake's story.

Want to learn more about Zee, the mysterious leader of the Fae? Her story continues in Insidious Magic. Buy it on Amazon.

But wait! There's more. Remember the wolf that Torix had under his control? There's more to him than there appears. His story unfolds in Treacherous Magic, available on Amazon.

Join Muse Interrupted Romance, my Facebook group, for daily shenanigans and sexy man chest pictures. Sign up for Muse Interrupted, my newsletter, for first access to new releases plus extra content, giveaways, sneak peeks, and first look at new covers.

If you have time, would you mind leaving a review on Amazon? Goodreads or Bookbub would be amazing too! Readers help other readers like you find books they love.

I appreciate you, and because I do, I've included an excerpt from the next book, Insidious Magic, right here for your reading pleasure. Turn the page to get started on Zee and Ryan's adventure.

~Nicole

INSIDIOUS MAGIC

MODERN MAGIC - BOOK TWO

Life in the Glade didn't change much for the Fae, but when it did, it brought Netflix.

Zee, Fae warrior, leader, and all-around badass, thought she was prepared for change. Ryan, human high school computer teacher and occasional badass, thought he wanted nothing to do with the Fae. They were both wrong. When the old magic breaks, can they find a common ground where human and magic meet or will their differences tear apart both them and the Wood?

CHAPTER 1

RYAN

THE LAST THING Ryan Nolan wanted to be doing was tromping through the Wood looking for a wayward fairy that didn't want to be found. Zee hated being called a fairy, so of course he did it as often as possible. A bare branch caught the sleeve of his favorite long-sleeved shirt, and he slapped it away. December in Texas wasn't exactly frigid, but he figured the less holes in his clothes the better.

"Stop playing with the trees and pay attention." Sera frowned at him again.

"They were playing with me. The grabby branches are getting worse. I think they're doing it on purpose" Ryan took a few more steps away from the forest they'd just left and toward the safety of the road, tightening the fleece he had tied around his waist.

Jake snorted. "I thought you liked grabby things."

An image of Maddie clinging to him in the Wood flashed across Ryan's mind, but making a joke about Jake's sister was in poor taste, even for him. "Can we not talk about this in mixed company?"

"Since when do I count as mixed company?" Sera asked.

"Since I don't want to get punched again, and you're a handy excuse."

She crossed her arms and gazed past him into the trees. "That's fair. Also, the trod is gone again."

Ryan glanced over his shoulder. "It always disappears when we leave the Wood."

"Yeah, but this time it was disappearing as we were walking on it, and did you notice the sprites?"

Jake swatted at a glimmer of golden light floating around his face. "What about them?"

"There were only a few on the trod. Usually there are enough to light the way for us."

"It's daytime, in the Wood *and* out here. Maybe we didn't need as many since we could see fine."

She shook her head. "That's not how the sprites work."

Ryan resisted rolling his eyes. Ever since he'd given Sera access to the Fae database, she'd become the de facto expert on magic and didn't mind lording it around a bit. Admittedly, there was a lot of useful information in there, but Ryan had never wanted to know more than was necessary. Magic, in the wrong hands, was dangerous, and the lure to use it multiplied exponentially. A quick glamour here, a little help there, and one day, the magic becomes necessary to everything.

Ryan could feel his mood getting darker as the sun went down. "Zombie bunnies." It was their safe word. Sera stopped lecturing them on sprites immediately. "Did we learn anything new this trip?"

Sera pulled her ponytail over her shoulder. "Same as all the last times. The trods are basically closed to us. Whatever

happened when I brought down the Fae barriers did something to the Wood, and until we can find Zee to find out
what, I can't get it to cooperate."

"What if we asked really nicely? Have we tried that?"
Ryan turned to the trees and spread his arms wide. "Oh
great and mighty Wood, have you seen Zee? We could really
use her to explain some shit."

Jake snickered behind him, followed by the distinctive
sound of Sera smacking him in the shoulder. Ryan obviously wasn't expecting an answer, smartass was his default
personality, but then the light changed deep in the trees.
The smirk dropped off his face as he lowered his arms. He
took a step forward, and a path appeared between the pines,
dotted with tiny glowing sprites. He looked over his shoulder, and Sera shook her head, eyes wide. Jake shrugged. If
neither of them had called the trod, then who had?

He didn't have to wait long for his answer. One second,
they'd been watching the sprites float around, the next, a
statuesque woman wearing wispy trailing scarves, complicated braids and not much else, was forcibly evicted from
the path. She didn't have a weapon, which was good for
Ryan because she was propelled forward, slamming right
into him.

She was damn near his height, tall for a woman, so they
nearly ended up sprawled in the road. Ryan managed to
quickly shift his balance and keep them upright, but reflex
had his hands splayed over the smooth bronze skin of her
back. Apparently, her sheer top tied around her neck and
didn't cover the back half, a style Ryan decided he heartily
approved of.

Her body was pressed against him from shoulder to
knee, and if he didn't do something, in a few seconds, she
was going to find out exactly how much Ryan liked her

top. And the scent of her skin. *Not helping.* He set her firmly away from him and removed his hands from her person.

Her green eyes were wide with panic, but recognition crept in as she straightened and studied the people around her. Ryan felt the weight of her gaze as she lingered on him. Absently, she looked down and noticed her clothes, then did a double-take. Her eyes narrowed in annoyance. He'd recognize those eyes and that look anywhere, even if the body attached to them was new.

They'd finally found Zee.

ZEE

Dammit, Chad. Zee was not happy. The trods had never been her favorite form of transport. They were draining and made her vaguely nauseous. Chad had assured her though that his newest trinket would speed her journey in the trod. Instead it appeared to have just changed her form and made the journey unbearably long. She'd left the Glade to join the battle against Torix, and at the time, she'd been wearing leather armor.

That had been hours ago.

She was definitely going to neuter him when she got back. The ridiculous dress she was wearing tied in a halter around her neck and flowed down into strips of fabric for a skirt. Not bad for movement in combat but terrible for protection. She could still feel the heat from Ryan's hands on her back when he'd caught her. Another thing to be embarrassed about. Fae warriors were simply not flung from the Wood to stumble about.

Ryan cleared his throat, and Zee met his eyes. He gestured at her. "Hey Zee. So this is new."

Sera piped up from somewhere behind her. "I've seen her like this before. New outfit though."

Zee considered the dream they'd shared and silently admitted it may have been Sera's vision that called the form instead of Chad's mistake, though no one should have been able to change anything about her period, and certainly not from outside the trod.

She studied the area around her again, more carefully this time. The humans stood outside the Wood, on the edge of a neighborhood street. Bare trees stretched high above them in front of the tidy houses across the road. Nothing like the cottages in the Glade, and not like anything she'd seen inside the Wood.

"Where am I?" Her voice was rusty, like she hadn't used it in weeks.

"The outskirts of Mulligan. Across the street from Jake and Sera's place... and Evie's place, I guess." Ryan was watching her closely with his hands in the pockets of his cargo pants.

The others were wearing pants and coats, and to her surprise, she had goosebumps breaking out all over her. She was cold?

How could she be cold? Fae could regulate body temperature with magic. She crossed her arms over her chest and shivered as a chilly wind blew right through the filmy dress. Everything was wrong, and she didn't even know where to start in order to fix it.

Ryan wordlessly untied his fleece and handed it to her. She slipped it on and immediately felt better. It carried his warmth and his scent, which was surprisingly soothing but also made her feel tingly and weird. Zee frowned. All three of the humans were watching her like she'd disappear if they blinked.

"What happened?" At least her voice was starting to sound more normal.

Sera and Jake shared a look, but it was Ryan who answered her. "We've been searching for you for quite a while, then I got sassy with the Wood, and it tossed you at me."

Zee blinked at him. "How long have you been searching?"

"Since Halloween, so about five weeks? Not very nice, by the way. We took care of your problem, and you all abandoned us."

Zee's eyes widened. Five weeks? When she'd left the Glade, it had been Samhain, what the humans call Halloween. The trods had kept her walking for what seemed like hours, but five weeks? She'd never heard of the time difference reaching such an extreme length.

"What about Torix?"

Ryan shook his head. "He got away, but Sera says he's powerless."

"How..." There were so many questions she had. She faced Sera. "What happened on Samhain?"

A soft flush stained Sera's cheeks, and Zee was reminded that humans had silly inhibitions about battle. "I fought Torix, and ended up draining his magic away. It's sort of what I do."

Zee didn't think her eyebrows could get any further up her forehead. "How did you get to him?"

Another flush. "Ah, I sort of took down the Fae barriers."

"The barriers my ancestors placed centuries ago and we've been reinforcing for generations? The ones instrumental in our pact with the Wood?"

"Some new information there that would have been helpful to know, but yeah. It released both Torix and Evie, who is stuck in her house by the way, because the world still thinks she's dead. We hoped you could help with that."

Zee didn't answer. She pivoted and strode right back into the woods. If she ended up stuck in a trod for several more months, so be it, but if the barriers were truly gone, then the pact was broken.

She'd taken several steps into the forest before she realized no path had emerged. Zee was crunching over dead leaves and pine straw, but no sprites joined her and she had to weave haphazardly between trunks. Also, her fingers were still cold. She pulled the sleeves of Ryan's fleece down over her hands and tried to use her magic to call on the Wood.

Nothing answered, and she stopped. The humans arrived seconds later. Where were the trods? Warning bells were going off in her head, but Zee remained calm. Warriors did not panic. She closed her eyes to block out the fading sunlight and the brambles, instead picturing the mossy green earth of the Glade. The circle set aside for teleportation. The symbols etched onto the surrounding rocks. She gathered her magic with intention and opened her eyes.

Ryan, Sera, and Jake stared back, waiting.

She was tired, sure, but she should have had enough energy to teleport once. It had to be after-effects from Samhain, but when she'd reached to gather her magic, she'd felt nothing. No corresponding power, no tingles, no sense of purpose. A horrible thought dawned on her.

Zee had left the Glade in her Amazon form, as Sera had dubbed it, but she could change shape at will. When she tried though, her will left her the same as before. The change should have been instantaneous. As soon as she wished to be a small flying creature, she should have been. Instead, she remained a tall woman in a ludicrous dress.

The humans shuffled uncomfortably, and Zee's eyes landed on Sera again. She belatedly remembered Ryan's mention of Evie in his explanation. "What have you done?"

Sera visibly straightened under Zee's scrutiny, and Jake's arms came around her from behind. "I did what I had to do to stop Torix and protect our world." Her eyes glazed over a bit as she stared, and then she gasped. "Your magic is gone."

Zee trembled inside, but nodded. She'd begun to suspect as much. Sera had broken far more than she knew. "I have to get back to my people."

Ryan sighed. "Good idea, but we couldn't get to you *or* your people even before the Wood dropped you on me." He ran his hand through his short hair, and a crackle of deep red magic zipped between his fingers like static. "Plus, you owe us, and we need your help before you just take your toys and go home."

Insidious Magic

ALSO BY NICOLE HALL

Modern Magic

Accidental Magic

Insidious Magic

Treacherous Magic

Impulsive Magic

Rebellious Magic

Chaotic Magic

ABOUT THE AUTHOR

Nicole Hall is a smart-ass with a Ph.D. and a potty mouth. She writes stories that have magic, sass, and romance because she believes that everyone deserves a little happiness. Coffee makes her happy, messes make her stabby, and she'd sell one of her children for a second season of Firefly. Her paranormal romance series, Modern Magic, is available now.

Let Nicole know what you thought about her sassy, magical world because she really does love hearing from readers. Find her at www.nicolehallbooks.com or Muse Interrupted Romance on Facebook!

Want to find out when the newest Nicole Hall book hits the shelves? Sign up for the weekly Muse Interrupted newsletter on her website. You'll get a welcome gift, the *Modern Magic* ebook, plus new release info, giveaways, exclusive content, and previews of the new books especially for fans.

facebook.com/nicolehallbooks

instagram.com/nicolehallbooks

amazon.com/author/nicole_hall

bookbub.com/authors/nicole-hall

Printed in Great Britain
by Amazon